BORROWED MOONLIGHT

THE WITCH WAYS

BOOK THREE

HELEN SLAVIN

ABOUT THE AUTHOR

Helen Slavin grew up in Lancashire and now lives in the West Country. She has written for television and radio. When not writing she's out in the lanes and byways looking for magic.

If you'd like to hear more from Helen, visit her website, www. helenslavin.com

 twitter.com/HelenSlavinBook

ALSO BY HELEN SLAVIN

The Extra Large Medium

The Stopping Place

Cross My Heart

From a Distance

Little Lies

After the Andertons

To the Lake

Will You Know Me?

THE WITCH WAYS SERIES

Crooked Daylight

Slow Poison

Borrowed Moonlight

THE WITCH WAYS WHISPERS

The Ice King

Breaking Bones

Whyte Harte

The Hedgehog Child

Helen Slavin

Borrowed Moonlight

For Dad, always

1

STEPS

It was the wrong path that Anna had taken. She could feel it beneath her feet. The moon was high but hidden, silvering the edges of the clouds that obscured it, and Anna's lantern faltered with a wink as if it might go out.

Emz was following behind their Guest, who had arrived an hour or more ago, already tired but anxious to move on through the Wood under their escort. No offer of tea or rest or refreshment was enough. The Guest looked, to Anna, in need of some real help. They had been walking for a long time in silence.

"This is the wrong way," the Guest said, her tone as flat and weary as her face.

"I think…" Anna halted and took in a breath. She reached around all her resources. What should she do? What were the options?

"I think we should head back to Cob Cottage. It's dark and you need…" she turned with an uncertain smile, but the Guest rounded on her.

"No. How many times? There's no time for teacakes. I need to be shown the way and head off. I have to be at Day's Ride before dawn. Just do your part and show me to Day's Ride."

The Guest was visibly distressed, the shards of it sparking out of her voice. Anna could not think. Nothing at all was coming to mind except for the idea that this was the wrong way.

"Wait here," she said and looked with a nod at Emz. The Guest gave a frustrated grunt.

Anna walked along the path ahead; the wood here appeared darker and more tangled than she had ever known it. The path was all bramble, almost a defensive wall, and this turn just knotted together with rowan and hazel, the trunks of which had twisted together so that it was no longer possible to tell them apart.

She had never heard of Day's Ride. Her memory was clicking through every possible day she had spent in Havoc Wood, and couldn't recall the place, and yet, she knew, Day's Ride must be here somewhere. She turned to the left path, *no*, a different vibe came from there, something off and unwelcoming, and, to the right, the wider path, no, again, a wrong feeling, not quite as bad as the left path but not promising. She needed Charlie. Charlie would know. Anna pushed her irritation and anxiety aside. This was not helping. She took a step, her foot tracing against a small flattened-down curve of undergrowth. A fox path. *Where did that go?* She lifted the lantern. It traced out the snaking line of the thin route. As it did so, the light strengthened, a weight lifted from Anna's chest.

The path was slender but gave them speed, cutting, as it did, in a neat diagonal across to the ridge. Anna made mental notes of this route. It had not occurred to her that they might ever find new places in Havoc Wood.

They began to follow the rise of the land towards a ridge, she was uncertain which one, but just below them she could hear the trinkling sound of The Splash, one of the skinny tributaries that criss-crossed Havoc. They were to the South, she thought. She would be able to see more clearly from the top of the ridge.

Up, up in a long steep effort, the trees dense and dark until the path broke out into a long holloway. It was domed over with hawthorn, the branches as intertwined as Celtic knotwork. In each direction, the vanishing point of shadows, the shimmering sound of leaves in the wind.

"At last." Their Guest pushed forward from the banking, her coat catching a little and tearing, but she didn't care as she strode off along the green lane. She had not taken five steps before she was hidden by the shadows. Gone.

"Where are we?" Emz asked. "Do you know?" Emz stepped closer, and Anna shook her head.

"Day's Ride, I suppose."

"Yeah. I know that. But, you know, where are we? Exactly." Emz examined the landscape around them.

"No idea. Let's get up onto the ridge and find out," said Anna. They stepped across the holloway to pick up the rest of the fox route.

They walked higher and the trees broke a little cover, a sort of viewing point so that they could look East to Crow Houses and further East to Yarl Hill.

"What do you think?" Anna asked.

"I think we're a long way East here. Beyond Frog Pond." Frog Pond sounded a familiar note for them, and they felt, at once, more settled. Yes. Of course. It was just a mile or so down into the valley if they hung a left.

"Do you think there's a quicker way back?" Anna asked, scanning the trees. In the distance, Emz could just make out the north tower of Woodcastle Castle. It was a good landmark.

"Probably, but we don't know it, so let's just retrace our steps. Yeah?" Emz was already taking steps back the way they had come. The two made their way back across Day's Ride and along the fox route that had led them here. They walked in silence, neither admitting that what they were doing was hurrying, that what they were feeling was afraid.

.   .   .

BACK AT THE cottage Anna moved to put the kettle on, her usual safety mechanism. Emz did not even take off the black waxed raincoat she'd habitually worn since their grandmother's death before heading down the hall.

"I'm going to bed. G'night." Emz said, the sound of her door shutting before Anna had chance to reply.

"G'night," she said, almost to herself. She pottered in the kitchen for a while longer, trying to organise her mind along with the supper dishes, and then, as the clock ticked to midnight, she gave up.

Down the hallway, she knocked on Charlie's door knowing that there would be no reply. She opened the door anyway, peering in, half hoping that Charlie might be there, snoring gently and oblivious. The bed was empty, still ruffled from the last time Charlie had slept there, some days ago. Anna shut the door, shut out the hall light, then shut her own bedroom door behind her.

Cob Cottage creaked a little, and outside the wind whispered in the trees.

2

MORNING, BROKEN

Aron was calling Charlie, repeatedly. It was an embarrassment, made more intense by the fact that she was at Drawbridge Brewery inside the aged mash tun, in the midst of shovelling out, and the ringtone, which she had forgotten to turn off, was pinging out like sonar trying to find her.

"Is that your phone?" She could see Michael framed doubly by the office door and the small hatchway into the mash tun.

"Yeah." Her voice echoed around the metal. Charlie shovelled the mash harder, the scent of it drifting up, sending her messages of what might be missing, what needed to be added. The ringtone and Michael's annoyed voice were distracting her focus.

"Aren't you going to answer it?" Michael yelled.

"No," she yelled back, the sound once again making a bell of the tun. She breathed in more of the last scents of the wort.

Focus.

Focus.

Hops tumbled in her mind and she felt calmer. Yes. That was

it. Add that later. Exactly the handfuls required appeared in her mind, an instructional calculation of aroma and bitterness.

"It's bloody annoying," Michael shouted from the gantry, his footsteps clattering towards her. The ringing stopped. Charlie shovelled the last of the mash into the barrow and wheeled it out.

"Switch it off if you're not answering it," Michael chided from above. Charlie didn't look up.

She had been spending a lot of time with Aron of late, pretending to be cheery Charlie. Her real self lay protected behind the smokescreen of stupid banter and fake laughing that had peppered her conversation in the wake of Apple Day and Halloween. As she finished dealing with the mash, her phone pinged out again with a text from Aron. She checked it over, headed towards the office.

"Can you sort the phone issue please?" Michael asked, his pencil tapping at the spreadsheet in front of him.

"Issue?" Charlie felt her anger bubble. Michael had been scratching at her nerves as of late.

"Keep it on silent in work hours. Please. It's just bloody annoying."

She made a show of switching off the ringtone. Her real self, sitting in the dark, shook her head at all this. Words tickled at her throat, but she could say none of them. She turned away from him to check the wall planner, despite knowing every notation and reminder on it.

Michael tapped the pencil for a moment longer and flicked another page of the order book.

"I need to sort out the wort for the Leap Woods Brew," Charlie said, distracting herself with the business of brewing. The required ingredients for the new brew were popping into her head with ease, another distraction.

"Charlie?" chimed Michael's voice, quiet, but not so quiet

that it didn't reach her as she headed out of the office. She heard him throwing down the pencil too, but she didn't turn back.

When her shift finished a few hours later, she found Aron parked up behind her car.

"Get in," he said with a wry grin, and Charlie did. She didn't much care where they were going, just so long as it was away.

He had an evening-out planned, and she already had a change of clothing in her bag, so they headed to Aron's flat at the marina. It seemed to Charlie that it became barer the more time she spent there.

"I sold on a couple of gadgets. That coffee maker for a start, never use that." Aron reached for their mugs from last night and pulled a slightly aged kettle from the cupboard.

"Where were you this morning?" he asked, his hand trailing from the kettle to the small of her back, his head tilting in to kiss at her neck.

"Had to get in to work. You were sleeping."

"Had to get in? Got some emergency brewing to do?" He was smiling with a hint of snide.

"Yes." She spoke firmly, her eyes rising to challenge his and, as he always did, he backed down. "What time did you get up?" She didn't really want the answer, she wanted to shift focus from herself. Aron grinned.

"Later. Shall we leave it at that?" He glugged some juice and looked at her. "You getting ready?"

Charlie looked down at her work clothes. She was tired and hungry and out of sorts.

"Ready for what?"

"Anything." He grinned, a smoochy kiss, a pat on the bottom

shoving her to the bedroom and her stash of clothes. She watched as he picked at the few items.

"This all you brought?" he asked with a frown. She stared at him, his fingers like claws picking over the clothes. The energy of him was sharp and unpleasant, in the way of electricity coming through a fork jammed into a socket.

"Cinderella borrowed my ball gown," she said. Aron reached to open the tall white wardrobe door. The dress within was slim and a muted gold.

"No, she didn't," he grinned.

At the harbourside, Charlie turned right to head to their favourite eating-place, Chunk, a gourmet burger place by the swing bridge. Aron grabbed for her arm, tugged her the other way.

"Whoa, whoa, where you going?" he asked, edgy.

"Chunk. Where we always eat." If she was being honest then, Chunk, with its red-raw slabs of beef and venison, was not her favourite place to eat. It was Aron's favourite, but he was shaking his head.

"Not tonight. I've got something on." He put his hands in his trouser pockets, the line of his suit ruffling. It must be important, this thing, Charlie thought. She could see his best shirt, the Italian linen one. He flicked his wrist out, checking the time, and she noticed he didn't have his watch. He noticed too, and the look of pique on his face stopped her making a joke.

"Come on then..." he said. "Don't want to be late."

"For what?" she asked, and he didn't answer. He smiled and planted a quick peck on her cheek. He did not, she noticed, take her hand.

· · ·

THE ARK WAS A VERY swanky restaurant indeed, moored by the bonded warehouse wharf. It was a long wooden vessel of some age, the portholes winked with candlelight, and the doormen wore dinner jackets. The gantry was painted black and bordered with black coffin-like hoppers housing ebullient navy-blue hydrangeas so that anyone boarding could not be glimpsed from the harbourside.

"Are you jok…?" She didn't have a chance to finish the question as the doorman ushered them aboard with a nod.

"He knows you," Charlie said as they walked the planks to the inner glimmer of the boat. "You've been here before."

Aron did not answer, he did not hear her. His attention, she saw, was focused on the doorway to the wheelhouse. There was a burst of laughter from within, glasses chinked with a musical note, and underneath it all someone trinkled notes from a piano.

Inside, the tables were set with white cloths and crystal goblets. The candlelight burnished everything into beauty. The air was scented with savoury threads that Charlie picked up without thinking: *thyme, salt, saffron, rosemary, garlic.* They were the only genuine things in the entire room.

A dark-haired man turned from his conversation and, without apology, abandoned his companions and his champagne glass and walked towards them.

"Aron." His hand reached out, took Aron's scrawny paw, and pulled him into an embrace. "You made it. Good. Good to see you." He was pointedly not looking at Charlie. There was the smallest bead of sweat on his hairline. The candlelight winked it into Charlie's vision. Wink, wink, like a signal.

"This…" Aron stood aside a little, "is Charlotte."

The dark-haired man reached out to Charlie. She shook his square and heavy hand, the gold ring on the third finger giving off warmth and something more, a bursting of energy that spoke directly to the heart of her Strength; it was like a flock of rooks taking to the skies. Was this a warning? *Danger, Charlie Way.*

"Charlotte. Delighted to meet you." He smiled with his mouth as his eyes watched her, and she was surprised at their soft expression, the hint of nervousness they conveyed.

"This is Mr Herald." Aron spoke with a hint of reverence that made Charlie glance up for the halo or the possible crown. The dark-haired man's soft eyes didn't blink as they held hers.

"Call me Ivan," he commanded.

CHARLIE USUALLY HAD A GOOD APPETITE, but the sensation she had felt on shaking Ivan Herald's hand had rattled her. She had managed to fake the starter, cutting up the smoked salmon into pieces and breaking the tiny triangles of toast apart so it looked as if she had eaten something, so she wouldn't draw attention or seem rude. Rosemary-scented red wine pooled around the lamb shank, the bone sticking up accusingly at Charlie. She wasn't going to be able to fake this. Her stomach lurched a little. What was this feeling? It was like a physical alarm going off.

Call Me Ivan was sitting at the head of the table and had been making light-hearted conversation with the two women on either side of him about a recent holiday to Positano. Other subjects included golf and, for extra tedium, cars. Charlie thought that the wine might help, but, as she reached forward, the wine, jewel-red, looked like blood, and so her glass remained full. She glanced around the table. She noticed that the other few women in the room were wearing similar gold and bronze coloured outfits. The blonde beside Call Me Ivan wore a stiff-looking silk number, the fabric artfully draped so that she resembled a Greek statue come to life. The woman beside her in a wider skirt, a vast bow at the neckline so she looked like a gift. The fabrics and the dresses and the whole chinkling-china formality poked at a memory. *Of wedding fabrics and a veil. Anna. Emz.* She looked away from the thoughts that crowded. Every plate held bones. The air was hot.

THE AIR on deck had a tang of diesel from the small cruiser just puttering past, but Charlie breathed in deep anyway. The tears she'd felt struggling to get out now drained back downwards, unshed, and she tried to get her heartbeat into an easier rhythm. It felt like some kind of folk dance was going on in her chest. The dress was stiff and uncomfortable, and Charlie was tempted to slip it off and slide down into the water, swim away, underneath the swing bridge to where the rock banked up beneath the Pineapple Inn.

"Are you alright?"

Charlie jumped. Call Me Ivan sounded genuinely concerned. "My apologies. I didn't mean to startle you." He took a sip from his whisky glass.

"No. No worries. I was miles away." Her brain was sending mixed messages to her face. Call Me Ivan watched a smile wrestle on her lips for a moment.

"I could have someone get you some water?" He stood a little way off, in the golden light of the wheelhouse doorway. The doormen had stepped back a discreet distance, one checking his phone.

"I'm fine. Thank you." The urge to jump overboard surged forward, and Charlie's foot kicked onto the bottom railing and rested there, just in case.

"I like to take care of my guests." Call Me Ivan smiled. "Is there anything I can get for you?" He took a step nearer, stepping out of the golden light into the harsher, white light of the nearby marina streetlamp. "Anything at all?"

"No. Thank you. I'm fine." Charlie lied as her heart abandoned its earlier folk dance and took up kickboxing. Call Me Ivan reached that gold-ringed hand towards her once more.

"Here, let me escort you back inside."

He took one more step towards her. Charlie pushed upwards, one hand shifting the skirt of that terrible dress a little higher to free her legs and step up, up onto The Ark's railings. There was a flapping sound from the sail of a dinghy moored opposite, the chinkling of lanyards and rings.

"Woman overboard!" The words hit the water just as Charlie did.

Murk. A muscular form that might have been an eel curved away from her with ease. Keels. Anchor lines. Debris of decades. The water cooled her, her heart stopped racing. With a kick, she bobbed to the surface and struck out in a bold stroke. She had no idea where she was going, but each splash that took her further from The Ark and Call Me Ivan felt better, lighter, stronger. She glanced around and saw where a small ladder climbed out of the water on the quiet side of the swing bridge. Several more strokes and she was there, suddenly heavy as she pulled herself clear of the water. The dress, dragged at by algae and shimmered with diesel glaze, hindered her every movement. She'd lost her shoes. She hoped not on the deck. Had she dived in with them on? She couldn't recall, it seemed so long ago.

She turned to pick a draggled reed from her neckline and fling it into the water. Glancing back, she saw where Call Me Ivan raised his glass in a toast before turning back to the wheelhouse.

3
BUMP IN THE NIGHT

The dream was vivid, almost more vivid than real life. The colours were turned up too high, the leaves were extra green. Emz's dreaming self understood there was meaning to this but, if she tried to translate it, the thought ran away from her into the wood beyond. She folded the idea into the pocket of her grandmother's raincoat for later inspection.

She twitched in her sleep, the raincoat creaking as she did so. The sound was in her dream, joining a chorus with the snapping of branches as she ran pell-mell through the wood. She was four-footed. What was that? Hoof. Flank. What was that? The extra green of the leaves fluttered with the extra gold of the sunlight. See, that was off, for a start. It was nighttime. She was asleep. Wasn't she? Her dream self moved back to the bed, to the folded crinkles of black that made up her Grandma Hettie's old raincoat. She just needed to push her arm through this sleeve.

She woke up before her hand broke free of the fold-back cuff. It was dark. There was a noise coming from the kitchen. A thud. Emz held her breath. There, again. She jumped up and headed through the door. Was it a Guest? A Visitor?

"What are you doing up?" Charlie was shutting the fridge

door. The bowl of risotto left over from suppertime had a fork stabbed into it, and Charlie was buttering some of Anna's spelt bread. It was the kind with pumpkin seeds in it. Anna had made it late that evening.

"I heard a noise," Emz confessed. "Cut me a slice." She nodded at the bread. Charlie took a bite of her own and sawed off another for Emz, pushing the butter dish towards her. "What are you doing?" Emz asked.

"I live here." Charlie was offended.

"We know that." Anna's voice came from the darkness, her physical self following after with a yawn as she too reached for the bread knife.

"I meant, what are you doing in the kitchen in the middle of the night?" Emz rephrased her question. Charlie gestured at the risotto.

"Er? Duh?" She pricked up a forkful. Anna moved the chair out from under the table.

"Why don't you sit down?" Her eyebrows rose a little. Charlie's gaze locked with hers. Anna was unrelenting.

"This isn't a stand-off." Her voice was low. "Sit down."

Charlie sniffed hard, the fork in her hand like a half-hearted weapon, and she did not sit. Anna took a spoon from the draining board and scooped up some of the risotto. Emz did the same, and they ate in silence.

"You look soaked. Is it raining?" Emz asked after several minutes, noting the draggled state of Charlie's hair and dress, the whiff of water.

"I went swimming." Charlie threw out the small fact.

"In Pike Lake?" Anna's eyebrows were once again rising upwards.

"In the marina, in Castlebury."

"In that dress?" Anna was staring at the gold brocaded dress.

Emz reached to feel the luxurious fabric. "Is that *your* dress? When did you get that?"

Charlie shrugged. "Aron bought it." She looked down at her food as Anna and Emz exchanged a look.

"Whereabouts in the marina were you? Near the big pontoons or…" Anna waved her hands a little as if conjuring up the marina.

"Does it matter? Is this TripAdvisor?" Charlie was gruff.

More risotto was consumed, the forks chinking against the side of the bowl and making a strange music.

"I swam to the Pineapple from the pontoon." Charlie's voice faltered.

"What were you doing? Has Aron bought in a boat?" Emz asked with a puzzled look. Anna looked at her with a wry smile.

"Aron buy a boat? He doesn't like the outdoors on dry land, never mind the water."

"Yeah, but one of those big boats is like his car, isn't it?" Emz reasoned. "You're in the technology, like a spaceship. I was thinking of a cruiser or something. Like a Mercedes on water. I didn't think he was bobbing about in a rowing boat or a three-masted schooner."

"I jumped off The Ark." Charlie slid the information in under Emz's chatter.

"For a dare?" Emz asked. Anna was quiet. Charlie's eyes brimmed over, and she wiped at them angrily. More fell into the silence between them. Charlie lobbed her fork into the sink and turned down the corridor.

"I'm going to bed." She turned towards the hallway, but Anna was quick to block her, her hand raised.

"No." Her voice was a stone, cold and hard enough to make Charlie pause and Emz hold her breath.

"I'm tired. I'm…" Charlie did not look up at her sisters.

"We needed you tonight." Anna was calm.

"I doubt that." Charlie took a step.

"We got lost."

"No, you didn't," Charlie sneered. "You're here. Snoring." She gestured up the corridor to Emz's room. Emz threw her own fork into the sink with a clang, her anger rising.

"You ever been to Day's Ride?" Emz glared.

"What?" Charlie was cornered, her face tight.

"Day's Ride. That's where we had to go tonight."

"Where we got lost," Anna chipped in.

"Did you get there?" Charlie challenged her.

"Eventually," Anna replied.

"Therefore, you didn't get lost." Charlie was on the defensive. "Bloody guilt-tripping me."

She made to go to her room, but Anna stepped forward again. "Guilt-tripping? What the…? What is going on with you?" Anna asked.

"Personal stuff." Charlie was giving nothing. Anna's temper lost its last thread.

"Are we not personal stuff? Is Havoc Wood not personal stuff? Do you not think you've got a responsibility to the wood?"

"There are three of us. We can do shifts. Tonight was your shift."

"We made a mistake once before. We don't need to do that again." Anna's voice was low and hard. "We need to patrol, we need to…"

"…escort Travellers to Day's Ride." Emz was peevish. Charlie rounded on her.

"*We need to escort Travellers to Day's Ride,*" she mimicked Emz's tone, adding a layer of whine to it. Emz and Anna were open-mouthed.

"What is wrong with you?" Emz's face was crimped into a frown.

"You can't be like this, Charlie. We need you here. We need the backup. You can't just…" Anna halted, her breath caught in her throat, her voice breaking.

"I can 'just' be however I want. I was out with Aron." Charlie's voice had cracks in it. She looked, with tired eyes, to each of her sisters, her gaze roaming back and forth as if waiting for a blow. Anna looked thin, too thin, and at the sight, something in Charlie broke.

"I'm scared." A dam of tears broke in her and, as her face crumpled up, so too did her sisters', Emz clapping her hand to her mouth too late to stop the words coming out.

"Me too."

"I'm scared too."

They spoke in unison, the words fading into a silence broken only by the sound of Charlie's sniffing and Emz's hiccupping sobs. Anna wiped soft tears from her face, ran her hands through her hair.

"The only way I can handle it..." Anna took in a relieved breath, "is to patrol. To go over the wood. Over and over the wood."

"I've been walking home by different routes, trying to cover all the ground. I can't cover it all," Emz confessed with a shake of her head. "It's too much."

"I've been running away." Charlie said. "It's like I'm scared of the dark. Of the trees."

Anna nodded. "I'm scared of my own shadow... in case it isn't my shadow." There was a tremor to her voice.

"I'm scared of who might come to the wood. Of *what* might come to the wood." Emz confessed. "The whole thing with Mrs Fyfe makes me feel that I don't know Havoc anymore."

There was silence for a few moments as the sisters pondered these confessions. It seemed an admission of defeat, but the mood in the cottage lifted.

"Do you think it was like this for Grandma Hettie?" Charlie asked. The sisters considered, Anna nodding.

"Yes. I think this is the job," she said. "Keeping watch in the wood, making sure what comes here doesn't get out. That's the job."

"A job we're not qualified for." Charlie's voice distorted with emotion. "Since Mrs Fyfe, since Apple Day. Since Halloween. I don't think I can do it. I'm *too scared.*"

"It's okay." Anna wiped at her eyes with the end of her sleeve. Her face eased out of relieved panic into calm.

"*No.* Don't do that." Charlie was shaking her head and waving her hand for extra emphasis. "It's not okay, because we don't know what might come out of the wood."

"But… you know… we did deal with her. It was frightening and mad, but we did it." Emz added, her arms folded tight so she could feel a little bit safer.

Charlie let out a scornful laugh, a harsh sound that seemed to shave at the exposed beam above them.

"She's got a point," Anna insisted, her arms folding in solidarity.

"I get that. Yes, alright, we did it. But it was terrifying and… I'm struggling with that."

Anna caught at Charlie's waving, negative hand and reached out for Emz who came to nest under her sister's arm.

"And that is okay." Anna put her finger on Charlie's mouth before it could open in protest. "No, Charlie. Listen to me. Listen." Charlie quieted at last, Emz hiccupped with her last sob. "It is okay, because now it's out in the open… we can be scared together."

4

OUT OF THE WOOD

Borrower awoke with a start from the dream. It was vivid and as iridescent as a starling in sunlight, the sound sharper. It had intensified in the last few weeks or so since Halloween. It had been a long time since Halloween had crackled with such strong, dark magic; it was reasonable, he supposed, that it still lingered in the air like smoke. He stretched in his roost in the elm tree and considered. What was odd about the dream? He often found himself in the minds of the animals when he and they were asleep. It was part of his bargain with the wood; more than that, a legacy from the line of his fathers.

He felt disgruntled. He enjoyed his rest, and this had put a ruffle in his usual mood. There had been something different about the dream. It mocked him from the boundaries of his mind, and then he saw it. The path the deer had followed — it had taken him out of Havoc Wood. In the dream, he had over-stepped the bounds of Havoc. Interesting. He dropped down from the tree, took a few steps to Frog Pond, and splashed his face with the water.

But, for the briefest instant, the reflection had not been his own. He shot to his feet, stepping back, stumbling against his favourite rock. His mind struggled to dredge the image from the dripping water. Brown hair, the same colour as his, but not his, longer. Different eyes looking back, green eyes.

He gathered his courage and leaned back over the still surface of Frog Pond. The face that looked back at him was the usual: slightly weatherworn but in a handsome, dashing fashion. He admired himself as his thoughts sifted over the green eyes of that other reflection. Did he know those eyes? He could spend time searching for them through his vast landscape of memory, but why bother? Next time he slept, he would be in the dream and he would find them.

5

PLANS AND OTHER NUISANCES

"Your boyfriend is here," Michael said without looking at her. These last few weeks, since the Apple Day events caused by Mrs Fyfe's ancient and magical slow poison, he had not looked at Charlie at all. He had, Charlie could see, been careful to bring a piece of paperwork to the brewhouse door, a practice that had become like a terrible white flag of surrender between them. She thought she might be upset by this turn in events but, in truth, Charlie was grateful.

She glanced beyond Michael's retreating figure and saw Aron, one man moving away from her, one moving towards her, and her heart squelched.

"You made a splash the other night," Aron grinned. She had not expected this. She had expected to be upbraided and have a fight, one she was looking forward to as a means of venting her fears and frustrations. She could yell and scream at Aron and pretend it was about stupid dinner dates. She took a breath.

"If you've come here to be pissed off at me…" she began, intent upon pursuing the fight. Instead of flaring up, Aron grinned his easiest, sexiest grin. Charlie was taken aback, shrank down inside herself, even more afraid, because she really did not seem able to interpret anything anymore. She was lost, wherever she was.

"Pissed off? Yes, that I missed you tipping off The Ark," he laughed, rich and throaty, his eyes flashing. "Seriously, Chaz, it was the prank of the decade."

"Prank?" There was a scent beginning to drift into the brew-house. It was unusual and it snagged at her. "It wasn't a prank. I needed to get out of there." The scent drifted deeper, and she traced it to Aron, something in his aftershave probably. He loved his extravagant aromas. He gave a sympathetic shrug, the smile stretched and deepened, and the eyes now had their old sparkle, winking at her from the memory of their secret kissing corner at school. A bike shed had been involved, of course. Later, after the bike shed was redeveloped, they shifted their lunchtime trysts to the curved sidewall of the new drama block. Charlie yanked her mind back into the present.

"Yeh. It was a bit intense. Not our usual stomping ground I grant you." He took a step or two towards her, his fingers reaching for a twist of hair that had worked loose from her ponytail. His fingers, light as they pushed it behind her ear, her skin shivering at his touch as it had always done. She couldn't help herself. She rushed him, folded herself into him, her face crushing into his neck, the curves of which seemed to fit her face exactly. His arms locked around her.

"Hey." His voice was soft, his lips moving against her ear. Aron, who knew her better than anyone in the world. "It's okay. Mr Herald wanted to meet you. He wants me in on a new business venture, and he needs to know I'm a safe pair of hands, that I've got a strong woman at my side. This business thing, it's about the future, and you're part of that future, Charlie." He clasped her tight; Charlie closed her eyes, not listening to the words, just feeling the sound of his voice vibrate through her. "Like I said, you made a splash. Extraordinary was the word he used."

Charlie was vaguely aware that there was a notion here that required attention.

"What? I didn't botch it all for you?"

Aron laughed and kissed her, his twinkling eyes casting downwards as he pulled away.

"You did not."

He didn't look at her again. He glanced back out of the doorway and gestured to his car.

"I thought we could maybe try again tonight? Head out for a quiet dinner. Something special. Just the two of us." His eyes focused on his fingers, which were reaching for her cheek, a soft stroke upwards. It reminded her of Anna's finger moving to her lips last night to hush her: *"It's okay"*, when it was very far from that. Charlie tamped down the sense of panic. Going out with Aron was the easy path, the escape route. The harsh scent wafted in again. It was metallic and a little bit chemical, and Charlie needed to get it out of her brewhouse.

"No. Sorry." She hadn't meant to sound harsh. It was something to do with the metallic scent, as if it was adjusting the acoustics of her voice. She could taste it as she spoke. Bitter-edged like frost. "I am really sorry," she tried again with no effect. The scent was tainting the tone of her voice. An alarm bell was ringing in a distant part of her head. What was this alarm? There was only one way to find out.

"I have Havoc Wood stuff on tonight." She expected his rancour, but he just nodded, leaned in to kiss her.

"I get it. I've said before. I totally get it. Family stuff is family stuff." His hand traced a tender line at her neck. "I sprung it on you. We can take a rain check." He kissed her again and began to move out. "I'll see you later."

"I'll text you," she promised.

But on the way back home, she switched her phone off and felt the layers of doubt and fear settle around her like a cloak.

6

FAMILY TRAITS

The flock of Canada geese had landed overnight and were dispersed across the field of winter barley.

"They've not done too much damage." Winn made the statement as she and Emz crossed the rutted field in company with Logan's mum, Etta Boyle.

"Yet," Etta said darkly. "They only landed in last night. Made a hell of a racket." They moved towards the clutch of geese. "Took a detour from your place?" Etta asked. Winn shrugged.

"We've had a couple of flocks in already. You could be right, though. This is a lovely spot though." Winn looked around at the wide expanse of field freckled with shoots of winter barley, the river running through it, another field beyond, and, at the edges, the orchards. Etta Boyle looked at her muddied Wellingtons.

"If you say so. We've never had them land before."

"Who knows, who knows?" Winn mused as she looked back towards the gate through which they'd come and assessed the ragged incline of it down to the river.

"So, Winn, can you take them?" Etta asked. "'Cause if you can't, Mike will be up here with Logan and the shotguns before the week's out, and he's even suggested having a shooting party at the weekend, charging folk for bagging themselves a Christmas goose."

Winn looked round with a nod. "Yes. I understand. They are the epitome of Wild and Free Range." She took in a huffing breath. "Right. Yes. We need to get the trailer nearer. Can we open that gate at the edge of the orchard?"

The gate was opened, and Winn manoeuvred down through the orchard. It was one thing organising the transport, it was quite another persuading the geese to accept the lift. Etta, Winn, and Emz herded and flocked and chased and, at the end of an hour, had precisely three geese in the trailer.

"I could do with a coffee," Etta sighed, as they watched the geese huddle at the river's edge. She took out her mobile and texted back to the farmhouse for refreshments.

"And a big net," Winn said.

The sky darkened with rain clouds and the air chilled further as the sound of the quad bike buzzed over the field towards them. Emz turned from their fruitless efforts at goose gathering to see Logan Boyle at the controls. He pulled up and took out a basket from the back of the quad bike. He was first to have his hand in it and take out a sausage roll.

"Consider that your tip," his mother said, as she handed out mugs and began to pour coffee from a flask.

"No luck then?" Logan smirked at his mum who pulled a face in return.

"Don't start, smart arse." She sipped more coffee and handed out a tin filled with sausage rolls.

"I said I should come and herd 'em." Logan was leisurely. "Dad's got the dogs, but I've got the quad bike, and it's the same principle." Logan looked at his mother and then, with a more polite expression of respect, at Winn. "What d'you reckon, Winn?"

The quad bike growled into action and, after ten minutes, had driven the geese further down the bank onto a patch of mud at the river's edge — some were on the water, none were moving off the farmland. There was an electricity in the air being generated by both the nervous geese and the encroaching storm.

"STOP, STOP, STOP!" Etta chased after the quad bike. "You're just churning up the bank… pack it in, pack it in." She flagged him down, frantic, and Logan tore up the farthest edge of the bank, the quad bike slithering a little in the clag of mud before it gripped and dragged over the rising ground to the edge of the field.

"Have to let Dad shoot them." Logan did not leave his seat. "We could do a Saturday shooting party. We'll be minted." His smirk was itching at Emz. *How might it feel to slap that face? Her palm stinging against his skin, his hand rising to snatch at her wrist and then…* as fantasy Logan turned to look right into her eyes, so the real and genuine Logan turned to look at her on the river bank. Emz felt heat flash through her.

"You could donate the cash to Prickles," Emz flared back, hearing the blade in her voice. Etta and Winn looked at her and then at Logan.

"We're not shooting anything just yet." Etta was conciliatory, and her phone began to ring out. Logan laughed.

"That'll be Dad." He turned meaningfully to Emz. "What do you stuff a goose with?" That smirk again, it was so pleased with itself. Emz turned to the geese. The wind was getting up, she could hear Etta's half of the conversation and hear the bullets in it from the farmhouse end. Logan started up the quad once more, the engine puttering and growling.

Emz turned to the geese. No. No one was shooting any geese, not on her watch. She saw them huddling together, their necks graceful, their heads lifted and watchful. Beyond them, the river whooshed. In less than an hour there would be rain. She could taste it in the air. She looked at the birds. Black. White. Brown. Buff and bronze and bark. Feathers layered. The weak light catching at odd edges and giving them a silvered edge. Wings, flapping, strong; feet, black and leathery, soft triangles of skin. Eyes. Jet beads. Look.

Look. Into the heart of them, where the beats fluttered and drummed. Into the heart of them. This way. This way. Emz walked, the mud of the bank no problem to her leathered goose feet. This, this, this hiss way, hoo, thisthisthisthisthis, here.

The geese began to move, their necks turning as if at a signal, towards the trailer. With a few flapped wings, they began to speed up, a waddling sea of goose, *thisthisthisthis way. Thisthisthis way.*

Winn jumped to open the trailer. The three geese inside were calm and wary as the leathery feet began padding towards them, the feathered bodies shuffling in and jostling together, *thisthisthis way.* No sound, no honking panic, a soft susurrating hiss like a whisper.

Emz shut the trailer up and realised she had not been breathing. She took in a deep breath now.

Etta Boyle regarded her for a moment. "Take after your gran then."

Winn cleared her throat and fussed with the keys as she headed to the Defender.

"Better get them gone." Winn climbed in and started the engine. Emz looked at Logan and then, with a frantic wave of her arms, rushed at him shouting "SHOO!" before turning to jump into the moving car.

In the wing mirror she saw Etta Boyle laughing, patting Logan on the shoulder. Logan, no longer looking so smirky, overtook them on the quad bike moments later, spurtling through the mud at the field's edge, away, to the farmhouse.

7

THE WAY HOME

"Do what?" Anna was part way through cooking their dinner, the pots and pans a clanging distraction from her thoughts. She had kept her eyes on the cooker, not glancing out of the windows at the twitch of any and every branch, her heart leaping into her mouth at what wildlife she might spot there.

"Show me Day's Ride." Charlie threw Emz's jacket at her, followed by her boots. She moved to switch off the oven, but Anna stopped her.

"Don't be daft. Leave it on and it'll be ready when we return." Anna wiped her hands on the tea cloth and headed into the scullery for her jacket.

They walked in silence. Havoc Wood itself seemed to hold its breath as they passed, the sound of their trudging feet an arrhythmic heartbeat. Anna and Emz took turns in leading this way and that, their feet sure as they navigated through the wood once more. They stuck with the route they had returned by, making quick time to the foot of ThinThrough so they were all breathing hard with the effort of the steep climb.

"Where is this?" Charlie was slightly freaked out by their

location. She knew her way around the wood, she was the Pathfinder after all, but this was off their usual track. She couldn't recall being here before, and yet there was a hint, a scent of the familiar. If she'd been here, it was long ago, a dusty childhood memory.

"Not much further... is it? Emz?" Anna looked to her youngest sister for confirmation. Emz was marching ahead.

"Here. Just here." Emz picked up the pace as they reached the line of trees that disguised the green lane of Day's Ride.

This time they did not break out of the trees onto the wide path; instead they felt the need to hang at the edge, each sister looking up and down the route. It appeared quiet.

"No traffic," Charlie said at last. She had been deep in thought, aware that her fear was like a zipped-up parka. It was giving her tunnel vision and making her unable to see the way through the wood. At the edge of Day's Ride, she felt something lift. It was written into her sister's faces. They had found this place once more, they had done this. The seemingly small and simple task carried a different momentum. There was some-thing about Day's Ride. She was afraid. Grandma Hettie had always said, *"You aren't brave if you aren't afraid."*

Charlie took a deep breath, shut her eyes, and let the fear she felt slide away. She stepped forward onto Day's Ride and opened her eyes. It was a green lane, like many others that ran through and around the wood, an ancient trackway, sheltered on both sides by trees that reached towards each other, making a tunnel of branches and leaves. Except that this one was broader, straighter, than any she had previously seen, stretching out into the distance in both directions.

The path glowed before her. The light it gave off was like seawater in sunlight, the fallen leaves and detritus of the wood making a golden surf. As she looked, she could see other path-ways branching off, but Day's Ride flowed onwards. There was a breeze, a scent carried to her of herbs, sorrel, and lemon balm, from this direction. She turned and inhaled the mousy scent of hemlock, the fust of foxglove. There was a lesson to be had, and she learned it.

"What is it?" Anna asked. Charlie stepped out of her Pathfinding thoughts and looked at her sisters. They wore anxious expressions and remained on the raised bank in the trees. Emz, she noted, had her hand on the bark of the nearest trunk.

"Different scents." She spoke in a calm and cool way because, for the first time in weeks, that was how she felt. "Lemon balm." She pointed in the first direction. "Hemlock." She pointed in the opposite.

"Useful," Anna nodded.

"Maybe we should take a look at what's growing where?" Emz suggested. "They might be markers." Emz stepped down onto Day's Ride, and at once Charlie saw where the light altered, darkened into starry night, a ribbon flowing from Emz's feet. Anna was swift to step down and Charlie watched. The light burned a burnished gold. She looked at her own feet. Dirt beneath.

"What is it?" Emz asked, looking down at her own feet. "Did I step in something?"

As she moved her feet Charlie saw the velvet-sparkled dark shift and quiver. Why was there only dirt beneath her own feet? Charlie let the cloak of fear slide back up again. She turned quickly.

"Nothing. This is the way back. The quick way." She hefted herself up onto the bank again and began to walk along a clear path down through the trees, her sisters following.

At Quinn's Gate, the rabbit twitched under the gaze of a predator. There were many predators in Havoc Wood, but not many wore a tweedy waistcoat, flecked with what looked like burning embers and sending out a scent that was woodsmoke tinged with honey. The rabbit understood that this villain was not someone she could hop away from into the brambles, but she had no other strategy. A hop, a leap, and she was done. But the brambles twisted and snared her because this creature *was* the brambles. Except that, with a breath, the thorns of him released her, and she bounced away like a shot fired from a catapult.

Borrower, looking up from the lost rabbit, sensed the edges of Havoc Wood tugging at him. Ordinarily, he would have cursed whoever disturbed his hunt, and he had been looking forward to the meal of the rabbit, but this feeling was not ordinary. It was something older than himself, yawning, stretching, becoming alive.

The paths he followed were his own, taking him down to the lake in moments. The lights were on in the Gamekeeper's cottage, so he gave it a wide berth, though his senses told him that the Gamekeepers were at large, out in the wild of the wood. He would keep himself one step ahead to avoid trouble.

He crackled inside with a new energy and wandered further from his bounds than he had in centuries. He understood that his feet were taking him, unbidden, towards the town. He had not visited Woodcastle in many hundreds of years, not since the last time. He brushed cobwebs from the memory. What had he done? His mind conjured the memory.

HETTIE WAY HAD BEEN GAMEKEEPER, the latest in the line, and Borrower was not ignorant of this fact. He had understood the vows and covenants on both sides. Long ago, the first of the Way women had helped his father, and, in gratitude, he had made a bargain with her. And here Borrower was, centuries later, still paying.

It was his heritage, though, and she ought not to begrudge

him, was his thought on the afternoon that the girl had wandered into Havoc Wood. He hesitated, for a hare's breath, when he picked up her scent at the lane's end. But what would his father say to such timidity? His father who had taught him to track such delicious strays?

When the Woodcastle women were lost, the panic made snare drums of their hearts. Such pleasing music drew him onwards. He had met her at the stile, offering his hand and the smile of a gentleman so that this little pretty would trust him. *Are you lost, dear heart? No matter, I will show you the way home.*

By the longest route, of course, and with stolen kisses, and when at last they had reached Banner Hill, he asked only a small tithe, a fingerbone, from the middle finger of her left hand, not a finger she would miss. The whistle he had fashioned from it blew a high piercing note, and at its call she must come to him. Each time. Running.

He saw her bare feet in the wood, the mud on her petticoats, the moon on her skin, and he might have drunk her tears till his thirst was slaked.

Until the evening when he had blown the note and it was no petticoat that snaggled in the brambles at the edge of his clearing. It was a black cape, weathered and proofed and cracking with doom, over the shoulders of Hettie Way.

He had never been so fleet as at that moment. He had launched himself up into the branches, borrowing the skill of flight from the crows, enough to take him footstep by footstep into the canopy where she could not follow. On and on he had raced, borrowing the speed of the weasel, heart in mouth, ahead of her, out further still, from Hackett to Hare's Ell and settling at last in the crook of the Old Elm to laugh at his lucky escape.

Later, he had been unwise enough to stroll up to Frog Pond to rinse the sweat of pursuit into the cool dark waters. The black cape, weathered and waxed against the elements, disguised her until it was too late, her hands in his hair, dredging him from the black depths to lie stranded, gasping on the stone as she cowed him with her magic, set Bounds about him so he could go so far, no further, in Havoc Wood.

He had tried to escape, here or there, but each instance he was dragged back by her binding spell, and Pike Lake spat him out onto the shore.

She had known his history, his lineage. She had honoured the bargain with his father. That was all that saved him. She had known, too, that they called him, amongst other names, Borrower.

It was known that the things he borrowed were never the same once returned. They were "turned", some said. He had turned them towards Havoc Wood, he had awakened desire and wanting. They were not grateful for his gift.

The young women of Woodcastle were made of sterner stuff than Borrower's own kind. They were flirty and fighty rather than tricksy and self-seeking. The females of Borrower's own tribes were like himself: too cunning, too conniving, eager to use him for their own ends.

The women of Woodcastle were odd and vital; muscles and hearts and breath, exotic and intriguing. The bones broke of course, along with the hearts and also those flickering lantern minds they possessed.

THE GAMEKEEPER HAD PUT a stop to it of course. He let his mind wander back. But what woman would not want to be his for all time? Cossetted in squirrel furs, her hair tied up with cobwebs?

Was that the message of the dream? That the Gamekeeper was dead, that the Bounds she had set him were broken? Or had Halloween set something else free? Was it time to go out into the world once more and borrow himself a wife?

· · ·

Borrower had taken the wrong route. He saw it as he approached the edge of the wood. The way was not open to him, and he understood why at once. This was not the path trodden by the fleeing deer. He paused, mulled over the dream. With a laugh of triumph, he turned in a different direction, towards High Foxes.

Already, he could see ahead to where the bounds of Havoc flickered. This way. That way. Stepping into the trees at Knoll it was a moment's work to emerge, elsewhere, within the stunted copse of birch trees whose ancestors had shaded the back of the Highwayman Inn for centuries. He was uncertain and, as a precaution, anchored himself to the furthest tree, his fist clenching around a branch, in case. Here, at the border, town met wood in a ragged bit of ground covered with something that looked, to Borrower's eyes, like black cinder toffee.

He stretched his other arm forward, felt his fingertips leave Havoc Wood. He was startled enough to dart back. He checked his hand. Nothing diminished. He could see where the boundary was thinned, not open, just the deer's path through. He stepped forward, the bounds bent and opened to him, and, with a wry grin, he stepped forward into Woodcastle.

He breathed in. The air made him cough a little and the music from within the inn was not the fiddle and drum he might have liked. It rattled the head, this sound. He inhaled once more and caught the scent he wanted.

Bridget Quinn had said she wanted a cigarette, but, in reality, she was going to do a runner. Outside, the air mixed with the bad wine she'd been drinking and made her head spin a little and not in a good way. God, Lyle was a boring gorm, and, after tonight, she was never answering a text from him again. About the only thing in his favour was that he had never sent her a dick pic and that, somehow, had seemed charming. Yawn. The phone chirruped as she held it, Lyle asking where she was and a kissy emoji. That was it. She was going home.

She could cut across the car park and into the allotments and be home in no time. She was not afraid in the winter dark. She liked this sneaky route beneath the trees, skirting the edges of town. It was frosty too tonight, everything sparkling in the soft light from her phone, even the tarmac of the car park. She cheered up, found she was humming a tune as she walked off the edge of the car park and under the trees. There was a stile here for the public footpath and she hopped over it, admiring her new boots with the chunky soles as she did so. Red boots. She was beginning to think that she'd found her style nirvana at last, and it involved red boots. Not that she could wear them for work, of course. In the Town Council admin department at the Moot Hall, she had to stick to 'appropriate dress'. Mr Wheeler getting his perv on with office chic. She grimaced to herself. What another tragic loser he was.

She was deep in the trees now, the branches still holding some leaves. There was the bare unkempt ground of Ditching Yard beyond and then, in the near distance, the edge of the allotments. The ground was hard underfoot, the glistening frost even making her breath seem like it twinkled in the velvet dark. Ha. Clearly, she'd had one glass of wine too many. No. What was that?

She halted. The air was twinkling, and she felt she must have drunk more than two glasses of rosé to make this effect. She took in a deep breath, and, as she did so, the man reached for her hand. He was smiling, she thought he was, it was hard to tell. There was a blur of face, of a tweedy looking waistcoat. His identity didn't worry her, it was the strength. She could barely move under his grip. She twisted, fighting, and then afraid and then remembering: she had her red boots on.

She kicked. Hard. Accurate. He vanished. She was shocked. As she turned, his arms were around her waist, like a suitor or dance partner but wrong, vice-like, overpowering. With all her strength, she lunged forward, away from him, her leg kicked out behind her. The chunky sole missed his leg, and he was pulling her back towards him, grinning with greediness, lifting her off her feet. *No.* She was not doing this. She kicked. She flailed. She punched. That connected. She felt his teeth slide behind the mashed lip, and the grip he had on her released instantly. Bridget fell back onto the ground, scrabbling to right herself before he might pounce. No. This was not going to happen. She kicked out once again, hard and certain. Her boot found nothing but cold air.

He had vanished.

8

THE SHADOW OF TREES

Vanessa Way recalled the day that she and her mother, Hettie, had rolled out the oldest of maps on the table at Cob Cottage. She could smell the smoky, fishy scent of the Cullen Skink simmering on her mother's ancient stove, in what could only be described as a cauldron.

Cream. Potatoes. Onion. Smoked haddock. A ladle of stock. Her mother chose fish that had been smoked naturally, supplied by her good friend Douglas from his small white van which drove into Woodcastle, Knightstone, and Castle Hill each Thursday, fresh from his brother's boat at the coast. The sea, Vanessa recalled, was only half an hour's drive from here.

Vanessa listened to the kettle boiling. Its blue light like starlight, cool to the eye. You could not see the coast from here, of course, too far away, and besides, Yarl Hill blocked the vista. You could, however, see all of Woodcastle and the greater part of Havoc Wood. Half-Built House, as Emz had christened her mother's new home, was placed at the edge.

Hettie had perused the map for a long time, her bright, brown eyes scanning every last legend and landmark upon it. Havoc Wood itself was marked out by deep green and ornate

41

copses of trees. The map was hand drawn, by a cartographer who had travelled a very long way to embark upon the task.

Unrolled, the parchment smelt of lanolin and oak gall, of burnt earth and charcoal. Beetles had bled for the red inks.

"Here, this shows the Bounds…" Hettie's finger traced over the document.

"The Bounds?" Vanessa's memory dinged distantly, she'd heard this word before.

"The edges and boundaries of Havoc." Hettie was focused on her task. "Where it frays and also where it is strongest."

"Who knows the Bounds?" Vanessa had asked.

"The oldest. The most rooted. The paths that tread out amongst the houses and gardens can only be trodden by the oldest."

"Is that a problem? Aren't the oldest disappearing?" Vanessa had a scientific thirst for empirical evidence. "Surely we can discount them."

Hettie looked at her daughter.

"The oldest are the worst, they are the best at surviving." Hettie had paused for dramatic effect and then resumed her quest across the map. She pointed a finger at last, let it rest on a lone bit of territory at the top end of town — it was bounded by trees at the rear and overlooked Woodcastle.

"Here. You'll be out of bounds here." She tapped at the map. "This is the best place. It's a blind spot."

"We could walk up there if you like?" Vanessa felt like making a peace offering after her churlish enquiries. "Check out the energy?"

She looked out of the window now. Her mother's shade, a darker piece with the winter night, stood with its back to her looking down into the town. The black waxed raincoat gave her the demeanour of a watchman. Vanessa did not blink, held her mother's ghost in her gaze until the kettle clicked off and the brief spell was broken.

She took her mug to the black lounger chair and sat on its edge. It was growing twilight and the sky was a beautiful gilded-pink in the setting sun. It had been a tough day again at the De Quincey Langport laboratory, and Vanessa needed to clear up her thoughts.

SHE WAS uncertain these days of what Far North had unleashed. On her return after the disaster at the Arctic research lab, a debriefing session had been followed by the offer of a job and funding for her PhD. She knew then that it was bribery, to keep her on side and silent. When the wreckage and debris were shipped back from the Tundra, however, questions were asked.

"You hold the answers," Dr Fell said, a greedy look in his eye. Vanessa worked hard not to give anything away. Each time, just when she was suspected of not cooperating fully, when Dr Fell's professional patience wore thin, she would vanish to Far North and everything would return to a default of grasping for knowledge. They wanted to know, they wanted everything, what did she discover this time? She let them have so little, only scraps to keep them at bay.

Nearly thirty years later, her own work had spawned the Dark Laboratory complex where small teams worked on eclectic and fantastical projects. Science melded with the supernatural, looked more closely at the paranormal, nothing was dismissed, nothing was out of bounds within Dark Lab. Vanessa worked hard to keep her secrets. She walked a line of misinformation.

Her mother had warned her, time and again.

"You are not in control of Far North, Vanessa. You can't find the way back, it finds you."

Her mother was right. Ever since Hettie's death something had skewed. Vanessa understood that all her efforts to conceal and hide were nothing. Far North could look after itself. It only told its secrets to those who owned them.

Sleep. Since her mother died it had come fitfully. She was so drained physically that one afternoon, in a lull as Rufus set up the baselines for their Shadow Matter experiment, Vanessa dozed off on the lab couch. When, an hour later, she woke up and was told of the power spikes and alterations in the magnetic field around the lab, of twitched electronics, she and the team pulled focus on her and her REM dream state. Sleep now was induced, under laboratory conditions. She had never been more tired or more exhilarated than today. She had begun to see that patterns were emerging within the data they gathered. Something was building, a storm possibly; the next few weeks would tell.

She sat in the perfect silence of the living room at Half-Built House and breathed deeply. It was a good place. The energy had been right from the moment that she and her mother had strolled up here. Hettie had been light of foot and mood at once, flitting around the space, her gnarly hands touching bark and branch of the thin line of trees before stepping out into the space beyond. They had looked out across Woodcastle together.

Vanessa's mind did not clear. Instead it ran over the dreams she'd had under the laboratory's strict conditions, the images prickling at her.

Dreams were gone when you awoke, but, for Vanessa, they were written into the scratchings of the encephalograph, and today, at the lab, they had resembled lightning on a distant horizon. Troubling.

It troubled Eleanor, her chief scientist. Late in the afternoon they had spent too long arguing, Eleanor unconvinced by the old technology. Surely the computers were more than enough, more accurate? Vanessa insisted that the skinny finger of the encephalograph, the roll of paper, made her feel more comfortable. "Think of it as my blanky," she'd said. "Something comforting that helps me sleep."

"Something's altered," Eleanor thought aloud. "Only I can't see what it is that's happening." And Vanessa had looked away, her eyes tracing over the jags and spurs of the readout.

There was no blind or curtain across the window at Half-Built House and, if Vanessa did not move, if she looked with the very farthest corner of her eye, she could see him in the shadow, watching her as he had always watched. Her sleep rolled her deeper and the snowflakes drifted, freckling at her out of the pewter-clouded sky. In the breaks here or there the aurora glimmered, now green, now sulphurous yellow. It was cold in the snow.

The wolf padded towards her, its breath on her cheek awoke her.

It took a moment for Vanessa to work out where she was. Home? Or the lab? Her neck cricked from her doze. She rolled her shoulder, kneaded her fingers into her nape. Home. She was home. Half-Built House. She looked down to where the wooden flooring shimmered and danced with the shadows from the trees. They were lacework, an intricate filigree of light and darkness.

Except that there were no trees outside the window, no sunlight to cast such shadows.

At once, Vanessa Way understood. Everything had altered. There was no time.

9

FOR WANT OF A RIDER

Charlie sat in her car for a few moments, aware that there were no lights on in Cob Cottage, which signified that Anna and Emz weren't yet home. Her phone buzzed in her pocket and, as had been her habit today, she ignored it. Charlie sniffed into the chilly November air and pushed her thoughts around, tried to bring forward the ones that concerned brewing and what she might forage from the fridge for her tea. She was hungry. At least her stomach had been growling at Drawbridge, and she'd thought of a big buttery baked potato and a scoop of Anna's homemade coleslaw and possibly a grate or three of cheese. Sitting in her car at the rear of Cob Cottage with the wood dark around her, it appeared that her stomach had changed its mind. It was churning rather than growling.

She pipped the horn with a sharp, determined gesture and, at its brief fanfare, stepped out of the car. She shut the door and took in a deep breath. The scents of Havoc rushed her: leaf litter and squirrel breath, boggy earth and wormwood. Her feet were attempting to rush her to the cottage, to head inside and shut the door, but she dragged them towards the garden and made herself walk around her territory. She began to feel more at ease; the scent of frosting grass beneath her feet reached like a small hand to hold her. She knew this place. This place was home.

The sudden waft of horse and leather almost made her sneeze. What? She sniffed, her nose making mousey twitches. Charlie almost tripped over the wheelbarrow as she rushed for Cob Cottage.

It was shadowy and dark inside, and she switched the light on and reached for the kettle. She did not take her coat off. She stood by the sink. Her breath was coming in short and shallow, and she concentrated on making herself take in better breaths. Slow. Deep. There you go, the sound of the kettle, the scent of water, coffee, the cure-all.

With her mug, she felt compelled to stand in the kitchen doorway. She was watching out. She understood that she was, of course, watching out for her sisters who were heading home, weren't they? She'd had that text and a missed call from Emz earlier. She checked her phone once more, sipped coffee, which could not mask the smell of horse and leather, a sound of bridle. Charlie held her breath. She didn't dare look up, not yet. Count to three maybe? After two she looked into the edges of Havoc Wood that stood just beyond the garden. Twilight had darkened into evening and the shadows huddled. Charlie let out a breath through her mouth and took a step away from the cottage door. The faintest chink of bridle. *There.* She took another step. *Another.* Within the treeline, a grey shadow shifted and with the movement came another heavier scent of horse and leather. A short rhythm of hooves and branches cracked, the ground pounded as the horse cleared the treeline and stumbled, uncertain, into the garden.

Charlie gasped. It was, without a doubt, the most beautiful horse she'd ever seen. It was strong and sturdy and tall, the grey hide was speckled with black and white, and a deeply grey mane draped across the powerful curve of its neck. It nickered and snorted, stumbling backwards, its head rearing as if to look at her and not liking what it saw. She had no experience of horses other than feeding an occasional apple to the trio who lived in the field at the foot of Two Hills Farm.

"Hey…" She kept her voice soft and low. "Hey…" She took a step and the horse stepped away from her with a desperate whinny. She looked at it, the wild rolling of its eye and the sweat that had gathered at its flank. It was uneasy, a hoof raising and stamping at the earth as the tail whisked. With a brief high nicker, it turned and disappeared back into the trees of Havoc Wood.

What she ought to do, Charlie understood only too well, was to follow it. She thought about this as she drew the bolt on the back door at Cob Cottage. She was breathing hard. What did she know about horses? Nothing. It was a beast. Powerful.

It bore a saddle but no rider.

Charlie Way was a Gamekeeper of Havoc Wood.

Shouldn't she be out there, following the horse? Finding the unseated Rider? Someone had fallen off their horse. They could be hurt.

Her fingers held onto the bolt, felt its cold iron. The inside of Cob Cottage creaked a little with, yes, Charlie heard it, disapproval. Her heart was running for Yarl Hill, beating so fast she could barely breathe.

The bolt slid back, the door pulled open. It appeared to be her fingers and hands doing the work. Charlie heard her footsteps chugging through the soft detritus underfoot. She was breathing in knife blades as she trudged towards the gap between the trees where the horse had gone.

Gone. No sign. She glanced down at the ground looking for hoofprints. The leaves were frosted, the air sparkled. Her breath clouded before her and she saw, through the fog of it, a glimmer of track. It flickered like lights in a power cut. Charlie took two, three steps and no further. In her mind, unbidden and instinctual, another path lit up, bright and clear.

She was rushing now, her breath fast-paced with exertion, the fear providing enough adrenalin to keep her moving forward. She knew where she was going and that something was happening. Something had come out of Havoc Wood and gone back in again. She strode on through the undergrowth. If her sisters wanted to look for her, then her trail was easy to pick up, and because she knew where she was going, it seemed reasonable that they might pick up on the same sign.

Day's Ride. A horse. A Ride. Charlie's boots bit into the soft ground as she made her way up the ridge, the bronzed bracken broken in her wake. In a matter of steps, she was at the edge of Day's Ride and at once slowed her pace. It was a magnificent horse, but, like all its brethren, it was easy to spook. It had come to find them, surely. It had come to lead them back to its lost rider? She took care.

At the edge, she paused, kept herself hidden in the trees as she looked up towards the lemon-balm scented direction of travel. In the near distance there was a movement, a shiver of mane and the drum of hooves. Charlie weaved in and out of the trees alongside Day's Ride. It was important, she knew, to keep out of sight and, more important still, not to tread upon Day's Ride itself. Instead, the pathway ran like a river beside her, the light travelling in the direction of the lost horse.

Eight hundred yards or so and she had made no ground on the animal. It remained tantalisingly out of reach. As the bells of St Brigid's began to toll out for midnight, the horse stepped out of sight into the darkness of the trees on the opposite side of Day's Ride.

Charlie took one step onto the path. It felt different from the night she had come here with Emz and Anna, and she was uneasy about taking the steps necessary to follow the horse further. She stared hard. The trees thickened and closed, the air sparkled with frost. Her gut yelled that it was the wrong thing to do, and Grandma Hettie had warned them all their lives to follow their gut.

Charlie turned back through the trees and, without thinking of her actions, took a different and much swifter route back to Cob Cottage.

IT WAS a measure of her own fears and misgivings about Havoc Wood that Anna had been driving to and from work in her old runabout. Before, the car had been parked along Keep Rows gathering leaves and occasionally rolling her out to the cash and carry at Castle Hill. Almost never had the battered and ancient little Peugeot ventured along the tarmac, gravel, and dirt drive of Cob Cottage.

As Anna left the Castle Inn, she noticed the left nearside tyre was looking a bit flat again, and so she stopped off at the garage on the way home to fill it with air.

It was a delaying tactic. Driving was a way of avoiding walking through Havoc, a commute that had previously been nothing short of lifesaving. After the loss of Calum and Ethan, Havoc Wood had been the only place she felt safe. One step over its boundaries had, if not eased the grief, at least shared the burden. Havoc Wood had taken her troubled mind over with its shadows and sunlight. It could still do that. She knew it in her heart. It was holding its breath, patient, waiting for the sisters to find it once again.

Not right now. Anna turned in at Old Castle Road, the bumping of the pocked tarmac surface lending her heart a heavy beat, which worsened as the balding tyres snaggled on the gravel and clunked into every pothole in the dirt.

Charlie's car was already parked at the side of the cottage. There were lights on and the door was wide open. As Anna rolled up, Charlie and Emz emerged from the kitchen.

"Hey," Anna managed a greeting. Clearly, they were as anxious to get their evening patrol over and done with as she was. "Ready for…"

"Something's kicking off." Charlie was forthright, her hands digging deep into her pockets, her jacket zipped up into the stand-up collar, which she hid inside.

"Kicking off?" Anna controlled the dread in her voice. Charlie lifted her head out of the collar.

"There's a horse," Charlie said. "Riderless."

"A horse?" Anna felt a small wave of relief. Not a werewolf then. Was a horse anything they should fear? No. Just a horse.

"Did you ring round? Ask Carrie or Winn? They'd know whose horse is whose. Did you find where it got in? Is there a break in the…" Anna asked.

"There's no break. It didn't get in. It came out," Charlie clarified, and Anna fell silent.

"It's riderless but saddled up," Emz said. "What do you think?"

Anna's mind whirled like a carousel. It was populated at the moment with unicorns and Pegasus. She took in a breath.

"Saddled. Okay."

"We're thinking that someone fell off?" Emz suggested.

Charlie nodded. "Seems logical."

"So… search and rescue patrol might be what we should do?" Anna felt easier. Search and rescue sounded doable, helping someone in trouble. Except, who might that someone be? Did anyone good come out of Havoc?

"This way then." Charlie was striding ahead, tramping through the undergrowth rather than choosing an older, more worn path.

Anna struggled to keep up. Emz was overtaking her, keen and focused. Anna was already having misgivings about the horse.

"Wait. What are you doing? Where are you going?"

"This is the quickest way."

"Quickest way? To where?"

"It headed to Day's Ride," Charlie yelled without looking back.

A stone settled in the pit of Anna's stomach, as cold and blue-black as the waters of Pike Lake.

SOME TIME LATER, the Way sisters paused on their side of Day's Ride. They caught their breath, pretending to be winded so that no one had to speak or, worse, be the first to take the step across.

"You feel it?" Charlie asked.

"The horse?" Anna said, not wanting to look directly at the other feeling.

"The block." Emz was open, observing the opposite side. "Where the trees are tangled. We can't go there."

Anna was not looking at the trees and the darkness, they were breathing at her.

"Anna?" Emz asked. Charlie looked at her.

"Yep. She feels it," Anna confessed and felt instantly better. Charlie grinned.

"Can't see the horse," Emz said, making exaggerated head movements as she peered forward and to the side.

"No," Charlie considered. "But this is where I followed it."

They all fell silent for several moments, the wind cracking the few leaves left on the late November trees, the bare branches rattling like bony fingers.

"You think it's a coincidence?" Anna asked.

"That we discover Day's Ride and then this horse wanders out of Havoc and heads up here?"

"It's not a coincidence," Emz stated the fact.

Anna rallied, the exertion and the company of her sisters gave her that.

"We have to take a look," she suggested, and, as if with one thought, they all stepped down onto the path of Day's Ride.

"Not sure about this." Emz shook her head, scowled at the opposite bank and its tangle of ivy and bramble. The thorns hooked into them, the ivy tangled at their feet.

"No," Charlie said.

"Back." Emz hopped.

"Stop," said Anna, her jacket ripping on a whiplash of bramble.

They retraced their few steps and stood looking at the impenetrable undergrowth.

"That's a definite no," Charlie sighed. "Loud and very clear."

Anna and Emz were silent.

"Let's move. Now." Charlie was edgy, her hands reaching for Anna's sleeve, tugging at Emz's black waxed raincoat. They hurried back across Day's Ride and slipped themselves between the trees of Havoc Wood, Charlie ahead, Anna breaking into a run so as not to be left behind.

"Wait. Stop." Emz paused to catch her breath when they had skidded and slid their way down the steep slope at the edge of Hackett. "Why are we running away?"

"Because we're scared," Charlie admitted.

"You saw the brambles, the thorns…" Anna's voice was rising to a screech. She pulled at Emz's raincoat; the black waxed fabric cracked and protested.

"Havoc Wood doesn't work against us," Emz insisted.

"Well, it stopped us following the horse…" The logic of this hit Charlie and Anna at once.

"It'll have a reason." Emz was sure. Charlie groaned.

"Oh God, it's bound to be something dark and dangerous." She rubbed her face as if freeing it from cobwebs of thought. "It's not going to be the Horse of the Year Show is it?" She groaned deeper, folding over at the waist so that Anna and Emz thought she might be sick. "We won't need a curry comb.

We'll need a pentagram and a rowan branch." She made several more groaning noises. Her sisters regarded her for a moment.

"We need to get over to the forge at Knightstone and get some horseshoes," Anna said with no apparent humour.

"What? To shoe the horse?" Charlie's face was crumpled.

"For protection," Emz reminded her. There was just a beat before they all burst into laughter. At the same time a breeze blew hard through the trees and the leaves clattered around them.

"Now I'm freaked out," Charlie said.

And in a tight knot of uneasy laughter and thudding, heavy footsteps, the sisters hurried back to the refuge of Cob Cottage.

ON THE WAY, they resumed their search and rescue, sticking close together as they roamed the patrol paths and checkpoints that had stood them in good stead during their visit from Mrs Fyfe in October.

"Not a sausage," Charlie declared as, drizzled by cold rain, they pushed open the door to Cob Cottage at last.

"You think whoever it is might be hiding?" Emz threw out the suggestion and Charlie gave a deep sigh.

"Yep. So I won't be sleeping tonight." She pulled off her boots.

"If they're hiding, they don't want to be found. Maybe they aren't injured, perhaps they're just passing through." Anna was trying to wring out all the positives.

"Like Mrs Fyfe was just passing through." Charlie stood up, moved out onto the porch, wiping a hand through her mizzle-soaked hair. Anna and Emz followed.

"We don't have to go round again?" Emz did not look enthu-siastic. "Do we?"

"Mrs Fyfe got in under the wire." Charlie looked out across

Pike Lake where it was pitted with the persistent rain. "We can't let that happen again."

Anna shook her head.

"Take my hand." She offered her hands eagerly.

"We're not seven, Anna." Charlie was over-tired and felt seven years old inside if she was being honest with herself.

"No. I know that. If we join hands, we can pool our resources, reach out."

Charlie looked half-persuaded, and Emz took her sister's hand, eagerly offering her own to Charlie.

"Come on…"

"What next?" Charlie took their hands with reluctance. "A bit of skipping?"

"Reach." Anna's voice was decisive. Charlie took in a sharp breath as their Strengths fused together with a hard rattle-like electricity. Charlie was going to close her eyes but stopped herself as the Wood blurred and halted, blurred and halted as if being shaken up.

"Reach." Anna sent out the request once more, and it was taken up by the wind. At once, three pinpoints of light lifted into the air above them.

"Reach." Anna's voice was low, stretching the word out, and the lights followed, glinting fireflies that ranged out in an expanding triangle. Charlie was reminded of radar pinging back signals. She focused on her own, bright and silver, showing up the paths and tracks through the wood, the map floodlit in her head, as clear as when she was little, and her Strength was free. The scents of the wood lifted towards her.

The paths were clear, only Day's Ride sent back an echo, as of something distant or lost.

Anna's mind flew over the treetops picking out breath. The traces of fox and badger, the distinct places where the horse had trodden, a small silvered track of swished mane and heavy breath.

Emz stared. Fox. Badger. Horse. Saddle. Ice. The horse's long face looking at her from Day's Ride, a whinny close to her ear.

And here. And over here.

"Frog Pond." Emz pulled her sisters towards the alteration, the green-weed glow that burst and then was lost. "Something definitely twitched at Frog Pond."

It was a matter of fifteen or twenty minutes before they reached Frog Pond and it was abandoned.

"Feel anything?" Charlie asked Emz. Emz shook her head, uncertain.

"What is it?" Anna pressed her, it was clear that Emz was ill at ease.

"Don't know." Emz looked about; the water drew her eye. The surface was cold and still and very dark.

"Bad? Good?" Anna did not push.

"Odd. Skewed." Emz felt off, as though she was looking out from somewhere else, watching them and afraid. At her neck, the pendant she'd made of the small silver shard Carrie had taken from the deer back in September felt cold. The leather thong it hung from felt warm. Emz was confused.

Charlie was impatient.

"Nothing specific?" She glanced around at the scene, the black rocks that bounded the pond, mossed to velvet, the bare trees overhanging, the tall rock face behind where, when the River Rade was in spate, water would cascade. Now, icicles were daggers drawn at its edge.

"No." She couldn't find the anomaly. The feeling intensified a little. "It's like… hide and seek… that feeling when someone is standing right over your hiding place."

The sisters listened. Charlie began to move around the space, kicking aside brush and stones. One rolled into the pond with a sonorous plop and the feeling vanished.

"Gone," Emz conceded. "But whatever or whoever fell off the horse is around here. Or was. We're on their trail."

"This could take all night," Charlie sighed. Anna noted the dark circles under her sister's eyes. Beside her she saw where a switch of the nearby rowan tree had snapped off and lay at her feet.

Anna reached for the stave of rowan.

"Nope. We can leave a marker." She stepped forward, stabbed the stave into a soft patch of mud pooling by the edge of the pond. "Whoever it is will know we are onto them."

With no further words, the sisters moved off down the path, Charlie choosing the quickest way for them, and none of them looking back.

10

THE REACH

The trees rattled like bones before Borrower understood what was coming. Ancient as an old friend, it clawed at his back, breathed on his neck so that he felt like prey. It was a three-cornered snare, a Reach unlike any that had searched through Havoc Wood in years.

It creaked with the weight of old magic, as he leapt and bound his way back to Frog Pond, borrowing, as he had of late, the particular fleeing run of the deer. Higher. Faster. Ahead of the Reach by only a footstep, slipping over the mossed stones of Frog Pond into the cold haven of its water.

Ice pricked around him for a moment, and he wondered if he was caught. No. A cracking whisper shuddered by him and down into the depths.

Three Gamekeepers, come to seek him out. He had chanced everything by stepping out of bounds and gained nothing save bruises. He recollected the pretty face and its bunched fist, the enticing, if vicious, red boots. If he survived this hunt, then might there not be further sport? Could he evade the wrath of three Gamekeepers?

He had witnessed their search of the clearing and the pond.

Were they looking for him? None plunged their hand into the water to drag him out by his hair as Hettie Way had once done. None summoned him out. His heart stopped its war cry.

It was clear that while they had the Reach, they had not identified their quarry. The Reach had been thrown out, a vast net, but he was not caught.

Still, he had watched as they left the stave as their marker, clear and true in its message.

He waited until after dawn before lifting himself clear of the water, sat dripping dry on the whetstone at the pond's darkest edge. The stave had already begun to scratch at him. He must find another way past it.

As morning rose, light filtering through the trees, Borrower looked upwards to the rock face. Ivy trailed in gnarly ropes and, by means of this and nicks and breaks in the rock, he lifted himself up and over the falls.

Change rustled at the boughs of Havoc. Hettie Way had toiled alone for years. She and Borrower's kin had occupied Havoc as the fox and badger did, each keeping to their chosen paths.

What had shifted?

The Fyfe woman, a rogue and vagabond with her poisoned apples. The Witch Ways had dealt with her in the oldest manner. Their stave circle had made the castle sing for the first time in centuries.

Something ragged tugged at his mind, but he could not snatch at the thread of it. He stood up, slicked back his hair, and gave a wry smile. He would wait until nightfall and then, once again, follow the deer for a game of his own choosing.

11

THE ICE KING'S RANSOM

THERE IS NO TIME

1991

The laboratory complex reminded Vanessa of a snowy landscape even in the height of summer, the white corridors drifting into white cubicles and, whiter still, the clean rooms.

The remains and remnants from the disaster at the De Quincey Langport Research Station in the Arctic, some four years before, had been transported back and resided, in the manner of museum artefacts, in Room 70C. Most of the Dark Lab complex was one level, mostly underground, hidden from observers on the rest of the science campus by bankings and tall grass. Black gates shut behind you, so thick and so densely matt black it was like vanishing behind some hidden corner of the night sky.

"In dealing with this incident, we've often used the 'needle and haystack' analogy." Dr Fell was not sitting in his chair. He was looking out of a window, one that offered a view of the bio lab where students in haz chem suits handled phials and flasks, a scene candlelit with Bunsen burners.

"Perhaps we can alter the analogy? This quest is rather like looking for a mammoth in a glacier." He laughed at his own humour. "You're no closer I take it?" His gaze towards Vanessa Way was severe. Vanessa wanted to take him to Far North and offer him up to the wolves.

"No."

"I do suspect that even if you took a stroll through the forest at Far North every day you probably wouldn't report it." He was sour. Vanessa stared him down. He would not be stared.

"Your child. How old is she now? Four? Five?"

Vanessa stilled, let her breathing shallow, thought of her last days in Far North, the ritual of the runes being inked into her neck, the pain and patience, the rhythm of the tapping.

"She is nothing to do with De Quincey Langport." Vanessa kept the shake from her voice.

"I disagree. It appears to me that the infant Alison is entirely its product." Dr Fell stepped behind the desk, still avoiding the chair. Vanessa did not correct Dr Fell's mistake about her daughter's name. A childhood in Havoc had taught her the importance of keeping your name safe. Dr Fell, pleased with himself and his logic, continued.

"If you had not been employed on this project then she would not exist," he smirked.

"You could say the same about Graham's new baby," Vanessa parried. Dr Fell snarled out a laugh.

"Graham's brat was conceived at an office Christmas party." He licked his lips. "He is not a biological specimen brought back directly from Far North in the incubator of his wife's womb."

Vanessa felt the ink beneath her skin, the tap tap of the hammer doing its work. Sweat. Woodsmoke. The skins she lay on as it was done.

"I could go public with what I know about the Arctic laboratory. I could tell the whole story of the disaster."

"They'd call you mad." Dr Fell's eyes glinted.

"A madwoman could make life very awkward for De Quincey Langport."

Dr Fell's eyes glinted once more, and he took in a deep satisfied breath.

"Health and safety is a precarious business at a research laboratory. On occasion, we have no idea what we are dealing with. Wouldn't you say?"

Vanessa continued to stare him down; her neckline burned with the old pain.

"You have eight weeks to find and open the portal to Far North. After that time, De Quincey Langport will lay its claim to the child as our rightful intellectual and biological property."

Vanessa nodded.

You can try, she thought as she left the room.

SHE WAS CURRENTLY HEADING up three projects related to the disaster in the Arctic lab that had resulted in Anna's birth. Only one team was a problem: the one with Christopher Bird at its head. He was, Vanessa knew, in league with Dr Fell to oust her. They wanted the keys to the archive. They wanted Anna's DNA.

The threat to Anna was a burr beneath Vanessa's skin. Something must be done. She made her way along the corridor to the archive.

There was no CCTV at this end of the building. This small security measure both protected De Quincey Langport and threatened enemies. The security cameras literally looked the other way. Any terrorist or industrial spy foolish enough to break in could be disposed of within five minutes of the crackling of a security guard's walkie talkie. It was a dark zone, a black hole of secrets.

There were rumours, for instance, about exactly what behemoth of a monster Dr Merchant had created in 109b. It had hatched, unexpectedly, out of some find or other. Vanessa did not ask questions so that her colleagues might extend her the same courtesy.

It was her duty to destroy the Arctic archive, and she was doing it one yellow contaminated sharps bin at a time. In only the last month, she had filled and disposed of almost a dozen, going through every scrap of paper, broken bottle, every last strand of wood or fibreglass, and nothing had connected to Far North. It was, she understood, something, a place, completely beyond.

The loss of the archive was her back up against the threats of Dr Fell. It was true, Anna was a relic of her journey there, but that did not give Dr Fell a licence to take her. Vanessa feared the consequences any such attempt might trigger. With Anna's ancestry, who knew what forces might be unleashed?

As she loaded up the latest sharps bin, Vanessa considered that what Dr Fell needed was a walk through Havoc Wood.

She recalled all the paths she had trodden through it, all the dives into Pike Lake she had risked to find the way back. Nothing had offered even a distant glimpse of Far North.

She put the bin on the facilities management trolley at the end of the hallway and, by a circuitous route, headed to her own laboratory.

It was a long day of anomalies and a paperchase of printouts from their latest electro-magnetic experimentation. Nothing affected the small compass that Vanessa carried; the needle was stationary, welded, it appeared, to its pivot point.

"You need a new compass," Alistair joked as they packed up for the day.

Nothing was ever left unlocked. They were careful with the most sensitive or important information so nothing found its way into Dr Fell's hands.

"I could take this home." Alistair patted the stack of paperwork, his calculations, Vanessa's proofs and theorems. Vanessa shook her head.

"No. I don't want to make you vulnerable," she insisted, and Alistair nodded.

VANESSA DROVE HOME, the car trundling into Woodcastle long past everyone else's bedtime. The castle itself loomed out of the summer night casting a cloak of shadow over her. She turned in at Petersham Street and saw the black car at once. It was parked, again, in what was assumed to be the shade of one of the cherry trees. Moonlight chinked off the front wing like a warning beacon.

Vanessa drove past the vehicle, turned out onto Wisheart Road and then by a process of right turns, she was brought out on the corner of Old Castle Road.

Tarmac. Gravel. Dirt. She saw her mother, three-year-old Anna at her hip, already waiting on the porch.

Hettie Way was not panicked, only angry at the threats and intrusion into her daughter's life.

"Dr Fell will learn the hard way," Hettie warned. Vanessa was uncertain of Dr Fell's power and influence.

"There's only so much Havoc Wood can do," she ventured, and Hettie laughed.

"I wasn't talking about the wood." She winked and helped Anna turn the page of her story book.

VANESSA SLEPT HEAVILY AND, as a consequence, was late setting off for the lab.

"Why didn't you wake me?" she moaned to her mother as she grabbed toast, and Hettie handed her bag and keys.

"You needed the sleep," Hettie reasoned.

Vanessa drove off. The wood burst with birdsong, the trilling terrors of the dawn chorus, except, as she listened, she felt the calls were altered, were not the wild chorus of territorial claims, instead they held alarm, a warning.

She was part way along Old Castle Road when the first snowflake fell. It lodged behind the windscreen wiper, a flake as big as her hand revealing a maze-like, and arresting, crystallisation. She held her breath, not just because it was August, but because she felt the compass in her pocket begin to spin.

Another flake fell, others drifted behind. The filigree patterns of light speckled the interior of the car as her breath steamed in front of her. The light whited out. She reached for the door.

She stepped onto the creaking ice of the lake. Above her, the aurora glimmered in green shutters across the sky as, across the lake, the wolf waited.

THE CAR WAS FOUND, and questions were asked by some of the more serious news outlets. De Quincey Langport was not a liked or lauded company, and the media leapt at the chance to pick over the mysterious disaster at their Arctic lab some four years previously. It was only twenty-four hours, however, before the small-town scientist's disappearance was superseded by shenanigans in Parliament, by fire and flood and inflation rates.

Hettie Way hunkered down in Havoc Wood with her grand-daughter. They ranged miles in a day, Hettie hoisting Anna onto her back when she grew tired, held there with the shawl she had used to cart her own daughter with her on Havoc business.

She heard the black cars before she saw them. Gears ground, bodywork was scraped and pranged, and so, Hettie reasoned, the passengers ought to realise that Havoc was making them unwelcome.

Hettie and Anna stood on the porch. Dr Fell and his hired

help on the shoreline of Pike Lake below, three men in black suits looking incongruous in the woodland setting.

"Hand over our property." He gestured to Anna whose hand squeezed tighter around her grandmother's.

"Get off my property," Hettie ordered. She was, she thought, very polite in the circumstances.

"I have a very low tolerance for this kind of resistance." Dr Fell forced his face to look world-weary, but Hettie glimpsed the small beads of sweaty desperation at his temple.

"You've still time to get away." The threat in Hettie Way's voice was small but deadly as a stiletto.

"Take the child," Dr Fell instructed to his nearest companion. The man he addressed took in a surprised breath.

"Take her," Dr Fell commanded, and the man jumped to it, rushing towards the porch.

Anna stepped forward; her small face looked stark enough to halt the assailant. She let go of Hettie's hand, tipped her head back, and howled. It was a primal sound, stopping the other suits in their tracks.

"There's still time to run," Hettie warned.

"For pity's sak..." Dr Fell strode towards Anna, shouldering his confederates aside.

This time, the howl did not come from Anna. It came with the wolves, from out of the trees.

"Too late," said Hettie Way.

It was spring when the snowflakes fell on Hettie Way as she and Anna made their way down from Ridge Hill. It fell, the first, like a lace doily, and at once Hettie packed up their picnic and they began hurrying homewards.

By the time they had hurried back to Cob Cottage, the sky was grey and heavy, the lake freezing over in front of them. The ice creaked and groaned, and Vanessa, heavy with child, walked across its snow-white surface, coming home.

A FEW WEEKS LATER, Hettie was once more the midwife, as Vanessa gave birth on the shore of Pike Lake.

A girl. Kicking and screaming, and named Charlotte.

12
DEER

Logan Boyle had borrowed his brother's car for their date.

"Are you joking me?" Caitlin snarled when he rolled up in it.

"You getting in?" He leaned across to open the door. Already the evening seemed doomed.

"Did someone shit on this seat?" Caitlin pointed to the brownish stain on the passenger seat, her face as pointed as her finger.

"No," Logan lied. His mother's old dog, Ninja, had crapped there on his last visit to the vet. Logan thought of the body in the blanket in the boot on the way home, his mother crying all the way, and the spades of earth he'd dug in the yard.

Christ, this date was not going well. His brother's car wheezed a bit on the hills, but it would get them to the party at Knightstone.

She'd come to the party with him, and then she'd pretty much ditched him, so Logan recognised that he was basically Caitlin's Uber driver. While others might see them as "together", Caitlin did not. He could see himself slipping in the boyfriend rankings. He was suitable for school purposes whereas, here in

Knightstone, it was Adam and Oliver who were the focus of her lust.

Logan sat and drank his beer slowly as the music throbbed around him, and he saw where Caitlin and the rich lads were definitely on for a threesome. He felt jealous and uncomfortable, and was reminded of Emz Way, his mind flashing up the white image of her face that night at that other terrible party in September, when she'd been sent out to the summerhouse at Tasha's place to catch him at it with Caitlin. He winced at the thought.

This was a bad idea. All of it. Everything he'd ever done with Caitlin was a worse idea, but he couldn't stop himself when she lit him up with desire.

The beer was sour, and he felt a bit sick as he glimpsed Caitlin. Yep. He was going to be sick.

Puking did not make him feel better. He sat on the floor of the bathroom wiping his mouth and thinking of Emz wrangling the geese. He saw her expression of concentration and confusion in Maths. He saw something there and it frightened him, it made his heart creak.

With Caitlin, nothing mattered, it was nothing, like a cheap chocolate bar you scoffed down. He pushed his way through the party into the conservatory.

"I'm going," he announced. Caitlin cast him a smug glance. Adam or Oliver, he couldn't remember or care which smug rich git this one was, was filling shot glasses with tequila.

"I'm not." She was dangerous. Logan saw she was cruel and wild.

"G'night then." He gave a dismissive wave.

"Logan." Her voice was commanding. He halted.

"Bye," he said. He could still taste the vomit in his mouth.

"Logan, what is going on with you?" She stood up, squeezed from her seat between Adam and Oliver.

"I'm going." He didn't engage with her.

"How am I getting home if you go?" She was put out. "This is shitty. Stop being shitty."

"Bye." The keys rattled in his hand as he moved away.

She was pissed off at him, and he didn't care, not looking at her as she chased him up the driveway spitting abuse. He didn't open the door as she tugged at the handle.

"I thought you were staying?" His voice sounded harsh, but he was shaking inside. She banged a hand at the window, and he reached to unlock the door. She got in with a curse and they drove off.

"What was that? How dare you talk to me like..." Her yapping voice disappeared if he just wound down the window, and he could hear the night whipping by. After this, after tonight, he was never going near Caitlin again. Never.

When the car broke down at the edge of Leap Wood, Logan thought it was the only way the evening could have ended. His phone was dead.

"You are such a fucking loser," she growled and walked off towards town. He watched until she crossed the road and began the long trek to the bus stop.

13

DREAMLIKE

Racing, Emz's heart fast as the deer's own heart, the land a blur but Havoc Wood still.

Wild fright filled her deer heart, but her human heart thrilled at the movement. Looking out through the doe's brown eye, she saw Havoc as another realm. The green so sappy, the bark scent, the forest floor beneath her hooves, and the leaping, bounding escape of it.

She was not alone. Breath caught in her throat at the thought, and she woke up. Emz had rolled out of the duvet and was cold, but she felt too rattled to lie back down in bed. Instead, she pulled on her sweatshirt and her socks and padded down the hallway to the kitchen.

For once, no one was here, and she was glad of the quiet dark. She didn't turn on the light as she ran the tap for a glass of water.

Anna was asleep after a long day catering a conference at the Castle Inn. To make certain, Emz wandered up to her door. She could hear her sister's gentle snoring, a sound like a cat purring. Charlie had had a text from Aron and gone out to meet him.

Her door stood open, and it was unlikely she would return tonight.

Things had felt better this morning. They'd all three been in better spirits and then the day had worn down and they'd all returned, tired and anxious once more. Perhaps that anxiety was what fuelled the deer dream. Emz sat in the spoonback armchair by the window and pulled her legs up under her. She contemplated the surface of Pike Lake for several minutes, trying to settle so she could properly consider the dream.

The trouble with dreams was that they vanished quickly. She held to the edges of this one. The deer, like before, racing through Havoc Wood. It was definitely Havoc Wood. She scratched through the ragged remnants of the dream; could she remember where in Havoc it had been? The pendant around her neck was cool against her skin. She reached to touch it. She'd worn it lately as a talisman. As she lifted the piece to take a closer look, it flashed like moonlight. Just once. She turned it. The moonlit effect did not repeat itself and she let the pendant drop. Was she even awake?

There was a message in the dream, she felt certain, but she was distracted by the physicality of the deer. She took a few deep breaths to stop being annoyed at herself. If she let her mind drift it might wander back to the dream. Or a better plan would be to go back to sleep, find the dream that way. That was the most difficult plan. She was wide awake.

She sat in the dark for a long time and listened. In the distance, a car on Castle Hill Road, nearby, the lapping of the edge of the water, in between the trees whispered with the night breeze and then fell silent.

Emily Way asked herself a simple question. *Am I afraid?* She was surprised at the answer.

. . .

THE MARINA WAS VERY quiet by the time Charlie arrived. The bars on the opposite side of the harbour were closing up and people were moving further into the city to nightclubs. Charlie had parked down by the river and walked up. Aron texting her to come to the Marina had been an easy exit strategy, a way to run away from the fresh fear that had settled over her as she returned to Havoc after work.

She called him. Her phone pressed to her ear listening hard to the ringing tone as if it was sonar detecting his presence. The voicemail message clicked in for the third time.

No matter. She was here. The second floor had recently become something of a jungle of tropical plants as the new owner of the flat there put out pot after pot of palm and fern. On sunny days the atrium was a scorching heat sink. This evening, as Charlie took the stairs two at a time, she noted that the plants lent a sharp green dampness to the usually arid air of the entryway. It reminded her of Havoc, as if the wood was reaching out to her. She hurried on upwards to the third floor and then onto the fourth.

It was quiet and dark. The frosted glass panel in the side of the doorway was dark, but Charlie checked her watch. It was not impossible that Aron had gone to bed. After all, he was working tomorrow. Still, having asked her here, he might have waited. He knew she didn't have a key. Charlie rang the bell.

There was no movement from within. No light switched on. The bell echoed out once again, Charlie able to hear how empty it sounded. She had no key. For several weeks he had promised to have one cut, and he had not got around to it. She checked under the mat and found nothing, not even dust thanks to the maintenance charges that provided a cleaner for the communal areas. There was nowhere else to hide the key. There was no letterbox. That was in the entrance lobby on the ground floor. Ha. Idea.

Aron's post box was locked, and she did not have a key to

that either. A cursory rummage through the flap seemed to suggest it was empty both of post and of spare keys on strings. Charlie tried Aron's phone once more. And again. Was this a prank for blowing him off the other night on Havoc business?

She was more upset than she had thought. The tears were hot on her face in the chill November night, and, when she was back in her car, she had to take a minute to gather her thoughts and settle herself before turning the ignition. She watched the river roar by for a few minutes, and, still feeling rattled, she got out of the car and stood by the rails.

The river was rushing, the air was sparkled with water, and the sound was like taking a deep breath after running. It reached up to Charlie and the breeze ruffled her hair. She took in several deep breaths. Above her, the sky was starred and inky. She felt lost.

Driving home, she opened the windows wide and let the scents blow into her. Her mind cleared as she inhaled the bitter scents of fuel and heating clouding the city. The cold damp of the river, here, where it rusted the edges of the bridge. The bitter crush of leaves, the frost biting into the earth. Soap powder at Portobello House on the main Castle Hill Road; Woodcastle, the farthest, rawest edge a brew of lichen and damp stone, jackdaw's breath, blood, dirt, bone, fur.

The deer sprang out into the road from the edge of Leap Woods. It was a creature in flight, Charlie's foot braking before her eyes registered hooves and flanks. It landed and she was afraid she had hit it but no, as she jumped out of the car, it turned to glance back as if aware of her. They locked eyes for a moment before, with ballerina leaps, the deer took off across the road, dodging over the boundary wall that marked the northern edge of the Hartfield estate.

Charlie took a few steps in pointless pursuit. All that remained of the encounter was the scent, the pungent animal musk and a smoky, honeyed drift beneath. Charlie stopped.

Woodsmoke. Honey. It called to mind the vanquished warrior that Ailith had brought to Havoc to be Bone Rested. That was the scent he carried, one of old magic.

For a moment Charlie was afraid, a thick, choking fear that made the sky darken despite the stars. She heard the soft, strangled noise escape from her mouth, and it jolted her.

She did not get back into the car. She crossed the road, looked at the leaves and loam by the wall, taking several moments, trying to push the fear to one side, before she saw the tracks. She hesitated, heart pounding; there was no way of not being afraid, she understood that. She leaned down and picked up the dirt that held one hoofprint.

At first the fear clawed at everything, then Charlie shifted her mind to the grains of dirt, the feel of them against her skin. She crushed her hand tighter and the leaf litter she held crumbled and gave up its scent, breathed into her.

At once, she saw the path, not simply where the deer had run, but also, glancing back, where it had come from. The trail was a thin, velvet-dark line, glittered through with stars. Charlie held her breath. Where had she seen that before? At Day's Ride, when Emz had stepped down. What did that mean? Just a link to Havoc? The deer was a Havoc deer, the velvet-dark trail its marker, perhaps. At last, she let the handful of dirt drift and the trail winked out.

Charlie sat in the car for several moments until she stopped shaking; the key glinted in the darkness. She would start the engine and she would drive off, back home, but nothing would be the same. She was shedding an old skin. Something new was emerging, or was it, rather, something old, a forgotten, mislaid part of herself, returning.

Charlie put her keys in the bowl by the back door and did not switch on the light. Through the window, she could see Emz wrapped in a blanket and sitting on the porch. The kettle was pinging with recent heat.

"You're up early," Charlie said as the church clock chimed three in the distance.

"Kettle's boiled if you want a coffee." Emz lifted her mug.

"I'm ahead of you," Charlie said, lifting her own mug. "Let's have a toast… to early mornings." They chinked, and Charlie sat down beside Emz.

"You didn't stay at Aron's then?"

Charlie shook her head. She had, in the encounter with the deer, forgotten the mystery of the missing Aron. She avoided the topic.

"Why are you up so late? Bad dreams?" Charlie joked and then, from the expression on Emz's face, wished she hadn't.

"Odd dreams," Emz confessed. "I dreamt I was a deer."

Charlie spluttered out a fountain of coffee.

14

THE HEART MURMURS

With a gasp of air, Vanessa sat bolt upright, moving with such speed that the sensors that had been stuck to her temple and her heart popped aside. In the galley beyond, she could see a wave of panic wash over her assistants. Eleanor, grey-faced as Eleanor should not be, was through the airlock door and at her side in a whiplash of movement.

"Professor Way?" Her hand, cold and small, gripped Vanessa's hand that was, Eleanor made a mental note at once, ice cold. "Professor Way, are you with us?" Eleanor was already making facial signals to the meds team, and trolleys and heat sheets were being mobilised. "Professor Way, can you hear me?"

"Yes. Of course." Vanessa took in another breath, an easier one, and she felt her heart rate cease its gallop.

Across the ice.

Eleanor was tapping at her tablet with nimble fingers, her eyes darting across the information.

"Recording," she stated. "Time stat comparison." Beyond the glass Vanessa could see Rufus with his ginger beard tapping at the mainframe computer. Beyond them all, the doors were locked on other Dark Lab projects, unregistered. Further away on the campus, even more scientists and research assistants busied themselves with black holes and graphene. There was a team in the outer greenhouses breeding better bees. Vanessa Way's heart skidded a little.

Across the ice.

It was enough to make Eleanor's heart shudder in sympathy, her keen eyes watching her mentor. Putting the tablet aside, she reached for a light and looked into Vanessa's eyes.

"Dilation."

"What are you doing?" Vanessa asked in a soft voice. She felt surreally calm amidst all the tension. Everyone else's sinews seemed to be twanging so that they were giving off a kind of music like a mental string quartet. It was, Vanessa thought, rather pleasing to the ear. She could almost hum the tune, if she just adjusted that note, there. She was humming, the sound within her matching the sound that emanated from them, so that the room felt like she was an orchestra, it was enervating, energising. Vanessa gave a peal of laughter.

"That just headed off the scale." Rufus's voice cut through on the intercom as the medical trolley was held at bay behind the locked lab door. "Am I opening up the vestibule yet?"

"That's a negatory." It was Eleanor's favourite phrase, something she had picked up from her love of science-fiction cinema. It was humour and she used it, as a general rule, to attempt to hide the fact that she was, at this point in time, afraid and anxious. She tapped some more at the tablet's screen. Vanessa saw waves of black lines, like the steepest mountain peaks you might ever see.

"You'd better still be logging, Rufus." Eleanor had her finger on Vanessa's wrist pulse point and was hurrying to retrieve the sensor and its small rubber sticker. She was counting to herself and attaching it to Vanessa's skin. "Okay. Are we back online?"

"Yep." Rufus was tapping at the computer once again. In the distance was the sound of a soft drum. Vanessa began to hum once again, the sound of her colleagues, breathing it in, vibrating it out.

"Rufus." Eleanor reached to her shoulders to pull up her headphones. Outside in the galley, her colleagues were doing the same.

"What do we do?" Rufus asked. The meds team were getting antsy, shifting their stance and staring in through the window as they adjusted their headsets. There was much shaking of heads, and Rufus was waving them out of the main door. Leaving. Vanessa's hum was warming, like fire.

Firelight. Burning bright. Across the ice.

She felt sleepy and the soft drum began to have a syncopated beat. Somewhere, a horn sounded.

Across the ice. Whiteout.

EACH SLEEP SEQUENCE had been more erratic. Today, it had resulted in an adrenalin shot and, Vanessa could see, Eleanor was still grey-faced from the experience.

"Let's not talk about that," Eleanor decided. Rufus spluttered his coffee.

"Not if we want to keep our jobs." He was finding it difficult to look at Vanessa who was now seated in the galley at the table, everyone's tablet tuned in and the data scrolling before them.

"Can you recall anything from the dream?" Eleanor asked. "It might help."

Vanessa took a deep breath.

"This…" she tapped at the tablet, brought up the heart rate, "this was a drum, the rhythm of it. This was a drum and this…" another tap, the graph of her breathing, "the wind. A particular whistling sound through the ice. And this…" she swiped up the digital encephalograph data, "this correlates to the way the aurora was shifting above me in the dream." She stared at it, her eye seeking every last point on the graph.

"Almost exactly, small margin of error here and there, nothing more."

"This is new, but it is a pattern. Let me show you…" Eleanor was collating all the bio information from Vanessa in their recent sleep studies. "The physical effects from the dream state have begun to shown a marked increase. This…" she tapped and scrolled and tapped some more and brought up old information for her comparison. "This is where we were back in June. As against where we are now." She aligned the two sets of data. "There are just two other points in the records where the phasing veers out and takes on a new wavelength. Both those occurrences are several years ago. The most recent was…" Eleanor tapped and scrolled at the page.

"Nineteen years ago," Vanessa spoke softly. She took in a deep breath and continued. "The previous one; twenty-six years ago."

Eleanor stopped scrolling and looked directly at Vanessa, who managed a smile.

"Go on with what you were saying," Vanessa encouraged. Eleanor stared at Vanessa for a moment or two longer. "You'll forget your train of thought, El." Vanessa smiled again. Her assistant hesitated.

"It isn't just the alteration in the wavelength. There's a time issue. If you look at the timecode, it's as if you're not in it. This is too slow. This too fast."

"As if I'm slipping between," Vanessa said.

Eleanor stopped tapping at her tablet.

"This new phase began in July. It might be unscientific to point out that it was just after your mother died."

Vanessa nodded and kept nodding.

"Do you need a moment?" Eleanor asked. "I could fetch us some tea." Vanessa was about to refuse the offer, to concentrate upon the task at hand, but then she thought of her mother, of sitting on the porch at Cob Cottage with a pot of tea, and she nodded to Eleanor.

"Tea would be very good."

RUFUS CLOCKED off before Eleanor returned with the tea, and so Vanessa was alone in the lab, sitting at the table which, once upon a time, would have been loaded with paper and printouts. Now, everything was kept online, ethereal knowledge held in the memory of a computer. Vanessa was the only one who insisted on the paper encephalograph as back up. The machine, cranky as it now was, had come with her through all her years at De Quincey, and she was not about to part with it. She trusted its records more than any. She glanced now at where the sensor arm was halted, but ready.

The lab was very quiet except for the sound of the branches tapping at the window, a thin musical noise that caught in Vanessa's head. She tapped vaguely at the screen of her tablet, her fingers drawn to smooth over the intricate lacework of the patterns and shadows on the screen. It was so beautiful as it trailed over the desk in crisp white patches and down onto the floor so that, if you breathed in deeply, you were in the branches of a tree and above you, Vanessa looked up, the aurora was a ribbon across the sky.

Strip lighting. Ceiling. There was no aurora. This was electricity, cold and white and clear. Vanessa felt her heart rushing like water and her hand, paused over the screen, was shaking.

"THIS," Eleanor tapped at the screen, "is another anomaly." She did not look at Vanessa, only at the screen. "It's similar to what we saw the other day. The only way I can think to describe it is…" Eleanor's lips pinched together for a thought, "it's like a heart murmur."

"Murmur?" Vanessa liked the sound of the word. In her head a breeze blew through leaves. *Murmur.*

"This is your heartbeat and then alongside or behind it, every now and again, there is this other sound, like…" she paused, searching her mind for a way to explain, "well. A murmur, another heartbeat, an extra sound, extra activity. The only way I can get a grip on it is to suggest a heart murmur."

"Okay." Vanessa had no words to offer the troubled young woman.

"That doesn't explain it. It's not medically correct, and it's too simple for what this is. Only I don't know what this is." Eleanor's voice cracked. "Harmony perhaps. Counterpoint." Eleanor shrugged, edgy.

"That's a good analogy." Vanessa smiled. There was a moment, Eleanor gathering herself. "You look worried."

"I want to help," said Eleanor, serious.

"You have. Always." Vanessa reached for her tea.

"I asked before, what is happening, and your response was…"

"Interesting things."

Eleanor nodded and they exchanged a look. She pursued it.

"You know what is happening don't you? You know what all of this means?"

Vanessa gave a single, simple nod. The young woman waited for more, but it did not come. Vanessa sipped more tea to give herself a moment to consider everything. She had chosen this young woman for specific reasons. All her team had been hand-picked, not employed by any agency or drawn from the pool of students and scientists that De Quincey Langport kept on retainers, turning their hand to anything and everything.

"You have seniority here," Vanessa said. "I've arranged matters with Senior Management so that, should the need arise, you can take full control here. Beyond this project…"

"Beyond it?" Eleanor's grey colouring paled further to a ghostly marble white. "You're ending the project?"

Vanessa held her gaze.

"You asked me what is happening." Vanessa paused. From the corner of her eye, she could see the branching shadows dancing on the white lab flooring. "Plans must be made." Her voice failed her, and her facial muscles could no longer contain their emotion. She struggled for a moment to master herself.

"You mean contingency plans?" Eleanor's face was as white as the snow of Far North. Vanessa reached for her hand.

"Yes. De Quincey are not kind. I want to make certain that your future is assured. Beyond this project, I have recommended that you be allotted your own Dark Laboratory research project. Your dissertation on Dark Light has caught their interest, but the final choice will be yours. Everything that you have learned here you will take with you."

Eleanor stopped breathing, her eyes widened. She nodded, once.

"You've got a meeting with Professor Harcourt on Thursday at 2:00." Vanessa tapped at Eleanor's tablet screen, scrolled through the calendar to the date just so that the two of them would have something to look at other than each other, and the future.

15

HORSE

Today something itched at Winn Hartley-Hartfield, and it was not the fleas she had caught from the badger. It might be the prospect of the imminent meeting with that ghastly Wildwood woman and her committee. Winn looked at her hand. Oh bugger, she'd had the time written down on the back of it, but it was obscured now by the mud she'd acquired in her recent rescue with the accursed poodle. If Winn had a pound for every time she'd had to wade over to Quarry Tump to rescue the creature, she'd have enough for a new education centre. Mrs Marshfield insisted on exercising the beast in Leap Woods.

"Poodles are hunting dogs," Mrs Marshfield insisted. She was right, of course, in the dim and distant past, but not in Petroc's pedigree bloodline.

Winn had washed at the mud, and the slick green detergent had also done an excellent job of erasing the note she'd made of the Wildwood meeting. 2:00pm was chiming in her head, so it was probably 3:00pm. She should just scrabble around on her phone and retrieve the text.

As she rummaged on the scree slope of paperwork on the desk, the hairs on the back of her neck prickled. She stood up.

"Hello?" Was someone stealing from the gift shop? She moved through. Not a soul and yet there was an edge to the air. Winn sniffed. As she did so, a snuffled, huffing snort of breath could be heard. Had she made that noise? It fuffed into the air again. It was a horse, Winn was sure of it.

The horse standing just beyond the pens was vast, grey, and as magnificent a beast as any she'd ever seen. Winn loved horses but only from a reasonable distance. She'd ridden to hounds once with her father and still felt the nagging creak in her collarbone from the terrible fall. There was also no escape from the memory of the pistol, warm in her hand, and the heavy, cooling corpse of the bay, Springheels. Winn let it wash over her as the great grey horse gave a low nicker and stamped its hoof with impatience.

Winn reached a hand towards the reins, but the horse would not let her hold him, choosing instead to move off. The horse was saddled up and riderless and so, here we go, thought Winn, someone somewhere needed dusting off. She remembered to pop her phone in her pocket, useful for ringing the ambulance when she located the rider. Or would it be simpler to just take the tractor?

It was difficult to keep up. The horse strode ahead of her, so far ahead, in fact, that he almost moved beyond sight. Winn puffed and pushed herself, taking care not to stumble or trip in her haste.

She was troubled by the memories of Springheels. Of his horsey face always giving her a wild-eyed glare and the sheer power of such an animal. He'd broken her in the end, of course, her collarbone snapping like a twig in the hawthorn they had attempted to jump. It had killed him too, his own legs snapped as the ground was not where he had thought, the hedge giving way to a deep drainage ditch. Winn scrubbed the memories to try to erase them.

The trees here were slim and slender birches that frayed out from the edges of Havoc Wood. Winn halted, her heart racing, and watched as the horse crossed the boundary. She was not going to follow it there. She did not trust horses, and she had been too recently reminded, by her dreadful tenant, Mrs Fyfe, of what happened when you wandered into Havoc.

Winn took a step back and, as she did so, heard the groan. It was a light sound, disorientated, female. Winn took a cautious step forward. Where had it come from? There, the edge of Havoc. She took another stalking step and the groan rose again accompanied by a small, frightened sob.

"Hello?" Winn wondered who might be more frightened. "Where are you?" Just ahead, breath caught and snagged, and a distraught sob followed. Movement. There. Winn picked her way carefully. "Hello? Hello?" She saw the young woman lying on the ground, her clothes torn at and grubby. "You fell off your horse. Not to worry." Winn sounded cheery, but, as the young woman sat up, face bleary, hair a nest of ivy and dead bracken, she felt anxious. "Anything broken?" Winn halted about a foot away. The young woman sobbed a little, her thin arms wiping at her face.

"Where the fuck am I?" she whined.

16

BREWING

It had become a rather horrible game of hide and seek between them today. Charlie entered the brewhouse, and Michael Chance, within the fewest number of seconds possible, exited, heading off to hide in the office.

Charlie popped into the office. Michael was up and out of his seat and half way to the delivery yard.

Charlie let a few minutes elapse before she walked down to the delivery yard to test her theory.

After proving it, she hid in the workroom, closing the door on herself because she needed space, a small, enclosed space filled with herbs and glass phials and flasks and a whiff of alcohol. She wanted to push Michael Chance out of her head, to occupy the space with the deer, both the physical one she'd nearly run over last night and the dream one Emz had talked of.

They had compared notes on the porch, but neither was sure what to make of this synchronicity of incident. Here in the workroom, Charlie was no better off, her head rattling with thoughts about Aron and his absence last night and their recent closeness which had an edge to it that she didn't want to consider.

There was a dusty mental carpet in Charlie's head, and she was adept at hiding awkward or troubling thoughts and emotions beneath it. Not today. Aron. His face flickered in her head. His smile had been wrong that night at The Ark. The whole mood of that evening had been off kilter. There was also last night's mystery. Where had he been so late? The blanks and holes of her Aron thoughts were matched by the strands of her Michael thoughts. He was avoiding her at all costs. The memory of the kiss they had shared to cure him of Mrs Fyfe's Slow Poison should have signified something, shouldn't it? She didn't know what she'd expected in the aftermath. Did he even remember? The answer to that question was plain in the fear he breathed out. *Focus, Charlotte Way, focus,* she chided herself.

Tonight, Charlie and her sisters had a plan to head out and look for the deer and see what further mystery Havoc Wood was going to throw at them. If only Emz had dreamt of the horse and its travels.

Charlie was so deep in her thoughts that she almost leapt out of her chair when Aron opened the workroom door, his grin wide and warm, but his eyes above it troubled.

"I knocked." He smiled, too hard, and brought his hand from behind his back. A vast bunch of roses, nothing so dull as red, instead a rich mauve purple Charlie loved. They were crowded into a metallic wrapper and clearly hand tied, expensive. She saw the fancy sticker from the Woodcastle florist, Mimosa, as he offered them.

"Big apology." His smile shifted to make way for his serious face, but, Charlie saw, it was the fake-serious version. He was operating all his charm. She could see his brain working so hard it almost ruffled his perfectly groomed hair.

"Big, big pile of sorry with some really sorry on top."

She would not take the bouquet, so he pushed it a little nearer to her face.

"I don't blame you for switching your phone off." He was slickly contrite.

"What?" She took the bouquet at last, as it became embarrassing.

"Your phone. It's been off all day." Aron smiled once again. Charlie reached into her pocket.

"Oh. Yeah. Right." She did not switch it back on. "So, what happened last night?"

Charlie had a bet with herself, which was ironic as the bet involved Aron and his gambling buddies.

"I got tied up with Mr Herald." Aron's face ran through a catalogue of pained expressions. "That project he wants me in on, there were some investors in town last minute and I couldn't get away."

"Couldn't text me?" Charlie pushed it.

"No phones in the meeting."

Poker game, she snarled in her head, but said nothing, her head nodding, not in agreement, but to shake away the thoughts. Charlie knew when someone was lying, but it was an inexact and frustrating skill. This lie was oddly gilded with truth so she couldn't break it apart. He had, she therefore deduced, got into some gambling with the investors at Mr Herald's behest. She hoped it was Mr Herald's cash they'd been raising and seeing.

"Let me make it up to you?" Aron's face held a glimmer that Charlie did not like.

"What's going on?" The question fell out of her mouth, and she witnessed the brief flinch of the muscle in his jaw.

"No hiding from you." He breathed in deep. "It's Herald. This is… this is so big, Chaz." Aron wiped a palm over his chin and took a deep breath. "Like, massive. This is like 'the' project. Ride or die stuff. If I get properly in on this, I can be on Herald's permanent team. This is me, made." His grin was too bright. "Us." He changed the wording. "This is us, made." He did not reach out for her, was still, she could sense, uncertain of her. "This is our future."

Charlie held his gaze for a moment. It was a face she had looked into so often. Once it had seemed a mirror to her own, the face of home and heart. As he folded her into his arms she held on tight.

"I will make it up to you. I promise." He kissed her hair, his hands reaching, one around her waist, the other to the nape of her neck, his mouth finding hers. "When do you get off for lunch?" he asked.

It was a short drive to Knightstone and the Tower House Gardens. The café terrace looked out over Woodcastle, and, as Charlie sat in the window, she was struck by how beautiful it appeared. Havoc Wood had turned through its autumn colours, the trees still holding leaves. It stretched out, and she saw, in the far distance, the bare ridge of Yarl Hill and thought of Ailith and her new career, riding out as a TaskMistress. They had helped her, in the end. It was not all bad, if Charlie looked back over what they had done. It was alright to be afraid, their grandmother Hettie had often said.

Charlie could see her earnest face reflected in the glass and smiled to herself. Trust Grandma Hettie to send the right thought for the right time.

"Hey." Aron sat down opposite to her. He looked smart and sexy in his suit. This grey flannel one was his favourite, made bespoke when he had earned a spectacular bonus last year as top salesman. Usually, he kept it for only the most special occasions. He put down the tray of tea.

"She's bringing the food over, all freshly prepared and all that." He winked.

Tower House Gardens had always been their place. As teenagers they had biked up here, sometimes with a picnic of thrown together sandwiches and packets of crisps. At other times, birthdays for instance, they had eaten in the café. It had always seemed so high end back then.

"So what is this deal with Ivan Herald?" Charlie asked as she poured the tea. Aron was loath to disturb the pretty logo on his latte and spent some seconds tapping the sugar sachet, thoughtful.

"Not sure how much I can say." He was cagey, not looking at her, looking instead at the view outside.

"What?" she laughed. "I'm not the competition."

"No. True." He tore the sugar packet, tipped the grains to stall further.

"Sorry I asked." Charlie felt uncomfortable. Was that his bespoke linen shirt too?

"No. No, don't be. I'm just trying to think of a way to explain." He smiled and looked out of the window, not at her. "It's just big. You know Herald, he's…"

"I don't know him," Charlie said. "I've met him once. It didn't go very well."

Aron gave a tight laugh.

"Actually you've met him twice," he said with a cheeky raise of his eyebrows. Charlie was flustered for a moment.

"When?"

"Halloween. Last year. At Pandemonium." Aron threw down the facts.

"I did not," Charlie resisted. She remembered every detail of that terrible night. "I think I'd remember."

"You weren't introduced, as such. He saw you. At a distance." Aron's cheeky demeanour wavered. Charlie was feeling out of sorts. Anger burbled and poisoned her.

"You made an impression on him," Aron laughed, growly and genuine. "I think it was those black wings you were wearing." He grinned. "And then, of course, the other night when you jumped overboard." He grinned wider. "He's never met anyone like you." His grin failed at last, too wide and stretched to be sustained. As it faltered, the waitress arrived with the food to rescue him.

They ate in silence for a few moments before Aron opened up.

"Herald wants to buy the old bonded warehouse on Tobacco Dock. Got massive, massive regeneration plans. Hotel. Casino. The fucking bollocks." He paused to wipe at his mouth. "He's got the Council in his wallet, pretty much. Just one or two that need persuading and, of course, price has to be right."

Charlie understood his edge now. Aron had always had ambition.

"If it goes, Chaz…" He paused. "I don't want to jinx stuff." He laughed once more, and Charlie nodded.

"I get it. Say no more."

They ate and chatted about nothing.

"Remember when we used to come up here all the time?" he asked. Charlie nodded. It had been on her mind during the whole conversation. "We should do that again, come up here more." He was lighter now, the burdensome secrets of his business dealings lifted. "Why'd we stop?" He was puzzled, his face creasing with the question.

"We forgot it," Charlie said. There was a beat between them. For a second Aron caught his breath and Charlie thought he might cry. It shook her.

"Don't forget," he said and reached for her hand.

17

GOLD DIGGER

Aurora Foundling was not the most popular of residents in Woodcastle. Her business, the florists, Mimosa, on Church Lane, kept going for two reasons. The first was that people remembered her mother, Daisy Foundling, who had been a bit ditsy and now lived in a yurt in Wild Warton on the other side of Yarl Hill. The second was that Aurora had a natural talent for floristry. There was not a wreath for grief better woven than by Aurora. Many were the bouquets hand tied by her that had stolen or mended hearts or sparked romances. Her wedding flowers took people's breath away. She could turn a venue from a bare and bleak marquee into a fairytale grotto with one snip of her secateurs.

But, by God, she was a diva.

THE CONSERVATORY at the rear of the Castle Inn was undergoing something of a temporary event makeover. Lella had given instructions for a deep clean, though had not actually wielded brush, mop, or power washer herself.

Aurora Foundling had rolled up in her van and brought half

a jungle with her. A very elegant jungle, that is.

"I'm not taking it in through here," she snarled. "You'll have to open the conservatory doors. I'll go via the garden," she ordered, surveying the low-slung interior of the Castle Inn, and so Anna had opened the conservatory doors and the beer garden gate.

"I need water. Fill that for me," Aurora commanded, handing Anna a watering can with the Mimosa logo on it. Anna was reminded of Aurora at primary school in Charlie's class. Her red hair had been plaited into a rope long enough for Rapunzel. Now that hair was a weapon to be swished and flounced and not argued with. It fizzed from her head with Pre-Raphaelite abundance and was, Anna thought, quite mesmerising.

"Did you hear me?" Aurora yapped. Anna took the can into the kitchen.

"How hot is it going to be in here?" Aurora asked with the tone of a general.

"Toasty," Casey said as she finished putting out the glassware.

"Are you being sarcastic?" Aurora pinned Casey with a glare, or at least attempted to.

"Yes," said Casey without blinking.

Aurora snapped and barked and organised the best ecosystem possible for the three arrangements of flowers and then left. Casey and Anna could not agree if her exit was a flounce or a huff.

"What is going on?" Casey asked.

"Business lunch." Anna shared the tiny amount of information Lella had given when they had been discussing the menu.

Lella arrived back from her errands shortly afterwards, entering the kitchen as Casey and Anna prepped for the 'business lunch' and the general lunch for those people parched and starved by the tourist delights of Woodcastle.

They were shocked by her hair.

"It's short." Casey had no edit function on her thoughts. "Looks lush though," she added as Lella fussed at the spikier edges.

"I needed a change." Lella did not seem confident of this change.

"It's a good change," Anna assured her. "I might do the same." Lella's face looked lighter, lifted. Anna reached up to where her own scraggy bun was working loose.

"I need to look professional," Lella justified the shearing.

"You do," Casey reassured her.

"Right. So. We're on schedule for lunch? No last minute hiccups?"

"Only if you drink the champagne too fast," Casey joked.

"That's not for pouring. That's on standby. In case." Lella looked flustered. "You didn't put the flutes out, did you?"

"Yes I…"

"Well, go and fetch them back. The champagne is just in case."

Casey headed to the conservatory to retrieve the glassware.

"What's going on?" Anna asked. Lella fussed with her hair some more. She was looking out of the window to the car park beyond.

"Is that his car? Shit." And, without another word, she was gone.

ANNA DID NOT TAKE much notice of anything beyond her hob and worktop. Pans sizzled, herbs were chopped, and she lost herself in the business of feeding a party of aromatherapists, who had walked up from a conference at the Moot Hall, alongside the usual tourists from the castle.

Anna was humming to herself. Her heart felt, in spite of recent Gamekeeper uncertainties, lighter. It was the first time since the loss of her husband and son that she had felt not unhappy. She took in a deep breath and accepted the small step. She accepted the stress and anxiety of their new roles as Game-keepers, too.

The kitchen door swung open. Anna turned, expecting Casey, but it was Lella accompanied by a dark-haired man in his mid-thirties and wearing an expensive looking suit.

"Oh. Sorry. I was expecting Casey. Hello." Anna smiled and looked to Lella for introduction or explanation.

"This is the kitchen, obviously. This is Anna's domain." Lella made a sweeping hostess gesture.

"My compliments to the chef." The man stepped forward with a warm smile and an offered hand. Anna shook it. At once her mind flickered with crowded images of black birds in flight, a rookery of feathers and beaks at once uplifting and distract-ing, before he let go of her hand. Anna's composure did not alter one eyeblink.

"Lunch was delicious. You have skill." His smile warmed further, like butter slicking over a hot pan. Anna nodded, grateful.

"Thank you."

Lella opened her mouth to introduce them, but the man stepped in.

"I'm Ivan Herald. And you are... Emma, did you say?" His brow furrowed.

"Anna," Anna corrected him. "Anna Way."

"Anna Way? You're not by chance one of Charlotte's sisters?"

Anna, unused to thinking of Charlie with her full and formal first name, had to think for a moment.

"Charlotte? Oh. Yes. Yes." She wondered how Charlie knew him. Brewery connection, possibly?

"I've met her through Aron Thorne," Ivan Herald clarified. "One of my business associates. She was at a dinner recently at The Ark." He gave what Anna could only read as an amused smirk. "She's an interesting young woman."

"Yes." It was Anna's only comeback. The rooks from his head clattered once more around her own and cloaked all thought.

"Right. So shall we head upstairs?" Lella brightened her smile by several kilowatts.

Anna brewed tea, and her thoughts drifted to Charlie returning home having jumped ship the other night. It must have been quite an occasion, not just, Anna reasoned, because of the venue, but also the guest list. She had no idea who Ivan Herald was, but his suit and demeanour suggested power, and he was linked to Aron. Ambitious, greedy Aron.

"Lella's selling up." Casey's doom-laden voice broke in on Anna's thoughts.

"What?" Anna was bewildered. What had Casey just said?

"Obvious."

"To you maybe. What is so obvious?"

Casey rolled her eyes.

"All this... This swanky business lunch." Casey swept her arm round. "The Grand Tour of the premises. Lella's showing him around, viewing the property." Casey reached for the cake tin and took out a consolatory wedge of yesterday's coffee and walnut cake. "Plus, he is Ivan bloody Herald."

Anna looked blank. Casey gave a weary sigh.

"Ivan Herald? He owns half of Castlebury... No, probably all of Castlebury by now, and most of Kingham and Knightstone, Castle Hill. Probably quicker to list what he doesn't own."

Anna was no wiser.

"He's the biggest entrepreneur in the area. The most success-ful, rich..." Anna's face remained blank. Casey threw her hands in the air. "I give up. Anyway, trust me, if Ivan Herald is looking round, Lella is selling up."

The small rag rug of hopes and tasks in Havoc Wood was whipped out from beneath Anna's feet. Dizzy, sick, she put a hand out to the worktop, for inside she was falling.

18

GOSSIP

No one was very hungry at Cob Cottage that evening. Anna had brought home leftovers from the afternoon tea, the sight of which only added to her rattled mood.

Charlie was late home from her shift at the brewery and did not so much as pick at the small hoard of Castle Inn goodies.

"Aron took me to lunch. Sorry, I'm full." Charlie's hunger had been sated more by uncertain thoughts of Aron and the future than by the food she'd eaten.

"What's he up to?" Anna's tone was judgmental, and Charlie's mood locked onto it at once.

"What do you mean 'What's he up to'?" Charlie frowned. Her own mind had been chewing at this question for half the afternoon, and she did not like to be called out on it.

"He's been wining and dining you a lot lately. The gold dress. The Ark dinner. Lunch today. What's going on?" Anna was stern and suspicious.

"Can you just dial it down there, mate," Charlie said. "What's your sudden problem with Aron? I didn't realise it's illegal to go out on a date."

"It just seems… I don't know, different. More…"

"More what? As if he cares? More as if we want to be together?" Charlie's thoughts were boiling over. "And that's suspicious is it?"

"I never said that." Anna was backing off, realised how she had stoked an argument and regretted it.

"I'm spending time with him because we're together, and that's what you do when you're supposed to be a couple." Charlie's voice rose in volume until it was loud enough to startle the sparrows from the bush outside the kitchen window.

Anna was silent.

"Oh. God. I'm sorry. I'm sorry." Charlie crumpled a little, her face white.

"For what?" Anna hugged her. "I'm sorry. Why should you be sorry for trying to live a life? I'm sorry for getting on your case. I've had an off day."

Charlie gave a short laugh. "Snap."

"When Emz gets here, let's just head out," Anna suggested, and Charlie gave a derisive snort.

"Yeh. Right. We can run away into the wood," Charlie sighed.

"Do you know a bloke called Ivan Herald?" Anna asked.

"Whoa, handbrake turn on the subject matter, there." Charlie looked startled.

"Do you know him?" Anna had softened. Charlie groaned.

"God, don't remind me." She sagged her shoulders. "He was at that terrible Ark dinner thing the other night when I jumped overboard." Charlie winced at the memory. "Aron's working with him on some massive deal or something."

Anna was stony faced.

"What is it?" Charlie asked.

"The massive deal. Only he was at the Castle Inn today and Casey is convinced Lella will be selling up."

"What?" Charlie was about to be outraged but the door burst open and Emz charged in.

"You won't believe it, Winn found a young woman in Leap Woods who'd fallen off the horse."

Charlie and Anna looked nonplussed at the news. Emz clarified her excitement.

"She fell off the Great Grey Havoc Horse."

THE WAY SISTERS walked through Havoc towards Leap Woods. They were en route for Prickles where Winn had put the Great Grey Havoc Horse into a pen and offered it refreshment. Emz had missed all the fuss of police and ambulance, just rolling up in time to witness the horse taking up the offer of a bag of hay. It had been a relief to see the beast in such an everyday environment, and the sight of Winn patting its vast shoulder had made Emz laugh. It was a big horse, but it was just a horse.

On the way to Prickles, the Way sisters had been delighted by the idea that the grey beast they had half-feared was, in point of fact, just a hack for one of the local horsey girls.

So they were not prepared for the sight of an anxious Winn hovering at the door to the education centre.

"Did you find it?" she asked. The Way sisters visibly sagged. "Is it with you?" With the Prickles pen empty, the hunt for the escaped horse was, once more, on.

"Why do *we* have to hunt it down?" Emz asked as they trudged back through Leap Woods, checking out every possible pathway and trail. "I mean, if it's just a town horse like we think, well, it'll wander back home, surely?"

"It is not just a town horse," Charlie insisted. "I told you. I saw it come out of Havoc."

"Just think it through…" Anna said. "If it is a town horse and wandered back *into* Havoc then it needs to be taken back out. If it's come, as Charlie says, *out of* Havoc, then we can't let it wander about Woodcastle."

"I see your point," Emz said.

"The real point is that it came out of Havoc." Charlie trudged harder.

"We can't have a Havoc visitor or a Guest or Trespasser or a Poacher or a..."

"Rustler," Emz teased. Anna and Charlie glared.

"It's not funny." Anna gave Emz a hard stare. "We can't mix plain, old Woodcastle horses with Havoc Wood... erm..." she struggled for the word, "...personnel."

Charlie drew herself up.

"I don't care about the girl who fell off," she said. "My theory is she fell off the bastard thing because she wasn't supposed to be riding it because IT CAME OUT OF HAVOC." Her words rattled around the trees to silence Anna and Emz. Charlie grabbed her moment.

"This incident is our responsibility. She could have been hurt. That Havoc Horse should not have been wandering about. We should have lassoed it to a tree or something, pinned it in a stave circle to keep it until whoever fell off or lost it came back. When they come back..." she took a deep breath, "we deal with them."

Anna and Emz nodded, chastised.

"We need to do a proper sweep of the wood. See if we can pick up where it went today. Find a lead." Emz began to stride ahead, keen to show she was on her top game. Charlie followed, Anna bringing up the rear, casting glances behind them in case there was any sign of the horse.

They took in their usual patrol routes and found nothing and no one, and finally they rolled round via Frog Pond to check out any activity. If anything, it seemed more abandoned than the previous visit. In the distance an owl hooted, and the three sisters turned in its direction.

"Where was that?" Anna asked. Charlie, without a thought, let her Strength loose and saw the flight path, speckled light.

"Up towards Mrs Massey's old place."

"Sounds like." Emz yawned. "We going up there?"

Anna took in a deep breath and looked at Charlie.

"What do you think?" she asked at last. "Check it out?"

Charlie shook her head. "I think enough is enough. It's gone midnight. Time to go home."

They began to make their way back down through the trees to where the lights of Cob Cottage could be seen in the distance.

19

THE NIGHT HORSE

Borrower had not reached far into Leap Woods when he scented the girl. Tears and anger fuelled her gait, and there was not a finer perfume anywhere. He tracked her to the old road, just at the bend where the Hollows of Havoc Wood met Leap Woods in a tangle of dead-nettles and frost-burnt brambles that those who lived in Havoc Wood called High Foxes.

She was beside a fallen tree at the wood's edge, cursing to herself and shaking forest bits from her shoe. The shoe dropped from her hand, and at once Borrower tugged at it so that it tipped further over the bank and rolled deeper into Leap Woods. At this, the girl cursed louder, the word like the beak of a woodpecker tapping at the air.

She was wearing some flimsy rag of white, so she had an elemental air that appealed to Borrower more than the violence of the red boots worn by the other maiden. This girl picked her way through the undergrowth with disgust, and Borrower laughed to himself at every curse and grunt she gave, and, with nothing more than a wink, he twisted the bramble to her.

As she tried to free herself from his snare, she was cut and prickled and sliced. He thanked the bramble for securing his prisoner and loosed her. She took flight, scrabbling up towards the banking, away from him.

"Need some help?" he asked, as she clawed at the earth, the bramble dragging at her hem, sinking its thorns deep into her calf at his bidding.

"No." Her voice no longer a curse, Borrower heard the whimper, all the fight gone from her. How to remedy that? Borrower rooted amongst her memories to find what he needed, a face he might use, a mask, a disguise, and, when the girl turned, he appeared to her as someone else: the boy she knew.

"What the fuck?" She was so relieved to see his new self. "What the fuck are you doing, Logan?"

"Rescuing you." He held out a hand, his mind edging her forward to him. She was pulled off balance, stumbled.

"What the fuck?" The curse was sharpened by fear. "Logan?... Logan, stop... Logan?" Borrower gave a low laugh and twitched her forward a few steps. She was too scared to cry, bewitched, unable to see what was real.

"Logan?"

Borrower dropped his borrowed face to startle her, and the scream was worth it. It was a skinned sound, and he used it to shove her backwards into the brambles.

Borrower stood over her, unfastening his belt. The buckle gave a louder chink than was usual as he licked his lips. He was reaching, pushing, his hand up her thigh, and the thigh was escaping him, the girl squirming, scraping her skin through the brambles to evade him. He laughed as he pulled at her ankle, dragged her back. She gave a frightened grunt, but the sound became heavy, disconnected, and, before Borrower could reason it out, he was kicked hard from behind, the pain slamming into his back.

Iron. The hoof raised against him so that Borrower was now

the one scrambling back from the prone girl, away from the angered horse.

It was a majestic creature, the head glowering down at him with a sense of strength in the curved muscle of its meaty neck. Borrower reached for it, his heart racing at such a rare find. A Night Horse, it must be. How long since the Night Horses had grazed Havoc? Too long. What had Halloween unleashed?

The Horse pushed him away, but Borrower dodged, his hand darting forward to take the dangling reins. The horse shook its head, the reins whipping out of Borrower's hand, leaving red welts across his fingers. As the horse shoved him forward, Borrower skipped back out of reach. Beside him, the girl lay on the floor, moaned as if in pain, and the horse gave a lower, deeper nicker that rattled at Borrower's heart.

He held up his hands in surrender.

"Whoa. Whoa, lad." He made his voice soft, his memory prompted him on what ought to be done. "Here, lad, come to your master." He claimed the Night Horse. Was that not how it worked?

No. The horse took a threatening step towards him. Borrower held his hands a little higher.

"Now, lad. I claim you. We shall not fight over a girl." He was his most charming, reaching into his borrowed bag of smiles. "Come, lad, help me carry her."

Borrower moved to pick the girl up, lifting her into his arms as she protested, writhing like a netted fish, her cries shrill and echoing through the wood, loud enough for any Gamekeeper to hear.

He flicked her upwards once, in his arms, as if she was a bolt of cloth and he was straightening her. At once the girl was silent and limp.

"Come, Beast, bend to your master," Borrower commanded. The horse stood taller. Strength rippled up through its neck as it reared. There was something other in its eyes, in the fall of the charcoal mane, as if the night sky and the stars altered.

Borrower did not drop the girl, unsure whether she was shield or talisman against the ire of the horse. His instinct shouted that she was the only thing between him and the hooves, and that she would have to be a hostage until he could run clear.

"I have her," he threatened and took a step backward. His escape lay behind him, back towards Hollows, and the Night Horse would not be able to walk free of the Bounds, Borrower guessed that much. He turned with his prize, ready to run.

In the three steps, the horse was on him, a hoof planted past his shoulder, the great cavern of chest pressing at his back, the breath damping his hair. No, not damp. It was ice, biting.

He dropped the girl, he cared not where, and ran, fleet as the wind, not stopping until he was out of the other side of Hollows, beyond Hare's Ell and high in the branches of the old oak trees at Grove. Pausing at last to catch his breath, he realised that the Night Horse was not in pursuit.

Frog Pond, staked out with its warning stave, offered no respite, and so he walked on further, winding his way through fox paths towards the highest western edge of Havoc Wood.

The old cottage, not much above a ruin now, offered shelter enough. There were no longer hens in the run, but a wood pigeon was woken from its bleary dreaming with a twist of Borrower's hands. Fire lit. Herbs gathered from the wild, and woody collection bequeathed by the long-gone old woman, and Borrower's feast was under way.

The fire, on his hearth of stones lifted from the crumbling wall, warmed his spirit. He was a fool to lie low at Frog Pond where it was damp and mossy. This cottage suited his temperament much better. He dug out a few of the potatoes running mad in the overgrown vegetable patch and was sorry there was no butter churned in the dark cool of the scullery.

His mind shifted back to the Night Horse. What could he do with a beast like that in his power... Travel would be nothing to it. He could escape Havoc, take himself somewhere, anywhere that was a day's ride from here.

Or he could trade it. A Night Horse was a priceless commodity. He lay on the soft, mossy grass by the fire and mused upon his wants.

A wife was top of the list. The taking of a wife would establish him within Havoc once more. They would have to wake up to his power after its long sleep. Borrower grinned to himself. With a wife and the Night Horse, he would be next to a King at the least.

The flaw in his plan was that he had never been a Rider. His domain had been forest and wood. He hunted on foot and, while he had borrowed many gifts and skills over his lifetime, horsemanship was not amongst them.

The plan shaped itself. He must find a horseman and borrow his skills, someone to give him sway with the great grey Night Horse. Then, thus armed, he could easily hunt down a wife, sling her over the saddle. He smacked his lips, wiped his pigeon-greased fingers on his moleskin trousers.

Denied access to Frog Pond and its perfect obsidian surface, Borrower scavenged in the ruined cottage. On a wall in the kitchen was a frame and a fragment of mirror within it, about the same size as his face. He grinned and took the shard out. Clearing spiders and mice from the old table he laid the mirror flat and thought of the hooves and haunches and breath of the Night Horse. The mirror awakened, winked with movement, showing him the beast. He grinned. Tonight he would rest and tomorrow he would triumph.

He settled himself on the mouldering sofa to sleep.

· · ·

Hours later he woke in a sweat and, convinced the shade of the old woman had tainted his dreams, headed out into the tumbledown garden.

He had dreamt, once more, that he was hunting the deer down, revelling in the speed of movement, the punching heart of it skittering through Havoc Wood. But he was not alone and, as the dream gathered, he understood that he was the one pursued. At every breath he must hide and conceal himself, the other presence close at his shoulder. He could not see them, not even reflected in the brown globe of the deer's left eye. All that visibly moved was a shadow cloaked in velvet night, punctured with stars.

20

THE PAPER PROPHETS

The driver of the skip lorry was not in a jovial mood.

"You know this place doesn't show up on the sat nav?" he grumbled. His severe look reminded Vanessa Way of the one the old primary school headmaster had given out at assemblies.

"It's a new build." Vanessa did not care to argue the point. "Apologies. I did tell your admin person." Vanessa could hear how defensive she sounded.

"No point telling *her*, love, she's not driving the lorry." The driver looked away with disdain and scanned the driveway, the wide gate. "Where are we going to put it then?" The lorry was partially backed into the lane outside. He surveyed the width of the gates and then the side access to the rear garden, a half-hearted tide of gravel swamped with mud. "Please tell me you don't need it round the back."

With the skip settled in the driveway, Vanessa had made the driver some tea and offered a piece of Anna's banana and chocolate cake, which was gratefully received.

"You on your own up here then?" he asked with a furrowed brow.

"Yes. Lovely and quiet." Vanessa reassured him.

"Out of the way though," he mused. "Do my head in being away up here, all them trees." He reached for the last of his chunk of cake.

"I used to live in town," Vanessa confessed.

"And you chose this spot to move to?" he laughed.

"Yes. It's the perfect getaway." Vanessa was summoning her mother's ghost to come along and supernaturally shunt him out of here.

"Oh. Wait. Wait." He stopped; the last bit of cake seemed to choke him. He swilled the last of the tea. "I know you. I know who you are." His tone veered at once from avuncular concern to fear.

"It's on the delivery slip." Vanessa glanced down at the tablet she'd just squiggled her signature over.

"No, you're Hettie Way's girl." There was a hint of awe replacing the fear. Vanessa did not often cause this reaction in people because, as a general rule, she stayed out of Woodcastle. "Your mam was the Gamekeeper at Havoc Wood," he informed her. Vanessa struggled not to feign surprise at the news. The lorry driver looked at the tea and the cake plate littered with crumbs, his expression questioning whether he might have been poisoned.

"You're not living at Havoc then? Not in the old cottage?" He looked around at the clinically bare kitchen.

"No, my daughters are the Gamekeepers." She had not said it aloud before, and a small bell tolled in her head, a mournful sound. It was a huge task they had inherited.

"Oh, right." The driver looked awkward, in schoolboy fashion.

"So. Thanks for the skip. I'll see you again in a couple of days when it's full?" Vanessa asked. She swiped at her own tablet, checking the calendar for the date she'd booked the return of the loaded skip. "You'll know the way next time," she smiled.

"Oh. Yes. Right." He set off towards the door. "Right. Yes." He hesitated. "How're they liking it there then, settling in?"

Vanessa smiled and nodded.

"Yes. They pretty much grew up there."

"Yeah. I remember. Your Anna was in my class at Brabazon school." He nodded and jabbed his hand forward. Vanessa took it, shook it. They were both sombre.

"I've given the wrong impression. My gran would be pissed off at me. She had a lot of respect for your mam. Lot of respect." He ceased shaking her hand at last and shifted into a sort of salute of farewell.

"See you next week," he said in a lighter tone, as he hefted himself back into the cab of his lorry. Vanessa looked at the skip. There was no putting it off now, so she turned to open the garage door.

The hoard of belongings was a mixed bag. There were many items from Way Towers, bags of the girls' old clothes and teenage clutter. There were flatpack wardrobes that yawed easily into the skip. Vanessa pushed on through it all, not stopping to hold up an old stuffed giraffe and reminisce about 'old, erm…giraffey?'. There was no time and no more room for holding onto things.

The Way Towers stuff was quickly despatched, a lifetime collection of crap barely seeming to make much of a dent in the belly of the skip. It was only as the last of those bin bags was slung out that she was confronted by the last few bits of her mother's belongings.

Anna would want that chair. The rest was the terrible bags of clothing, and Vanessa slung those out, quickly followed by a rickety bookcase to weigh them down. That done, there was just the chunky oak drop-leaf table already rejected by the girls.

"It pinches your fingers," Charlie had explained, and so it gathered dust in Vanessa's garage.

It pinched her fingers as she dragged it onto the drive, the small hinges proving vicious metallic teeth. She loaded it onto the wheelbarrow and rolled it up the planks. As it landed, the drop leaf snapped off leaving splinters and shaves of wood.

Nearly there. What was left? There was that odd, stumpy little chest of drawers at the very back.

It had been her mother's and it was not pretty. The girls had not taken it back to Cob Cottage after their abortive 'holiday let' scheme.

"The drawers always stick," Emz had said. Vanessa tested her theory and tugged the top left-hand drawer of the two-over-three-under configuration. The drawer opened with a squeak and there was nothing inside. She might as well check the other drawers just in case. It wouldn't do to send it to the charity shop loaded with her mother's old bank statements or stray underwear.

The other top drawer squeaked even more, though the long drawer beneath was quick enough and bare enough. Vanessa pulled open the next drawer down with no problems. The final, bottom drawer, however, refused to budge. Or, rather more disconcertingly, it budged about an inch and a half, far enough for her to see that there was something inside, a box of some kind, before the drawer grazed shut.

Vanessa held her breath. Had it shut itself? Or was it just stiff? She grasped the mismatched glass knobs again and pulled the drawer. Again, it slithered an inch and a half before snapping back from her grip. Vanessa looked at the drawers for a moment and was aware that, on some level, the drawers were looking back. This piece of furniture might choose its rightful owner.

VANESSA HAD TEXTED CHARLIE FIRST, hoping she might pop in on her lunchbreak. Now they were both in the garage.

"Nope." Charlie was down on her haunches peering at the

drawer. "It's like it's on a spring or something. Might be catching on something inside."

She tugged the drawer open again and was about to put her fingers inside to check for obstructions.

"No." Vanessa grabbed her hand just as the drawer clipped shut.

"Alright Mum," Charlie snapped, unaware of the danger she'd just escaped. "I'm not three." She glanced towards the skip. "Why are you bothering about it? Isn't it going in the skip?"

"Yes, it is," Vanessa lied.

"Need a hand getting it in?" Charlie surveyed the wheel-barrow and the distance between the garage and the planks ramping up to the skip. "I can load it onto the barrow…"

"Er. No. Don't worry. I'll do it later." Vanessa fobbed it off. Charlie shrugged.

"Okay. If you need help later just text me." Charlie looked restive and unhappy.

"Alright, I will. Everything alright with you?" Vanessa probed. Charlie brushed it aside.

"Yeah. Fine. Usual Havoc stuff."

"Tea?"

"No. Sorry. No time." Charlie gave her a farewell hug, and Vanessa watched her car disappear down the hill.

AN HOUR or so later it was Emz and Vanessa who were staring at the odd little chest. It looked darker. If Vanessa had not known better, she might have thought that…

"It looks like it's frowning," Emz said with a short laugh. "Those top two drawers are like grumpy eyebrows." She tugged at the left-hand drawer which whipped out so fast that Emz stumbled backwards. "I don't remember this from when we were kids." Emz said, attempting to slide it back. It resisted, the wood squeaking and creaking and then suddenly skidding into place so that Emz tripped forward.

"Maybe just leave it. There's nothing in there anyway." Vanessa was feeling edgy about the little piece and its odd energy.

"No, we can't not look," Emz grinned. "I mean, it's not just to make sure there's no treasure map or old knickers in there, it's just being plain nosey." She laughed and reached for the first of the long, bottom drawers.

It was stubborn. The glass knobs seemed greased and Emz struggled to get a grip. When finally she did, and yanked the drawer forward, it protested with a sound like an operatic cat. The middle drawer slid in and out with an oiled swiftness, catching Emz on the knees as it did so. The bottom drawer was defiant. After a great deal of effort Emz dragged it open a finger's width wide.

"Oh!" she gasped. "There's something in here… I heard it slide." She put her face to the small, shadowed gap. The chest of drawers made a faint wooden rasping sound that alarmed Vanessa.

"Be careful." She reached for Emz's shoulder to pull her back.

Emz leaned closer still, her nose touching the beeswaxed wood. She turned her head, this way, that, trying to peer in. "There's definitely something in—"

She straightened and reached her fingers down into the darkness of the bottom drawer. As she did so, the top drawer slid open, clipping her hard on the brow bone. Emz fell back, and the bottom drawer slid silently closed. Tight.

"It doesn't like me," Emz decreed. Vanessa slid the top drawer back into place, the wood giving a satisfied clunk as she did so.

. . .

LATER STILL AND it was Vanessa and Anna who were standing in the garage.

"I thought I'd give you first dibs on the footstool." Vanessa flipped up the lid on the stout, boxy bit of furniture. "It's got the storage bit, remember?"

Anna liked it but struggled to recall its place in Cob Cottage.

"Did she get this from Mrs Massey?" Anna traced her hand over the cross-stitched upholstery of the rectangular seat. The carved legs drew her gaze.

"Oh, that's a possibility." Vanessa had not thought about Mrs Massey.

"This was in her room. I remember. Sitting under the window. Yes, yes I'd love to take it." Anna was feeling animated by the designs of flora and fauna carved and stitched into the piece. "What else did you say there was?" Anna looked up.

Vanessa noticed that the stumpy little chest of drawers now looked honey gold in the afternoon sunlight and that the same sunlight caught in the mismatched glass knobs and refracted into small kaleidoscopes of colour.

"You're not throwing this in the skip?" Anna was outraged, and in this light Vanessa was beginning to doubt her own sanity regarding this funny little chest.

"It looked a bit… well… shit, earlier."

Sun-basked, it was transformed into a thing of beauty. Anna's hand smoothed over the grain of the wood.

"I'll have this. It can go in my room."

"There's just a bit of a problem with the bottom drawer…" Vanessa advised.

"Oh? Nothing a bit of candlewax won't fix," Anna said, and at her touch the bottom drawer slid gracefully open. Vanessa held her breath. Inside, a small cigar box slid backwards into the rear of the drawer.

"There's something in here." Anna reached for the cigar box. It was brightly coloured in earthy, ochre tones splashed with teal and a burnt looking red. Anna smoothed her hand over the scenes of ships and palm trees that graced the lid.

"Oooh, lovely box. I don't remember seeing it before." Anna opened it. Inside was a small deck of cards bound together with the kind of thick elastic band preferred by postmen. She paused.

"Cards?" her mother said. "Don't recall Mum ever bothering with…" She was stopped by the expression on Anna's face.

"It's the Paper Prophets." Anna's tone was hushed.

"The what?" Vanessa felt her neck prickle. She noted that Anna did not touch the deck. There was a lovely scent of cigar, of jam and cream and warm scones.

"Mrs Massey always kept them in her pocket. In that linen apron she always wore." Anna stared at the deck. Vanessa remembered the apron, but she had not been privy to knowledge of the Paper Prophets themselves.

"What do you want to do with them?" Vanessa asked. "Whizz them in the skip? There aren't many, not a complete deck."

"They're not playing cards." Vanessa heard the reverential tone in Anna's voice.

"Oh. Okay." Vanessa understood.

"You couldn't open the drawer?" Anna asked. Her mother shook her head.

"Nope, neither could Emz or Charlie." She watched as a glimmer of excitement flickered over Anna's face. It had been a long time since Vanessa had seen her daughter look anything other than sad or anxious. She slid the drawer back as Anna shut the lid on the cigar box and held it close.

"How about some tea?" Vanessa asked and, without waiting for an answer, headed into the house.

VANESSA HAD BREWED a pot of tea and microwaved more of Anna's banana and chocolate cake before Anna entered the kitchen. She looked flushed and bright and held tight to the cigar box with her left hand. When she took up her seat at the breakfast bar, the cigar box rested, not on the granite worktop, but on her lap, with her palm placed on the top of it.

"We could give Emz a ring. Maybe get Winn over here with the Land Rover or get Charlie to borrow the Drawbridge van. We can load up and get the chest and stool over to Cob Cottage."

Anna nodded, a fresh smile radiating, if not happiness, then, Vanessa crossed her fingers, something hopeful.

21

TRUTH AND LIES

Emz had not slept well last night. She was tired from the mental effort expended by the recurring deer dream. Once again, she had felt that sense of pursuit, but the predator was just out of sight. It was frustrating, and she found her mind was racing along the tracks the deer had taken her along.

She'd been sleeping, as was her habit, in Grandma Hettie's old black waxed raincoat. Emz had asked herself the question whether that raincoat might be protection, and the idea of a kind of black waxed armour surfaced with a mental pop.

She'd been disturbed enough to rise early and do a swift patrol of the east side of Pike Lake, picking up the trail and finding it led to a spot by the water where, when she looked out, there seemed to be a memory trying to surface but sinking just out of reach. She let the dream deer bob onwards on its path, and her own footsteps followed.

There was nothing out of the ordinary. No poisoned apples. No lost seamstresses to hint at danger or problems. Nothing stepped out of Havoc, save for a squirrel or two and a flurry of long-tailed tits, a buzzard circling overhead. No horse. No hoofprints.

Back at Cob Cottage Anna was just leaving.

"Need a lift? I can roll round that way."

Emz usually walked to school, but just lately one or other of her sisters had been troubled and needed the distraction of a detour and so, once again, Emz accepted the ride.

She was dropped off in the car park, on time for once, and so found that the sixth form common room was full and loud with chatter.

The second she entered the space it was like an electrical current, the energy as unpleasant a sensation as a fork in a plug socket. This, Emz recalled, was why she tried to avoid the place.

Her usual remedy was to shut out the negative energy by pulling out a book, but today the pages of *Wildwood* became strewn with the litter of other people's thoughts, the strands of chatter nagging at her. When she looked up, her heart lurched. Above the room was a web of black lines spinning and stretching like a web. She'd seen this before, at the terrible party at Tasha's house. The fibres of it hummed with a low-key drone. Emz tried looking back into the pages of her book, but the web and the sound it made would not be ignored. She began to tune into the conversations.

"…wrong. You're wrong."

"No. No, it was worse. I heard it was worse."

"He did not."

"From the car. Just kicked her out into the road."

"Into the road?"

"Left her."

"Left her there and then."

The web was vibrating around her. There was a message. Something was wrong, but she couldn't work it out. A feeling of panic crushed her. Phones clicked, screens were swiped. Emz realised she'd left her phone charging on the sideboard at Cob Cottage. The web was inescapable. Emz could hardly breathe, and there was nothing for it but to physically exit the building.

She was on the stairs as Mia and Katie were walking up. Emz was dismayed to see that the web was winding around them, black fibres connecting their mouths. There was a look exchanged between them, and, at once, Emz felt the sting of it, that it related, in some way, to her.

"Hey." Mia greeted her with an unwelcome expression of smugness. Emz, without thinking, glanced full at her, her Strength sliding the girl's everyday face to one side to reveal her real face, the one that showed her true self. It was a babyish, peevish tantrum of a thing. Katie's real face was small and pinched and vain. Emz ought to have felt surprise at this revelation but, in truth, this was how she'd always felt about these two girls. It was a strong sensation, too strong. She tried to switch off her Strength and failed. The web trembled, and her Strength was a white-hot piece of charcoal in her chest. The girls whispered together. Emz, unable to catch what they said, was using everything to focus on the charcoal inside her and keep it under control. She hurried past them.

"Where are you going?" Mia asked. Emz picked up her tone — what was it these girls thought they knew? She glanced at the web. Something was very wrong.

"History." Emz did not bother with a fake smile, or even to stop. She had reached the last step.

"Not going to see Logan Boyle?" Mia pushed. Emz saw where the web shuddered and halted.

"No, I haven't seen him. Are you looking for him?" Her heart was beating fast. The charcoal of her Strength was fierce. She felt the alteration in its energy. Why would they think she was going to see Logan? It didn't make any sense. Her heart stalled. Had Caitlin or Mark stirred up some rumour about that stupid night at the summerhouse? It was not beyond either of them.

"No," Mia snorted. "Thought you might be going to see him."

"I don't get it." Emz was strong, staring them down. "Why would I see him? Logan doesn't do History."

"He is history," sniggered Katie, looking smug.

"What are you on about?"

"Logan." Mia's eyes widened at the obvious gap in Emz's knowledge, at the pleasure she was going to get from telling her.

"What about Logan?" The white heat of her Strength glowed like starlight.

"He's been arrested." Katie's tone was glib. Emz was silent; the web vibrated around their mouths with a deep and unpleasant hum.

"No. He's not been arrested. He's 'helping police with their enquiries'," Mia clarified.

"Whatever." Katie was snarky. "He's at the police station either way."

"They're questioning him." Mia pushed the point home. Nothing like this had ever happened to Emz before. She could not feel the edges of her Strength.

"Questioning him? What?" Emz stared at them. "Why? What did he do?"

"He tried to rape Caitlin." Mia, having pulled the pin on this verbal grenade, walked off up the stairs, Katie trotting quickly behind.

A door at the far end of the corridor banged closed like a gunshot.

The History classroom was empty save for Mrs McInnes marking a set of books. She looked up.

"Oh, someone's coming in then." She sounded weary. "I did wonder." She glanced at her watch. Emz's thoughts jangled and wouldn't resolve themselves into action. She sat and reached into her Strength. It was calmer, so she tried to get a feel for what had happened. The web of gossiping voices, the sound it made, the violence of her Strength.

"Do you want to hand in the essay?" Mrs McInnes interrupted her thoughts. Emz rummaged in her bag for the papers, except they wouldn't surface. All she could see were images of

Logan Boyle, his hand on her arm at the turn of the stairs a few short weeks ago.

"Sorry."

"You alright?" Mrs McInnes asked with genuine concern. Emz nodded; the contents of her bag rustled and shuffled and were uncooperative.

"This Logan Boyle thing is very unsettling," Mrs McInnes said, chewing her lip. "You good friends with him?" she quizzed. Her tone was empathetic, not the vicious gossip of Mia and Katie or the mad burble of the common room.

Emz nodded, when in reality she had no notion of what her relationship was with Logan Boyle. What was she to him? She was not, she noticed, feeling anything in regard to the allegedly wronged Caitlin.

No one else turned up at the history lesson, and, after Mrs McInnes and Emily Way had exhausted the topic of the Chartists and the fight for universal manhood suffrage, Emz was dismissed and made a speedy escape in the direction of Prickles.

Or she attempted to. She was only half way across the yard outside the Humanities block when Tori, Keira, and Tasha exited the biology labs on the opposite side. There was no avoiding them and to turn back would be running away. Already she could see the web beginning to snaggle and wind as they approached.

"Emz, Emz…?" Tash was waving her hands in excitement as if flagging down a bus. "What the fuck is going on with Logan Boyle?" Emz was cornered.

"Why are you asking me?" she shrugged, and the look that she recognised from Mia and Katie flashed between this trio.

"Well. You know." Tash was pulling an odd face, one of insincerity. "We all know you like Logan."

Emz saw the knife of it, understood in one sentence how she was being drawn in.

"I don't know anything." She shrugged again, convincing no one. The group, no, the pack, Emz made the important distinction, shifted.

"You heard what happened?" Tori piped up from her spot at the rear of this hunting party.

"No, I didn't." Emz had not heard what had happened. She'd heard gossip and hearsay. The girls rounded on their prey.

"It's tragic." Keira was shaking her head. "Like, really fucking grim."

"You know he's at the police station? You know that's why he's not in school?" Tash was talking as if Emz was a toddler; one, Emz thought, who was about to be torn apart.

"Yes. Katie and Mia said." The pack faltered a little at her lack of reaction.

"He raped Caitlin." Keira dealt the killer blow. The web sang a high piercing note that joined with the starlight of her Strength. Emz felt odd, as if she ought to feel weak, but the energy flowed through her, swift.

"Left her for dead in Leap Woods. That old woman you work with found her." Tori folded her arms.

"He fucking raped her." Tash's eyes couldn't really get any gogglier. Emz looked at them. Her Strength was soaring, out beyond the idea of seeing real faces, further still to where the black web poured out of their mouths, tangled their hair. Did this black web signify the terrible news? The starlight of her Strength reached for the web and the two joined. Emz saw clearly.

"Were you there?" Emz asked. There was a ripple of shock.

"What?" Tori asked.

"What the fuck?" Keira was outraged.

"If you weren't there, you don't know what went on."

The three girls were open mouthed. More web spooled out.

Emz said nothing. Could she trust her Strength? Did she really know what she was doing?

"Caitlin told them he did it. Caitlin said he raped her." Tash's voice was hard. Keira took up the cause.

"They had a row on the way back from the party and he just raped her in the woods." Keira's real face was the most disturbing, as bland and featureless as a badly set jelly.

There followed a silence that could not be broken.

EMZ WAS ALMOST RUNNING to Prickles. Her mind was a roil of thoughts. She had not been in the loop for gossip for a long time. Once, she had been on Facebook and joined in with the group chats on WhatsApp, willing to chit chat and interact with the other girls, even the ones that she didn't like. It had not mattered. She could put up with them for the sake of a social life, to fit in. She'd always disliked cliques and drifted from friendship group to friendship group with not much thought or commitment. She was a freelance friend, Caitlin had once joked. Emz had not cared, always having Prickles to escape to, and could gossip to Charlie about parties and trips to town.

Until that terrible Halloween a year ago when Calum and Ethan died, and the bottom fell out of the world.

It was not simply the loss. It was the faked grief and ghoulish interest of some of the members of the sixth form on social media. It had felt as if they were feeding off the tragedy, and she could no longer fake caring about them and their petty social concerns, the backstabbing and bitch-baiting. She cut herself off, and no one had come along to fetch her back.

Caitlin saw her as an amusement, like a cat with a mouse. Did Caitlin love Logan Boyle? Did she? The other question filled Emz's head. Did Logan do this? It filled her head, left no room. She thought of the black web snaring everyone. Did she trust herself to understand its message?

Emz was tormented by the many images in her head of Logan and Caitlin and their exhibition kissing and, worse still, the terrible game at Tasha's party, luring her out to witness Logan and Caitlin together in the summerhouse. Emz had been played, and these thoughts were a greasy slick in her mind.

It hurt. All of it. It hurt like a thorn in her heart, and she had too much pain to deal with. Calum and Ethan, Grandma Hettie. There had to be no room for Logan Boyle. She had cut him out of her heart.

She was in quite a state by the time she entered via the back door at Prickles. Winn looked taken aback by her appearance as she put down the phone.

"Good God alive, sit yourself down." Winn pushed Emz into the saggy old armchair in the corner. "No arguments, you look dreadful. What happened? Are you hurt?"

"I'm fine." Emz could barely breathe for the seething emotions. It was taking all her energy to hold back the tears. "I'm fine."

"You heard?" Winn was straight to the point, her face a concerned frown. "That girl I found was from your school."

Emz nodded.

"Good friend?" Winn asked, as she clicked on the kettle and fussed with tea things.

"What happened?" Emz asked.

"I told you. Found her in the woods bit the worse for wear, and I thought she'd tumbled off the horse. I called the ambulance. End of story."

"She's saying…" Emz found herself unable to say Logan's name, "…she says one of the boys at school raped her."

Winn was silent for a long moment. The kettle boiled with panicked breath.

"All I saw was the girl and the horse. I assumed she'd come a cropper, no more, and she said nothing to the contrary. I certainly did not see a boy."

Emz nodded. It was not proof, it was not evidence of Logan's innocence.

"He might, of course, have run away." Winn made a case for the prosecution, and Emz scooped up all her thoughts. Tighe Rourke and Mrs Fyfe and all that Havoc Wood threatened seemed nothing beside this.

"Can't find out who owns the horse," Winn admitted. "I've rung round all my horsey pals and no one can even place it," she sighed. "Since it wandered off into Havoc, I wondered if…"

"It's our jurisdiction," Emz nodded. "Don't worry about it, Winn."

And Winn nodded.

"Fine and dandy." Winn's voice was a little odd, but Emz did not register the difference. She was also glancing at her watch. "Well and good. Yes. Right. Fine." The time on Winn's watch was, of course, wrong, and so she glanced up at the clock on the wall. "I've got a meeting with the Wildwood Society committee in about fifteen minutes," she announced. Emz looked at the clock.

"Shouldn't you be on your way there then? It's a good half hour to their offices." Emz was glad of the mental distraction. Winn considered this for some moments.

"No need. It's been, erm, rescheduled." She patted her pockets, finding her phone in the left and a hedgehog in the right. Putting the hedgehog by the back door, she headed out into the education centre.

22

CALL ME IVAN

Before breakfast, Charlie Way walked some of her more hidden paths to Banner Hill with a mind to tracking down the Great Grey Horse. It remained firmly out of sight, though, once she drifted out of her everyday thoughts, she caught scents of it in the wind here and there. A few hoofprints pressed into the mud made her halt and, as she touched the indentations, the path that had been taken lit up through the landscape. Except it led nowhere. Black velvet and sparkling with something like stars, it turned back on itself and pointed her back towards the shores of Pike Lake.

She made a mental note and then followed a curve of the trail up Banner Hill. Her fear, she noticed, was starting to curl back at the edges and she began to work out how to overcome it. Ignore it. Starve it. Whenever she felt most afraid, she determined to look in that direction as if the fear was a Waymarker.

Her calves stretched and aching, she turned to look back at Pike Lake from the top of Banner Hill. Her breath caught in her throat. There was not one path shimmering through Havoc, but a network. They curved back this way, stretched out long in that direction. At first, she thought it was the random wanderings of the Great Grey Horse, but finally she saw the pattern. It resembled nothing so much as a compass, as if the horse had written the points of the compass into the wood.

She felt the panic and fear rise, and, in doing so, blank out the compass. Charlie shut her eyes, took a step back. She inhaled the scents of the wood, used them to bank her fear, and opened her eyes. The compass was clear. What was this? The horse had clearly marked this out, but why?

She considered the direction of the compass points. Was it even orientated to a normal compass? She glanced across Woodcastle to get her bearings. Heron Step to the East. Yarl Hill to the West. Behind her, out of sight beyond the trees, was the southern ridge of Beacon Hill. This was North then, out towards Winter Hill. The compass that the paths had written into the wood was out of kilter in a way that she could not quite pin down.

Hurrying back to Cob Cottage, Charlie was eager to share her findings, but, when she arrived, Anna and Emz were already gone on their way, dishes draining by the sink. She scribbled as best she could on a piece of paper, anxious that her discovery would have to wait to be shared.

CHARLIE HAD SENT a text already telling Emz and Anna, "Found compass point path for the Horse. Talk later" and wondered if it was too cryptic and would cause them both to panic. She'd made a start on trying to draw the compass points on a piece of paper and was doodling at this when Michael's voice cut in.

"You're aware that it's a busy morning?" He sounded annoyed. Since Charlie had already been quite busy that morning with the latest delivery and the supervision of brewing, she wondered who he might be talking to.

She looked up from her compass diagram with the thought, *That bit is wrong...* drifting through her mind.

"Sorry?"

"I'm going over to see Midge Hills." Michael had to talk to her, but he couldn't look at her, his gaze concentrated on his tablet as he tapped at the screen. "And there's been a change of plan."

"What plan?" Drawbridge Brewery ran best on chaos in Charlie's opinion. Michael looked up. She was aware of a disapproving glance at her workwear.

"You should smarten up." He gestured to her jeans and Drawbridge t-shirt.

"I'm brewing beer, not walking a runway." Charlie was sharp.

"Well, this morning you're filling in for me with the Herald rep." He raised a pompous eyebrow. "So… brush your hair or… or…" He had glanced at her hair and found it too taxing, and so he was looking away again. Charlie was hurt and wanted, more than anything, to put her tongue out at him or, worse, give him the finger. The name yelled out in her head.

"Wait, what rep from where?" Charlie was confused.

"The whole mess this morning is your fault." Michael was already turning to leave. "You double booked the meeting with Midge Hills and the meeting with Tim at Montpellier."

Charlie was losing her temper.

"Montpellier wants to drop us," Charlie said. "They want the beer to be cheap and nasty, and we shouldn't be dealing with them. They've been really shitty with the Knightstone winery."

"Shitty they may be, but Drawbridge needs cashflow. They're a good contract to have."

"They pay late."

Michael slammed down the tablet.

"I forget where someone made you the owner of this business. I'm now juggling them and Midge Hills and having to drive half way round Castlebury twice, so I think the least you can do is spend an hour sucking up to this Bettina Wright woman who's coming from Herald."

A bell tolled in Charlie's head. Herald?

"What? Ivan Herald?"

"Yes. She rang last week. They want to increase their offer of locally supplied products, carbon footprint, etc, so they're checking out the local microbreweries. Christ, do you ever listen?"

Charlie watched him. He was all edges this morning. She did not remind him that she had been the one to chase up all the leads in the last six months.

"I'm off." He rattled his car keys out of his pocket. "Brush your hair, and don't bollocks it up."

He was gone with the slam of a door.

HALF AN HOUR LATER, Charlie, her hair resolutely unbrushed but a fresh t-shirt on, was waiting in the yard for the sleek black car carrying Bettina Wright to pull up. It was like awaiting royalty, and, as the tyres crunched over the yard, Charlie thought she ought to have a posy or a medal to hand. As she was amusing herself with this thought, the car door opened and, instead of Bettina, a middle-aged man got out. The cogs in Charlie's head clicked into place, and, plastering her best smile across her face, she stepped forward.

"Good morning, Mr Herald." She offered her hand. He took it warmly.

"How many times, Miss Way? Call me Ivan."

IVAN HERALD'S CLEAN, strong hand caressed the belly of the mash tun.

"Where did Chance find this? Surely it wasn't here already?"

"No." Charlie was unaware of the charm being worked upon her. She had been lost in the brewery and its workings, the very last detail of which Call Me Ivan had been interested in and asked smart questions about. "No. This was a flour mill. Michael got this when they closed Toppers."

The time had wandered by on slippered feet, and Charlie was talking about the brew and the malt and opening the workshop and revealing secrets and pouring samples and the words tumbled from her and fell upon attentive ears. She forgot the Mr Herald of The Ark and of Aron's greedy ambition. She forgot his connection to Pandemonium, that palace of pleasure and beauty that was inextricably linked to her own grief.

She let go. She lost herself in hops and herbs and felt connected to another person. Not even Michael knew as much about brewing as Ivan Herald. Their laughter made the hot copper in the brewhouse ring like a bell, bringing light.

"You're very passionate about this," Call Me Ivan said.

"Oh. Thank you. Yes. I love my work," Charlie confessed with a smile. Her mind replayed the toast he had raised on the deck of The Ark as she had reached dry land. There was a scent of cigar and leather and crisp Irish linen that was heady and felt like home.

"I'm sorry, I've kept you overtime." Charlie noticed the clock on the brewery wall. Call Me Ivan shook his head.

"No matter. This tour has been an education. Thank you."

"Thank you. I mean, you know your stuff and you're…" Charlie felt a hot blush light up her face as his eyes met hers. She was gushing, being unprofessional, and, as Michael had warned, probably bollocksing it up. She swerved back onto track. "And, just to be businesslike, Mr Chance will be back in the office after 2:30 if you need to call and ask him anything."

"I think you've covered all my questions. It's been a pleasure." They shook hands once again. His smile was easy and genuine, his eyes, she noticed, green-flecked with brown, exactly like the hazel in Havoc Wood.

23

CATS AND CARDS

I t had not been a great morning at the Castle Inn. There had been a fractious discussion after Casey attempted to make Lella spill the beans about the sale of the inn.

"Just because you don't like Ivan Herald." Lella was flustered. Casey was defensive.

"I didn't say I didn't like him. I asked if you're selling up." Casey stood her ground. "A question that you haven't answered, by the way."

Lella fudged it.

"I like him. The man has single-handedly regenerated Castlebury. He sees potential." There was a desperation in her voice that Anna didn't like to hear, and so she was grateful for the unexpected sound of bustle and custom in the restaurant.

Students from the EFL Academy in Castlebury had taken a walk along Rook's Ridge from Blackstone Height and arrived in need of emergency rations. Lella was curt.

"Lunch just finished." She shook her head to the weary-looking tutor. Anna was on her way to her own break.

"But, fortunately, Afternoon Tea is just starting." Anna spoke

132

up behind her. "What can we get you?" And she reached for some menus under Lella's gimlet eye.

WITH THE ARRIVAL of the EFL students, Casey and Anna had been in their element: eggs frying, poaching, scrambling, all manner of toasties and the soup tureen drained of its several pints' contents. There had been a cairn of scones to be consumed, an ocean of tea.

The day had fed into Anna's mood. The discovery of the Paper Prophets had switched something positive inside her. In a time when everything had seemed to be tumbling after each other, the arrival of the Prophets felt like a pulling together.

Their last search for the Great Grey Horse had not been successful, but Anna felt a cautious optimism. If she had to characterise it, it would be a small wood mouse of optimism. This feeling was prone to flee at the first rustle of leaves, but it had poked its nose out.

She'd felt so different this morning that she commuted on foot, striding down the shore of Pike Lake, her senses aware, sending out small pulsing Reaches, testing herself. There was no sign of the horse, but Anna could see that there was also no sign of anything else that might be untoward. She'd come along the Dark Gate path that edged beneath the old castle moat.

She'd come out on Dark Gate Street with only cats for company, and now, as she walked herself home again along the same street, she was aware once more of the spilling mew of Ginger and Tabby making their way to and from Cordwainer Street. This morning she hadn't thought much about it, but now, heading home, there seemed to be a lot of Cordwainer cats about, far more than was usual. She paused for a moment. The white one on the wall at the corner of Moot Hall Lane, three or four black and grey and tabby scampering their way up towards the back end of Market Drab. Ginger, patchy, and that rather sleek blue grey specimen that had eyed her from the top of the wall at The Twist. Anna paused at the corner of Old Lamp Lane and Long Gate Street. There were a lot of cats.

She ditched the idea of going home and headed towards Cordwainer Street. It would be exercise, both mental and physical, to patrol town. That was something they ought not to forget. Grandma Hettie had always been insistent that the Bounds of Havoc also stretched out across town; thinner, flimsier, but there nonetheless.

At the end of Cordwainer Street, Anna could see the roil of cats. They were everywhere, seething around the feet of a neighbour fetching shopping from the boot of her car.

"Shoo, damn you." She kicked at the coil of cats winding its way around her ankles and then looked guilty as she saw Anna.

"Have you ever seen anything like it?" she blustered. "Bloody nuisance. And the smell." She picked her way to her own wooden gate at No 7 and pushed it open. The cats did not sidle in with her. Anna observed their movements, which were focused on No 4. The ranks of them squeezed around or under the fence, jumped along the walls. Anna watched them head off. Where were they going?

She followed them to the car park at the rear of the Highwayman Inn, where they swarmed over the tarmac and wove themselves in and out of a stand of birch trees before streaming away back towards Cordwainer Street. It was odd. Perhaps there were more mice here.

She was part way to the Plainsong Chapel and so, with the cats milling around her head if not her feet, Anna walked onwards.

The chapel was almost complete. Painting and sanding was going on, and the door was open, the cold winter light of the late afternoon glowing through. Anna could see from the gate where the plain, squared panes made golden angles on the interior. Matt Woodhill and his team were almost done. There were rumours around town as to the ultimate use of the building. Boxing gym. Community centre. It seemed to offer hope and possibility.

As Matt lifted his safety mask, Anna thought of Roz. She had only seen her around town twice since the terrible incident of her possession by Mrs Fyfe. A brief nod of acknowledgement had passed between them, but nothing more. Anna made a mental note to go and visit Roz. She could use Matt's work on the chapel as an excuse perhaps.

She shuddered at the thought of red apples and turned for home. Digging her hands into her jacket pockets, she felt the small rectangle of the deck of cards and closed her fingers around it. Was it warm? Or were her hands just cold from the bitter November afternoon?

Finding the Paper Prophets had fired up memories about Mrs Massey and the afternoons spent at her cottage. As she walked to Old Castle Road, her mind drifted back to a long-ago afternoon. Grandma Hettie had let them wander and then, late in the day, asked for Anna and her sisters to wait for her at Mrs Massey's cottage.

The cottage was at the rear boundary of Havoc Wood, close, Anna realised, towards the vicinity of Day's Ride. She roamed within her memory of the cottage. It was nestled into the trees on the mid slopes of High Hill. They often stopped there, and Mrs Massey was kind and welcoming, the sort of grown up, like Grandma Hettie, who did not regard them as the twin perils of dolls or nuisances. There was always something in the oven at Mrs Massey's cottage, including, once, Anna recalled, a basket of kittens being kept warm and fed after their mother had perished in a fight with a badger.

Kittens. The link glimmered for a moment and banked down. Anna felt the edges of the cards, soft and worn.

The Paper Prophets resided, at all times, in Mrs Massey's

apron pocket. The day that put itself front and centre of Anna's memory had been in summer.

It had been hot at the bus stop and Vanessa had been patient with Charlie and Emz who were playing a game of rock, paper, scissors that involved Charlie punching her little sister's shoulder for the "rock" option.

"You can come along if you like?" Vanessa had frowned at her eldest daughter. "We'll go to the Cavendish after we wrestle Charlie into her new shoes."

Anna shook her head.

"I promised Grandma Hettie," Anna smiled. She disliked shoe shopping, they all did. Vanessa nodded.

"Wise move." She winked and leaned to kiss Anna farewell. "See you later."

The bus rolled up, and Charlie and Emz united in pulling faces at Anna from the top deck as it rolled away again.

It was hot. It was quiet, too, as Anna moved off along Dark Gate Street and picked her way up through the brambles and bracken into the town-side edges of Havoc Wood.

Grandma and Anna had not brought a picnic because Mrs Massey would have something baked or baking. Indeed, as they made their way up the little stone path, alongside the drone of bees in her hives, the kettle was already whistling its greeting from the kitchen.

Anna did not recall what gossip was exchanged that day. She remembered bees and birdsong and raspberry jam. She remembered Grandma Hettie being called away. Rainclouds rolled in, so they moved indoors.

Usually they spent their time in the kitchen, but, on this afternoon, Mrs Massey showed Anna into the small parlour at the front of the house. Anna had never been in there before, and as she took up her seat at the table with its velvet cloth, Mrs Massey fussed for a few moments with the drawer at the front of the dresser, so tall it appeared to stoop under the beams of the ceiling.

"Needs a bit of candlewax, that does." Mrs Massey turned suddenly, and her hand reached into her apron pocket and took out a small deck of cards. They were bound with a thick elastic band, the sort used by postmen. Mrs Massey also took out a small, pearl-handled fruit knife and a length of rusty orange embroidery thread.

"Been looking all over for that." She popped the thread back in her pocket and reached for an apple from the bowl on the table. The bowl was made of cut glass that caught the sunlight. Anna thought it very beautiful.

"You ever play a hand of Three? Your gran ever teach you?"

Anna shook her head. They often played card games, but this one did not sound familiar. Mrs Massey had given her an assessing look.

"Let's have a crack then, shall we?" She licked her lips and, with one finger, pushed the small stack towards Anna.

"How about you have a go at taking off the band." Her eyes did not move from the cards. Anna could see herself reflected in the lenses of Mrs Massey's small round glasses as she reached.

Anna took off the rubber band and held the deck. It was not really a deck at all.

"Oh. There aren't enough cards." She looked to Mrs Massey, whose mouth was pinched tight, her eyes still focused on the cards and Anna's hands.

"This is a very old deck. The Havoc Deck." She took in a breath. "Some call them the Paper Prophets." Her finger rested on the velvet of the cloth, and she nodded to the deck.

"Try and deal out three cards, just onto the table, between us." Mrs Massey's finger tapped the table three times.

There were pictures. Anna recalled the rich and lustrous illustrations, like illuminated letters from a manuscript: lightning so vivid it seemed to crackle as she laid the card down; a comforting wooden spoon in a herb-bedecked and practical kitchen scene; and, the final and most beautiful, a vision of water and weeds.

"Ooh look." Anna pointed to the view through the kitchen window above the white butler's sink inked onto the card.

"What do you see?" Mrs Massey asked, resting her head on her other hand.

Anna had seen several different things in that small image. A view of Yarl Hill lit by glimmering candles. A summer view of Crow Houses, the meadow bobbing with ox-eye daisies at one instant and, in a blink, the scarlet of poppies.

"Oh, they're so beautiful." Anna felt she could fall into these cards, they were so pretty.

"This one," Mrs Massey tapped at it, "is the Scorched Spoon."

The name made Anna look again at the spoon. It sat at the sink's edge in a blue flowered pot and, yes, there at the tip, the blackened bit where it might have caught on a hot pan. Or been struck by the Lightning. Anna's glance shifted at the crackle of electricity from the other card.

"What do you see?" Mrs Massey asked. Anna said nothing for a moment. There was something about the way that Mrs Massey asked the question. She locked glances with her for a second and then looked back at the card.

Lightning seared it, but, if you paused and took a breath, Anna could see the edge of Havoc Wood behind it, the hills of Woodcastle, and how the lightning showed it in a different, otherworldly light.

"The edge of Havoc." Anna chose her words carefully. Mrs Massey understood.

"Exactly."

The third card had altered at the edge of her vision. She could see where the water and weeds hid a pike.

"A pike." Her own finger pointing at the third card. "In the lake." She knew the black, deep, blue-cold water as if it ran through her veins.

After this first afternoon, there were other days when Mrs Massey had asked her to cut the cards and deal their game of Three, and it occurred to Anna now, as she walked up past Pike Lake to Cob Cottage, that on no occasion had Mrs Massey dealt the cards. Each time, so few now that Anna looked back, Mrs Massey had sat very still and upright, her left palm face down on the table, and her twinkling, clever eyes watching Anna.

No one was home, and Anna, without taking off her jacket, cleared the stray bills and leftover crumbs from the table and sat down. After a moment, she took the cards out of her pocket and set them on the table. She was uncertain what to do next.

She reached for the kettle and clicked it on, but the bright blue electrical light of it was wrong. She rummaged in the cupboard for a moment, pulling out Grandma Hettie's cast iron whistling kettle. She filled it, put it onto the hob, and, at the first hiss of the heat catching the water, an instinct twitched inside her.

Anna sat down and reached for the cards. The edges were foxed and feathered into something like mouse fur, and it gave the sense of being alive. Her fingers stretched the elastic band and released the deck. The old gilding on the backs glittered.

Anna paused. She was very tired. She was weary of worry and grief and afraid of being afraid and angry at distrusting herself. She sat for a moment, letting her eyes wander over the filigree patterns of the top card. The kettle whispered behind her. She made a choice.

Let go.

Let it go.

Anna shuffled the few cards. How many had there been? Thirteen, of course.

She dealt three, face down. The remainder of the Paper Prophets she placed face down on the table and focused on the sound of the kettle and the hob light, *phut, phut, phut.*

Let go.

She turned the middle card. The Castle. It was at once new and familiar. She recalled the intricate brickwork of the crenelated tower strangled with ivy that she did not recall in real life. The sky above it shimmered with green light.

Panic rose up like bile. Anna took a deep breath, and, instead of trying to fight the fear and the doubt, she reached past them, further down to where her Strength was trying to hide.

She opened her eyes and turned the right-hand card. This was how she had done it with Mrs Massey, and she was certain now that it had been a lesson.

The Stand. A cluster of trees, but it was different from the card of her memory. It had been elm and oak and everything Havoc, but this time it was a needled pine forest. Towering larches and firs reached up into another sky that shimmered green. The ground sparkled and was dappled with lacy shadows. The bark of the trees was textured with lichen. It took her breath away. She looked into the image for a long time, glanced back at The Castle. What had Mrs Massey said of that one?

"Secrets." The voice spoke close by, as if Mrs Massey was once more sitting opposite to her at the table. *"A fortress you see, a place to keep secrets safe. As well as being a home, of course."* Mrs Massey's voice acquired a dreamlike tone. *"Stronghold and target. There's a balance in all of the cards, the knack is knowing which way it's tipped."*

The kettle on the hob was more agitated now, whispering fiercely as Anna let go and let the card speak to her.

The Castle was sitting in snow. The window casement was frosted shut. The ivy looked more tangled in the green glimmer of the sky. The sky signified something more, and Anna thought of the *aurora borealis*. She had a strong sense that someone within the castle was looking out. She acknowledged this thought and looked down at the small wooden gate beneath. Oak, closed tight. *Secrets*, the kettle whispered.

The Stand. She was convinced it was not Havoc Wood, but it was alive and evergreen wherever it was. What was this card again?

"It's always Havoc, but in its other ways." Mrs Massey confused matters from her seat in the past. At the time, Anna had understood because, back then, she was knitted into the Wood like mended bone. The Stand was the way home, shelter, even more. There was something beyond the trees, waiting. Anna let her focus shift, dreamlike. There, to the right, just beyond sight, did it feel like a threat? She didn't blink. There was a sense of threat in her thoughts.

The left-hand card waited for Anna to turn it.

The Black Blank had been blank indeed the sole time she had seen it. Mrs Massey had shown it to her. Anna had never dealt it. She remembered this card was the Ace of the deck.

She stopped breathing as she looked at the card. It was no longer blank. The darkness was the backdrop to the stylised image of a heart, something bloodied and animal. At the edges of the heart was torn fur, grey and black, as if it had been recently ripped from a ribcage. The aorta twisted out of it, the open end of the artery pointed towards her. Anna did not want to lean forward, but she must if she was to see the scene pictured at the end as though through a telescope.

A white frozen lake; a wolf, black, making its solitary way across the surface.

The kettle howled wildly as Anna jumped up from the table. She reached a shaking hand to turn off the hob. The sudden silence was calming. She breathed deeply.

The wolf on the lake. One of her recurrent dreams and

always, always associated with her father. The missing, absent, Dr Lachlan Laidlaw. She was shaking and turned back to the cards with the intention of shuffling them away. The Black Blank was empty once more.

BEST LAID PLANS

"Did Mr Herald ring then?" Charlie popped her head around the office door on her way from the brewhouse. Michael was looking at the computer screen and pulling at his bottom lip, deep in thought. Charlie could tell he was not listening.

"Michael?"

He glanced up, put out.

"What? I'm slogging here, can't you see?" He looked back at the screen. Everything had become a slog of late for Michael Chance, and a dark thought crossed Charlie's mind that perhaps he had been permanently poisoned by Mrs Fyfe's apples. What if this current mood was a hangover from that?

"Never mind." Charlie ducked out of sight. The poisoning thought was tainting her mind. She could not remember if she had any of the antidote, her Blackberry Ferment, left. She might track some down and slip a shot into his coffee.

Her mind was being tricksy today. As she loaded the tun, letting the scent of hops and roasted wheat waft over her, she considered that a true love's kiss was generally a cure-all. Her memory flickered over the kiss they had shared in Michael's garden. He had been heavily under the influence of the Slow Poison, and that kiss had not worked. Or perhaps it had carried a poison of its own.

Charlie tore the thought up and set the mash to boil.

SHE AVOIDED the office for the rest of the day and, as was his habit of late, Michael avoided any interaction. Charlie left it until the last moment of her shift before entering the office and putting two shot glasses down on the desk.

"You shouldn't be here." Michael looked at his watch, but Charlie felt a shiver at the words.

"I'm on my way. But first..." She undid the stopper on the last ever bottle of Blackberry Ferment. There was a finger or two of the ruby liquor still remaining. Charlie had taken that as a good sign.

"Let's have a toast." She offered him a glass.

"We *are* toast," he said. "Quincey's have cancelled our contract."

Charlie's heart lost its sense of rhythm for a second.

"Well, let's drown our sorrows then." She chinked his glass as it sat on the desk.

"You're always so cheerful," he snarled. "It's annoying." As their eyes locked, she saw he meant it. Charlie drank the Ferment.

"I'll think of something." Charlie was bluffing her bravado. "See you tomorrow." And she left him poring over the computer screen.

CHARLIE WAS ready for a stride home through Havoc Wood, hoping to get trampled by the dratted Great Grey Horse or attacked by possessed squirrels, at the very least. It seemed a fitting ending to another tense day. Instead Fate threw Aron into the car park.

He was leaning up against an unfamiliar car.

"This is a different car from the other day, isn't it?" Charlie wondered why this seemed to matter to her. Aron shrugged.

"Courtesy car. The Mercedes is in the workshop."

It struck Charlie as odd that the Mercedes garage had offered a rather worn-out looking VW Golf as a courtesy car.

"What do you want?" She heard her curt tone and watched it slice at Aron in a way she had not anticipated.

"You." His voice had a vulnerable edge to it that, with everything else that was going on in her head, she could not handle, and so she laughed it off.

"I'm popular today. Mr Herald was here this morning." Charlie was disappointed to see Aron look caught out. "I gave him a tour of the brewery." Aron's reaction and the memory of the tour collided.

"Shit." The word darted from his lips. Charlie glared at Aron. He was trying not to shrink away from her, she could see. His arms were folded, defiantly relaxed. Charlie pushed a little.

"Why d'you say that? The idea was that he's looking for local suppliers for his alcohol," she said. "Isn't that a good gig if you can get it?"

"Yeh… yes… of course," Aron said. Charlie could hear an edge in his voice and could not translate it.

"Or was he just there because Quincey's dropped our contract? He's in for the kill already." Charlie felt prickly.

"That's just your paranoia." Aron lied.

"Is it? Is it really? Or is the truth that he wants to buy the brewery? That this is all part of his grand schemes? The Castle Inn? The Drawbridge Brewery? Ivan Herald, King of Castlebury." As Charlie spoke, Aron tensed, his brow forming an origami of creases. "Is that it? Is that the big project?"

"No."

"It is, isn't it? And I'm your contact, your foot in the brewery door. That's why the sudden interest in me. Oh my God, that is why Quincey's has cancelled on us."

"No." He was firm, resolute. She saw the veneer of sorrow that glazed him, and she stopped talking. There was a long moment, Aron's arms were folded tight, and, for a second, she thought that the only thing stopping him from falling on the ground was the car. He shook his head.

"The project he's into… is nothing to do with the Inn or the brewery. Seriously. Nothing at all." His voice was flecked with nerves. "Can I take you home?"

They drove in silence. Charlie felt a heavy sadness, like a body of water suffocating her. Aron did not turn the car in at the tarmac roadway. Instead he pulled into the verge.

"You know I love you." His voice cracked. Charlie was speechless, love was not a word that Aron bandied about, he was afraid of it. She looked into his face, saw where he was leaner, harried. He reached across, not to kiss her, but to open the door. Charlie hesitated.

"I've always loved you," Aron said.

She was all the way down the tarmac before she heard his car pull away, and she did not dare look back. As the tarmac cracked and broke into gravel, Charlie understood that, while Aron had said "love", Charlie had heard goodbye.

25
DATE NIGHT

Casey had dressed up for the blind date and felt uncomfortable and not herself. Her friend Mitzi had organised the disaster, for that was what it was shaping up to be.

"I've got this colleague at work." The conversation had begun and Mitzi, being forceful by nature, had already organised matters before Casey could wriggle free.

She'd had other blind and double dates with Mitzi and Jared, her hipster other half. Mitzi was a woman on a mission to find Casey a mate. None of the candidates had been suitable.

"You don't make enough effort," Mitzi chided. "Try and be more…" Mitzi had struggled for the word, "amenable."

Casey was not a difficult person by any measure. She was just unable to make herself be smaller or tidier or obedient to another's will, really. The dates that Mitzi arranged had all wanted something she could not give: less of herself.

Tonight, she'd decided to follow every letter of Mitzi's advice so that she could, perhaps, shoot her down properly next time. Casey did not doubt there would be a next time. As part of her Mitzi strategy, she had worn all the clothes that Mitzi had picked out for her online. She was wearing uncomfortable shoes and make up from a YouTube tutorial bookmarked by Mitzi.

As Casey sat in The Fiddle, Woodcastle's most posh pub at the end of Rook Row, awaiting her suitor, she realised that she didn't like Mitzi very much. They had been school friends, and, if she thought back, she hadn't liked her overmuch even then. It was just that Mitzi was hard to shake off when she latched onto you.

"You're my project," Mitzi had said last week, and Casey felt uncomfortable.

He was late, this date, Casey checking the text message Mitzi had sent including his phone number. What was his name again? As she was scrolling through the message to locate it, her phone began to ring.

"Hey, Carey?" It was not a good start. She'd forgotten his name, he'd misremembered hers. "It's Jason Burnett." Jason. Jason, of course. She pictured him wearing a golden fleece, arriving aboard the Argo.

"Oh, hey." "Carey" had considered and did not correct him, keeping her tone light and possibly fluffy.

"Listen, been a bit of a meltdown this end." *Oh, trouble with the Argonauts?* Casey thought and then paid closer attention "I'm really sorry to do this to you but…" clearly the Golden Fleece needed dipping, "…wondered if you fancied meeting me here, in town?" He sounded very pleased with his suggestion.

"Town?" Casey was confused. "I'm in town. I'm at The Fid…" Fake laughter and a lot of noise from Jason.

"Ha. No. No. I get that. I meant proper town. I'm in Castlebury. Up at New Town." He was having to raise his voice to be heard. "Mate of mine managed to get us VIP'ed at Pandemonium." It was a social coup, clearly one that passed Casey by. Although the place sounded like its name. "I thought we could hook up, you could get a cab or something and meet me here."

Casey visualised the forty-minute cab ride to New Town on

the far side of Castlebury to go to a club with a complete stranger chosen for her by Mitzi.

"Seriously, Carey, it will be a lot of fun. I promise."

CASEY WALKED HOME. It was a starlit evening, and she needed some air. The Fiddle was not her favourite of Woodcastle's pubs on the best evening. She found the Georgian rooms sombre and disapproving, and it was also quite a long walk home.

That said, tonight she wanted the long walk and chose the most circuitous route, because it would take her past the Castle, which was looking particularly majestic as she made her way up Barbican Steeps. She liked the cobbled walkway with its ancient setts. She and her brother, Seth, had always used them like stepping-stones and played at not stepping on the cracks. But the cracks tonight were in her ankles, twisting over in the horrible shoes. She took them off, and it felt good to feel the frost beneath her stocking feet. Felt free. She laughed to herself and began a light-hearted hopscotching step across the brown paving stones. Her brother had said they were brown because of all the bloodshed.

Step. Hop. Dance. Hop. This drapey dress that Mitzi had picked was not stupid at all, it was beautiful, the streetlight catching in the embroidered fancy bit on the swirly hem. Casey heard herself laugh out loud as the fabric twirled and rippled. Spin. Spin. Turn. The strong hand reached for hers, and she laughed until she was spun around, into the strong arms. Spin, spin. Turn. Turn.

SHE AWOKE at the foot of Banner Hill feeling bruised and hungover, her head spinning. She lay still so she would not be sick. She sat up and let her mind rove over her body, assessing damage. Grazes. Her dress spoilt, muddied, spattered with blood. From where? Her heart raced. A long cut on her leg, shallow and crusted over now. Bruises coloured her arms, and, as she looked at her hands, she had a wild memory of dancing at the castle, of strong arms spinning her. No. She couldn't go further. Not yet.

Casey scrabbled to her feet, stockingless and bare, grubby and with no sign of her shoes anywhere. She recalled taking them off at the castle. She took several deep breaths, but she could not stop shaking.

It was the longest walk home she'd ever had.

26

BAREFOOT BORROWED

The scent of heartache drifted to Borrower through the trees of Havoc Wood. It was like burnt earth, blood on his lips.

Whoever she was, this wife was different. He made swift progress, following, once more, the track of the deer, and there she was, outside the castle, like an offering from the town. It mattered little that the old bones of the place pushed against him, he shoved back, took the few steps needed across the stones to take her hand.

He felt the skills in her hands, knifework, the stirring of ladles, the wooden spoon of savour. He would not have to borrow any of this when she was his. He would take her back to the cottage and she would warm the hearth. He would make her Queen of the Wood. He twirled her around, put the steps of his dance into her feet, and she laughed as his arms folded tight about her. A snare of strong arms.

He was ravenous for her, lifting her over his shoulder and stepping up onto the banking to skirt the castle, the speediest route back. While he must follow the deer out, he could find his own way back into Havoc.

It seemed fated when, the moment he stepped into the trees, there was a rough nickering sound. Borrower turned to find the Great Grey Night Horse towering over him and, feeling that, this time, the Fates were with him, grabbed for the reins. The beast could help him carry off his Woodcastle wife.

It was not to be. The reins lashed him once again, twisting their leather around his hand so that he had to wrench himself free as the vast hooves stepped forward, intent on trampling him. Borrower hefted his wife higher onto his shoulder and ran. The horse pursued, forcing him this way, blocking that.

The trees did not greet Borrower, the branches creaked and switched. Leaves slapped at him like punishment, and the wind blew up and took his breath. A dozen times more he dropped his prey. Desperate to escape the horse, his hand sealed about her wrist, bumping her unconscious body over the ground.

No. This was not how it should be. Bark grazed him. Thorns reached from bramble and blackthorn and clawed him to the ground. The hooves grazed at his calves as he fled.

At the foot of Banner Hill, he was halted, the wood floor sinking and bubbling into a bog, the ground chewing him up, further and further the mire rose until he let go of the wife. At that, the horse whinnied, triumphant, rearing up to clatter its hooves on the ground with a sound like rocks falling, and Borrower stumbled.

On his feet at last he ran, the roots and hollows tripping him on his long path and nowhere was safe, there was no haven. Havoc Wood was spitting him out.

27

MAKING THE OWLS TURN THEIR HEADS

THERE IS NO TIME

Dr Fell had retired shortly after Charlie was born, and Vanessa herself had been asked to take over the inception of a new department.

"You are our greatest asset and our biggest liability," Hennessey had told her at a private meeting at his house. It was a big house, as befitted the CEO of a company such as De Quincey Langport.

"All I ask is that you find us something. Anything. A power, a force, some kind of supernatural commodity. I do not care what you find for us, only that you let De Quincey Langport be the keepers of the secret."

He had not offered Vanessa so much as a glass of water since her arrival. Her mother would be pleased at this, warning always of the perils of supping with the enemy.

"I work hard," Vanessa had repeated. Hennessey had smiled, wily as a fox. He understood there was no arguing with her, and so he let her go.

· · ·

THE LIGHTS in the laboratory fused for the third time that day, and Vanessa told the team to go home.

Alone, she looked back over the paper readout for the encephalograph, most especially the vividly spiked section that had continued to etch itself across the paper even as the power supply failed. Probably, Vanessa mused, this was the reason for the power outage.

She sat for an hour, more, her work illumined by the small pool of light from the anglepoise. She liked this lamp, the way it leaned over with a studious air. Her breath, she saw, was steaming in the cold of the room, making a fog in the lamp's bright light.

Bright as snowlight.

Vanessa switched off the lamp and reached for her bag. The compass in her pocket twitched. Her thoughts twitched with memories.

BACK THEN, Anna and Charlie had been staying with her mother at Cob Cottage. When Vanessa pulled in, she glimpsed them in the kitchen taking out the candles they had made earlier in the week; beyond, the porch door open as Charlie rushed out to place hers first on the edge of the deckboards. Anna followed, with more ceremony.

"Solstice," Hettie Way said as she came through the kitchen.

"Mum, Mum, Mum." Vanessa's daughters raced to greet her, a tumult of information and candles as they readied for marking the night.

"We have to light the candles to carry the day," Anna said, lighting a taper from the woodburner and sheltering it with her hand.

"Can I? Can I?" Charlie buzzed and hurtled back and forth between hearth and door. "I want to make the light last." And Hettie handed her her own taper.

The candles, set in saucers along the length of the porch, looked beautiful. Inside there were candles on the dinner table and a feast of a rich stew.

"It's happening, isn't it?" The last few days had carried a mineral scent through the air of Havoc that set Hettie's senses alight. She broached the subject as the girls drifted off to sleep, curled under woollen blankets on the big sofa. Vanessa pushed the hair back behind Anna's ear and kissed her forehead.

"Yes." Vanessa tugged the blanket over Charlie's foot, kissing the sole of it as she did.

"Do you have an idea when?"

Vanessa laughed at the question. "When have I ever?" she said. "I'm not adept enough to read the signs."

Hettie regarded her daughter for some moments.

"Stop staring," Vanessa half chided, shifting in her chair, uncomfortable.

"Sorry. But I'm not sure when I might see you again." Hettie's eyes were sparkling with tears. She controlled them, the two women sharing a warm hug.

"Let's get the kids into bed then." Hettie bustled a little. "No sense in taking them back to Way Towers with you now that it is time. Stay here. You know your room is always ready."

They bundled the girls into their blankets and carried them to their rooms. The small, cosy spaces softened the edges of Vanessa's mood.

"I ask a lot of you," she said as Hettie closed Charlie's door.

"I'm their grandmother," Hettie smiled. "I do what grandmas do."

Vanessa felt wired. Her mother put her hand on her shoulder.

"Rest."

Vanessa yawned.

· · ·

She woke, hours later. The digital clock by her bedside flashing in real alarm that, at some point in the night, the power had gone out.

In her pocket, Vanessa could feel the compass. She did not need to check how fast it was spinning, nor in which direction.

Her mother was already up, the two colliding in the hallway. Outside there was a disturbance.

"Horses," Hettie said as Cob Cottage rattled.

Vanessa moved through the kitchen, beneath the arch. Her mother was watchful at the kitchen window.

"They're coming down from Day's Ride." Hettie turned as the drumming of hooves beat rhythm into the building. The cup on the table jolted as the Riders thundered around the cottage. War cries.

Vanessa reached for the door.

"No." Hettie was warning, knowing it was futile from the look on her daughter's face. As Vanessa turned the handle on the porch door, the kitchen door wrenched itself open and a vast, bellowing grey horse entered, bowing its heavily maned head through the frame. It stood inside, panting, the scent of it thickening the air inside Cob Cottage. It glanced at Hettie then nickered at Vanessa.

Hettie moved out of the path of the horse as Vanessa hop-skipped onto the sofa, her hands twining into the strong mane as the horse stooped for her. As Vanessa hefted herself onto its back, Hettie darted forward to open the porch door, the great grey beast pushing past as she did so, so that she was flattened against the wall.

As the horse stepped out onto the porch, the door to Cob Cottage yanked itself free of Hettie Way's grasp and slammed shut.

"No. No. No." She rattled at the door, but it would not let her out. She looked up, Vanessa looking back for just a nod before the Great Grey Horse jumped from the porch. Hettie, her hand on the window, felt the glass freeze, the icicles like knives ranked at the porch edge.

The black horses, their Riders in black and furs, streamed from each side of the cottage, in pursuit. The Great Grey Horse took steady strides, the limbs powering towards Pike Lake. Hettie thought they would skirt around, but instead she watched the surface of the lake freeze before them with a sound like an animal, deep and mournful.

The Great Grey Horse was surefooted. The Riders crowded behind, spurring their charges on, and Hettie watched where the ice cracked behind the Horse, fracturing into splinters, melting beneath the hooves of the Riders, all swallowed down in an eyeblink.

A ripple rolled its silver ring of light across Pike Lake, then all was silent.

The Horse had left a calling card at the rear of the Cottage, a small cairn of cobbles of dung that Hettie used on the vegetable patch that following summer. The beans that year were particularly prolific, the flowers a deep purple, lipped with grey. She harvested them, but they sat in a bowl in the scullery for a good while until she decided to dry them and store them away.

"GRANDMA?" The voice was small and familiar in the dream. "Grandma. Grandma." It wasn't a dream, of course. Charlie was leaning over her face, her small fingers pulling Hettie's eyelids open. "Are you awake?"

"Yes." Hettie blinked and stirred. "Is it time for breakfast?"

"Mummy's here," Charlie said, wide-eyed with delight. "And she's really FAT."

.   .   .

A MONTH OR MORE LATER, and it was a full moon over Pike Lake when Emily Way made her way into the world, her first cries echoing around Havoc Wood, making the owls turn their heads.

28

SIGNS AND POLICEMEN

PC Williamson did not want to risk the patrol car on the gravel and dirt track that led to Cob Cottage, so he parked in the layby on the opposite side of Old Castle Road and walked in.

He had not often walked into Havoc Wood. No one did. He'd been possibly three times before, and always in company with his grandmother, his father's mother, Violet, who had "business", as she put it, with Mrs Way. As the tarmac driveway led him into the cover of the trees, he recalled that his grandmother had always brought a gift of some sort for Mrs Way, a basket of scones or something. The basket of scones could have been used to cobble the dirt track if memory served. His grandmother was enthusiastic about baking, but baking did not repay the favour. PC Williamson wished he had brought something. It felt wrong.

The trees were watching. It was a distinct sensation, the prickling at the back of his neck and the fact that, here and there, in the brisk November breeze, branches swayed down far enough to brush at his cap, almost knocking it off his head. *Don't look up. Don't be afraid.* He remembered his gran Violet's instructions. She'd not been afraid. What had she been? Respectful. It was a tenet of his grandmother's life, and, with that thought, PC Williamson took off his hat. The branches ahead of him bowed low, as if in approval.

The tarmac crumbled away into gravel, which seemed quite civilised once you were on the pitted and rutted dirt track. He looked down to where Cob Cottage sat, just up from the shore-line, and he could see lights on. This only served to remind him that it would be dark soon, and he was walking in Havoc Wood.

Anna Way opened the back door as he edged past the tangled garden.

"PC Williamson," Anna smiled uncertainly. "Want to come in?"

If the wood had seemed standoffish and aloof, the interior of Cob Cottage was a glow of warmth and comfort. There was something cooking that smelt of garlic and herbs and made PC Williamson's stomach grumble. He'd been so wrapped up in his investigations today that he'd forgotten to have lunch.

"How can we help?" Anna asked. Emz turned from setting the table.

"It's Emily I've come to talk to." PC Williamson tried to make his nod as friendly as possible. Emz looked trapped. This was always the problem with being a policeman, PC Williamson found, people were never really very happy to see you.

"Do you need me to leave... or should I...?" Anna seemed flummoxed. PC Williamson shook his head.

"No, no need for that. Stay." He decided to charge into the subject. "Emily, I wanted to ask you about the party at Adam Overton's home the other night. We're looking into the attack on Caitlin Milburn, and I need to get statements from anyone who was there."

"I wasn't there." Emily's voice wavered a little and her face was pale. PC Williamson felt that his police instincts ought to kick in and tell him that she was lying or covering up the truth in some way, but his instincts were quiet. It was odd. Perhaps, he thought, what was odd was that he was hearing the truth.

"Oh." He felt foolish. "I was told you were. One of the girls mentioned your name." He was trying to recall which of the sixth form girls had given him this information. He did not like this investigation and the way it was turning.

"No. Sorry." Emily's voice was even quieter, and PC Williamson visibly wilted.

"Wild goose chase?" Anna asked with some sympathy. PC Williamson nodded.

"I apologise. I might have misunderstood the information I was given. They might have said you weren't there, and I was not listening properly." He was feeling lightheaded and waved his notebook in surrender. "Sorry. I've got a lot of information and statements and interviewing going on." He checked back through his notes, the pages making a dry rustling sound.

"Did you speak with Winn?" Emily asked, her voice gathering a little strength. "She found Caitlin."

"Yes. She thought she'd fallen from a horse. Can you tell me anything about the horse?" PC Williamson thought that it might be important. "It was saddled up, Winn said," his mind was picking a path, "but no one can find the rider."

He felt the tension twang a little.

"It doesn't belong to Logan Boyle," Emz said, her face pinked a little. "If that's what anyone has told you. It's not his horse."

"No one suggested it was." PC Williamson was regretting the lack of lunch, he felt out of sorts and lightheaded. "It was worth throwing it in the mix. Winn said it was saddled up, so I assumed some poor bugger might have fallen off."

"Is it just gossip you're listening to?"

"Emz?" Anna stared at her sister, who was not to be tamped down.

"I'm serious. At school they're saying…" the name was impossible to say. Emz swallowed it down, "…he raped Caitlin. They all believe it."

"I can't tell you anything about the case."

"I'm not asking you to. I'm asking you to not go with all the gossip."

"Emz. Seriously." Anna was stern.

"No." PC Williamson shook his head. "I can reassure you that I am investigating this thoroughly. Hence my calling here tonight."

There was a silence. Emz backed down a little, nodded.

"I can say that Logan Boyle is no longer helping us with our enquiries. He's made a statement, and I'm following up any leads, which is why I ask about the horse." PC Williamson felt the tension release itself. He glanced out through the window.

"Shit, is that it?"

All eyes turned.

The Great Grey Horse stood at the shoreline of Pike Lake as if looking out admiring the view.

"Wow." It was the only word that had come out of PC Williamson's mouth since they had all hurried out of the cottage. "Wow. Wow."

"It is a bit," Anna said. The horse turned to survey its audience and nickered greeting. PC Williamson could not take his eyes from the splendid animal.

"That saddle…" he moved forward a step or two to take a look, holding his hands up as if in supplication, "…that's an expensive bit of craftsmanship."

"Is that a clue to the rider?" Emz asked.

"Probably. We should ask Marlow Whitburn up here, from Caracole Stables. She knows about saddlery and stuff," PC Williamson advised and then caught the look from Anna.

"When I say 'we' I mean you." He took in a deep breath and looked again at the horse. It looked, very distinctly, back at him, its head turned to focus its left eye upon him. He heard his grandmother's voice in his head, saw her lips move as she packed a brick of fruitcake into her plastic shopper.

"This..." he nodded to the horse, "this looks like Havoc business."

Anna and Emz looked at him. PC Williamson gave an uncomfortable smile.

"My gran knew your gran," was the only explanation required. "You're the Gamekeepers."

At this a look passed between Emz and Anna; PC Williamson cleared his throat, nervous.

"Yes. Right. So anyway..." he was fumbling a little. Anna rescued him.

"We've searched for the rider and come up blank," Anna confessed.

"You don't think they're connected?" PC Williamson asked. "When did this chap show up? Was he here before the first attack?" He pointed to the horse. Anna was quiet.

"I think we can safely say that the attack on Caitlin is police business." She was cool, uneasy. "She was in Leap Woods." Anna did not look at Emz, as a terrible thought drifted across her own head. The woods were sisters, frayed together at the edges; the question was how frayed.

"Right. Yes. Well, I don't want to step on toes," PC Williamson said. "I have my beat, you have yours," he conceded. "Can you keep me in the loop regarding the horse?"

Anna nodded.

"Marlow Whitburn is a bit..." PC Williamson was looking for the politest way to proceed.

"...of a bitch?" Anna finished. PC Williamson raised his eyebrows.

"I was going to say busy." His eyebrows flickered up again,

almost making Anna smile. "You could call Carrie instead. She'd probably have time to help." And he said his farewells.

"Carrie's on her way." Emz put her phone back into her pocket, while she and Anna stood looking at the horse as it leaned to drink from Pike Lake.

"It is massive, isn't it?" Emz was awed by the power of the horse. Its mane tumbled forward, the ends trailing in the water and making sparkled ripples in the waxing moonlight.

"Must be a Shire or some other sort of draught horse." Anna's voice was distant and dreamy. "Look at the colour of its coat." She reached forward, but this time the Great Grey Horse stepped away, turning its back on them and moving down the shoreline.

Emz was looking at the ground, at the pattern of hoofprints and footprints.

"Charlie might be able to make something of this," she said, as Anna looked down. "You think?"

Anna nodded.

"What's going on?" Charlie's voice called down from the porch. "I nearly ran down PC Williamson on the track. What's happened? Oh." She spotted the horse. "Still can't catch it?"

Anna and Emz shook their heads as Charlie joined them.

"Emz has given Carrie a ring. She's on her way," Anna brought her up to speed.

"Good shout." Charlie looked at the scuffed-up ground.

"What do you think?" Emz asked. Charlie did not reply for a moment, her brow furrowed.

"About what?"

Emz nodded to the prints.

"They tell you anything?"

Charlie looked up, embarrassed.

"No." She dug her hands deep into her pockets and looked at Anna. "Listen, I saw that Herald bloke again today. Gave him a tour of the brewery."

"Oh no." Anna was in catastrophe mode. Charlie shook her head.

"He wants to increase his 'local offering', as they say, for booze."

"You mean he wants to buy the brewery?"

Charlie pulled a face.

"Have to admit that was my instinct, after what you said about the Castle Inn." She grimaced. "Do you think Lella will sell?"

"Yes," Anna nodded. "She needs the cash, like everyone else these days. What about Drawbridge? Will Michael sell?"

Charlie avoided looking at Anna and nodded her head.

"Although Aron tells me Herald isn't buying the brewery."

"D'you believe him?" Anna could see the moment that she said it that the question stung Charlie.

"Why don't you buy the Castle Inn?" Charlie suggested, swerving the subject. Emz looked astonished, Anna, terrified.

"It's not impossible," Charlie said. "You could get a loan or a mortgage. Something." She was defeated. "Oh, you're right. Who am I kidding?"

Anna laughed, a light, high sound, and hugged Charlie.

"Hey. I appreciate the attempt to cheer me up."

Charlie did not look cheered and Anna took note.

"You know he might not be evil," Emz suggested, feeling defensive. "He might have genuine reasons for his interest. Saving the Castle Inn, maybe? Keeping the brewery going? It's not impossible."

Anna and Charlie regarded her with interest.

"I'm just saying. Maybe we're not the only people who love Woodcastle," Emz continued.

"You have a point," Anna agreed.

"Herald is in it for profit. He owns most of Castlebury, he's got pockets filled with councillors backing his every planning permission. And why are you defending him? You don't know him…" Charlie could hear her own voice rise in volume and took a breath. She was riled; the thought of Ivan Herald sparked like lightning in her head.

"Neither do you." Emz pointed out.

Any further discussion of Ivan Herald and his possibly evil plans was halted by the sound of Carrie's jeep chugging down to the cottage.

CARRIE, the local vet and equine expert, looked at the horse with undisguised admiration.

"I don't recognise it." She too reached out to the grey-black flecked flank, and the horse took a polite step back. "Oh my God. It is magnificent." Carrie once more stepped forward to try to take the reins. "Here boy, here you are, not going to…" The horse did not care what she was not going to do, she was chiefly not going to take the reins. Carrie sighed.

"Okay. I've got a halter in the car." Carrie was resourceful. "Let's give that a go."

They 'gave it a go', as Carrie had suggested, and several minutes later the landscape around the shoreline was dotted with divots of mud. Carrie and the Way sisters tried to catch their breath and check for bruises as the Great Grey Horse whinnied and stamped.

"Well, my bad, there. He sounds pissed off now," Carrie said as she shook some shoreline sand from her hair.

"He sounds amused," Charlie grinned and reached up to tighten her squiffy bun. Anna wiped a scuff of dirt from her face.

"I've had an idea." Carrie brightened, her tone dragging Emz's gaze from the horse. "There's that show in Castlebury, Wild Horses. Maybe it's a runaway from there?" She looked confident.

"Wild Horses?" Charlie looked puzzled.

"Yeah. It's like fantasy dressage, very theatrical. I'd forgotten. I was up at Caracole Stables the other day and Judith was talking about it. Well, disapproving of it, point of fact." Carrie grimaced a little at the memory. "But yes. It might have wandered away from there."

"Sounds worth a pop to ask them." Anna smiled but was aware of a dark look from Charlie.

THEY WATCHED Carrie's headlights disappear through the trees before Charlie spoke.

"It's not come from any stupid dancing horse show."

"It's out of Havoc," Emz finished the thought.

"It might have wandered in through Havoc." Anna was trying to be reasonable.

"It has never been to Castlebury," Charlie stated the fact. "It is not a dancing tart of a horse." She was severe. "Those hoof-prints in the sand, before we all rucked them up…"

Emz lit up.

"You did see something." She was delighted. Charlie was thoughtful.

"Yes. I don't know what it was."

"Describe it?" Anna suggested. Charlie looked as the horse lifted his head as if listening.

"Lines. Criss-crossed lines. Not like a random path. More…" she groped for the right word, "mathematical, I think. Or a compass." Charlie dug her face deeper into her jacket collar as she fumbled in her pocket for her recent doodles. She offered them to her sisters. Anna turned her page around as Emz's gaze switched between her doodle and the one in Anna's hand.

"I've seen it written over the wood, as if the Horse has mapped it out." Charlie said.

"What if…?" Anna began, feeling inspired, "what if we're looking at this from the wrong angle?"

"How d'you mean?" Emz asked.

"What if it's waiting for someone?" Anna said. The sisters exchanged a look.

"Good point, well made," Charlie said, her voice sounding lighter. She was about to speak further when the horse gave a snort and began walking away. Charlie headed after it.

"Charlie?" Anna took a few steps.

"I'll see you later," Charlie's voice lilted back through the dark.

"Do we follow them?" Emz asked. Anna shook her head.

"No, she's the one with the Maps and Compass," Anna said and then gave a small start.

"What is it?" Emz asked.

"Nothing." Anna shrugged it off, headed back up onto the porch. "Just a stray thought. Let's wait inside."

In the scullery, after putting a load of washing in the machine, Anna took the Paper Prophets from her trouser pocket. She felt the energy they gave off and paused for a moment to consider it. What sort of energy was it? Like an engine, ticking over.

She stretched the elastic from the cards and put it back into her pocket. Hurrying, she did not shuffle them this time. She took the first card from the top.

The Maps and Compass startled her. She had seen this clearly in her mind's eye as Charlie had started off after the Great Grey Horse, and here it was. The routes on the maps depicted were complex, intertwined, and seemed not to lead anywhere. She looked at the compass and held her breath. The needle was spinning. A crash from the kitchen made her put the cards away.

Emz was clearing away the remnants of a plate.

"Sorry, it slipped out of my hand." She looked uncertain.

"What's wrong?" Anna asked. "Is this about Logan Boyle?" and Emz folded into tears.

"You think he didn't do it?" Anna asked when the tears had dried over the tale of the sixth form's current rumour mill mood and the message carried by the black web.

"It feels wrong." Emz snuffed at her tears. "But I don't like Caitlin, so I don't trust myself," Emz confessed. "And I'm not sure about Logan. They've been going out, but it doesn't seem genuine."

"Why would she say it?"

"Revenge? Drama?" Emz felt heavy thinking about it.

Anna mulled it all over.

"What happened, do you think?"

Emz shook her head.

"What if the rider of the horse is the person who attacked Caitlin?" Anna threw the thought out. "It's possible. Whoever it is rolls up on their trusty steed, maybe they didn't even fall off, they got off on purpose to attack Caitlin."

Emz did not panic or protest. She stood for some moments considering.

"The horse protected her," Emz said. "Winn was sure. Said the horse came to Prickles to get her, led her back to Caitlin."

"So?"

"Well, if its rider was the villain, surely the horse would be transport? It wouldn't protect Caitlin, it'd have carried her off."

Anna felt relief flood over her.

"Good point."

Emz continued. "To be fair, it amazed me that Caitlin was

even in the wood at all. She's not outdoorsy, and she doesn't tend to do what she doesn't want."

"Puzzling. Maybe she just stumbled across the horse," Anna said. Emz shook her head.

"Or the horse stumbled across her. In trouble."

They thought about this.

"This is definitely a Havoc problem," Anna decided.

IT WAS over an hour later before Charlie arrived home looking cold and frustrated.

"What happened?"

"I followed it, and it was all fine until I got up to Quinn's Gate, and I thought I'd lost it so I… I just let myself, you know…" She raised her eyebrows, her voice conspiratorial.

"'You know' what?" Anna was being dense. Emz gave her a shove.

"She used her Strength, you tit." A smile illuminated Emz's face at this news. "Go on, what happened?"

Charlie shook her head. "It was all over the place. The path lit up in front of me, only there was this frost shimmer to it, so in places I couldn't even look at it directly. I had to look sort of sideways." She plonked herself down in the chair. "It was as if it was just out of sight, and, if I looked directly at it, I could see the compass points spreading out over the landscape and spinning."

Anna sat very still. Emz put her chin in her hands.

"Spinning?"

"Yes. Made me dizzy to look at it. I've never seen anything like that before." Charlie leaned back.

"Where is the Great Grey now? Did you bring him back with you?" Emz asked. Charlie revived for a moment, looking up with a smirk.

"The Great Grey?"

"Good a name as any," Emz shrugged. Charlie nodded.

"No, the Great Grey is not with me. He vanished into the trees. Again."

"Where?" Anna asked. Charlie wrinkled her brow.

"Can't you guess?"

"Day's Ride," said Emz.

29

ICE

It began with the clock hands spinning. No one really noticed, busy at their tasks, tapping at keyboards, and skimming mice over mats as, in the observation room, Vanessa Way slept.

When Eleanor looked back over her notes and memories long, long afterwards, she would recall the idea that Vanessa slept like a princess in a fairytale, lying on her back, one hand rested on her stomach, the other by her side.

Eleanor kept paper notes that she wrote with a pen. She had learned from Professor Way that paper could not be shorted out, ink would not vanish in a corrupted file.

A spike registered on all the graphs and charts, screens and monitors, tall as a spear, and the lights blinked off.

"Whoa." Dexter looked round as if someone had turned the lights off. "We're up. We're still online folks." He was reassuring, his hands and eyes doing their swift dance between keyboard and touch screen.

Heart. Brain. Breath. Vanessa Way's life signs etched and scratched themselves across the machinery.

The lights winked on, the computers blinking before the

sudden fall in temperature accompanied by a tight cracking sound. The lab darkened, silence from the team, Rufus and Dexter playing symphonies of keyboard clacks.

"Nothing," Rufus stated. "We're offline."

"No emergency backup." Dexter confirmed in a calm voice. "No recording. Nothing live."

"Except that." Rufus pointed to the arm on the old encephalograph, which had begun a new and frenzied transcription across the paper. The sound rustled into the silence of the room.

"How? There's no power." He looked to Eleanor, who nodded, continued her vigil of Vanessa. The light altered around them, the darkness pierced with white crystalline spears and branches. In the pale illumination, they could all see their breath, and Dexter checked the thermometer and barometer on the wall.

"Spinning," he noted, as the light altered.

"Shit." Rufus's voice was shaky. Eleanor held up her phone camera to the observation room window and checked it was recording, the light winking red.

She watched as, in the observation room, a green light rose from Vanessa in a shimmering curtain that whipped and furled above her. In the lab, Dexter called out a time code as the clock and barometer whirred round, unstopping.

"THERE WAS no power outage anywhere else in the building?" Vanessa, dressed in a white bathrobe, sat at the desk with Eleanor.

"Nope." Eleanor shook her head. "Not a hint of an issue anywhere else on the entire campus."

Vanessa considered.

"Did you work out the circuit loop? The extent of it?"

Eleanor pushed a schematic drawing across the desk. It had

been scribbled on with a pencil. Vanessa noted the boundary of the power cut. The pattern it made. Mathematical and angular.

"I even took it up to Anthony in Facilities Management. Their computer registered nothing out of the ordinary."

Vanessa nodded.

"Show me the footage again..." She gestured to where Eleanor's phone rested.

"Can I ask a favour first?" Eleanor was shaken, her face, several hours later, still ashen.

"You can ask." Vanessa gave nothing away.

"We're Dark Lab. I understand the protocols of that. We need, no — I'm going to be truthful, I need — I need you to give the team your ICE contacts."

Eleanor reached for Vanessa's own phone, swiped at the screen. "I'm not being funny, but there is nothing in here that is of any help in a crisis. There's me, there's Dex, and Rufus..."

"What did you say?"

"I'm saying you need ICE contacts." Eleanor was perturbed at the troubled expression on Vanessa's face. She looked grey. "You okay?"

Vanessa was very still.

"Ice?"

Eleanor was wary, unwilling to distress Vanessa, though she herself was struggling.

"In Case of Emergency. I-C-E. ICE." Eleanor forced calm through her voice. "We need your daughters' contact details. In case of emergency."

Vanessa stared at her for a moment.

"Show me the footage again," she requested. Eleanor was about to open her mouth and protest, but she knew better. Vanessa leaned forward, grabbing the USB cable. "Let's put it on the laptop." A couple of clicks brought the images onto the laptop, grainy, but clear enough.

"This light emission, is it electrons or...?" Eleanor knew

what it was but was struggling to pull her mind back into shape after the day's events. "It's the aurora, isn't it?" she ventured. The clip ended. Vanessa took in a deep breath.

"You know where my daughters live." She began reaching for a pen, dragging a bit of paper from the back of Dexter's notes. "Here are their numbers." She began writing Anna's number. "Only you, Eleanor. No one else. Not even Rufus or Dexter."

Eleanor nodded, wiped at the tears that were filling her eyes.

"Okay." Her voice was breathy and quiet as Vanessa folded the paper into her shaking hand.

30

HORSE SENSE

Borrower tracked the Horse from Day's Ride. Its path in and then out of Havoc signified its true status as one of the Night Horses; a fact compounded, Borrower felt, by the way that it had thwarted his recent attempted acquisitions of a Woodcastle wife.

It was vexing, but he did not mourn the loss. One had been pretty, one had breathed heartache. He had not chosen wisely when he picked the one with red boots. Borrower would have his way, and, as revenge, he was determined that the horse would bend to his will and help him. It would learn a lesson in obedience beneath his reins and take him on his travels with his new wife. A Night Horse had passage anywhere and Borrower could not recall his last foray beyond Havoc.

The beast, he now saw, took specific paths through Havoc. Its route from Day's Ride to High Foxes would tell him something of its origins, if he cared to look, but he did not need to know its history, only its future in his service.

When the Horse reached the darkest edge of Finches, Borrower watched as the Horse halted and looked up into the canopy, its mane tumbling like a waterfall over the muscles of that powerful neck. He held his breath as its eye turned directly upon him and he felt the pull, the drawing down, so strong that he was losing his footing in the branches of the tree. The Horse gave a low nickering sound that grated at Borrower. Was it mocking him? He was outraged and unsettled, his feet sliding, but his hand reached out for a switch of hazel as he fell. Draw him down? Ha. He would land on its back and teach it who was master.

He dropped. The air rushing him, the switch whipping in his hand. Again the low nickering sound rumbled as Borrower crumpled onto the leafy earth. He rolled himself over, angry.

The Night Horse had vanished.

With a spit and a curse, Borrower turned and wondered where he might spend the rest of this troubling night.

31

THE TRUTH WILL FIND YOU OUT

The rumours at school were no longer rumours. They had taken on the twist of truth by repetition. Officially no longer implicated or helping with enquiries, Logan Boyle had returned to his timetable and, for the most part, his fellow students had left him alone, scared that trouble might rub off on them like tarnish.

Only Mark Catton was openly hostile in the sixth form common room. Emz looked up to see the black web spooling from his mouth as he spoke to his former friend.

"Think you can keep your dick in your pants till home time?" was his withering jibe. The room fell silent, all eyes turned to Logan. It was clear, to Emz at least, that everyone in the room was suspicious of Logan. Some afraid, some gleeful at his downfall. No one, it appeared, as Emz scanned the real faces, considered that Logan might not have done this. The sixth form wanted the drama and gossip, not the truth, which was that the police were not interested in Logan. That a man with a tow truck and two of Logan's brothers were witness to Logan not having done anything except wait at the roadside for assistance.

He hitched his backpack onto his shoulder and left the room.

Mark Catton looked smug. "Who the fuck does he think he is?" Mark brayed, but most of the students looked away.

Emz made her way to Maths where Logan was sitting at the back in the furthest corner. He did not stay for the whole lesson, Mrs Kumar casting only a slight glance as the door closed behind him.

Emz had reason enough not to frequent the sixth form common room. She placed herself firmly outside the circle of girly politics and clique in-fighting. She knew Mark Catton always hung out there, viewing the slightly shabby first-floor room as his court. If the weather was bad, she hid in the library, but her usual hideaway was by the wildlife pond.

A small copse of birch trees and a range of shrubs had been allowed to grow wild, and, even in November and rimed with frost, the branches tangled above her head and made the place feel like a nest. She skirted the edge, which bordered the back of the Science block, and cut in through the gap between the hedging.

Logan started up from the bench concealed there, his face pale and thin-looking as he snatched up his backpack and turned away.

"You don't have to run away from me," Emz said. He hesitated and then put his bag down, retook his seat. Emz sat on the opposite end of the bench. There seemed a hundred, possibly a thousand, things she wanted to say to him, but she had courage to say only one.

"Need the notes from Maths?" she asked. He looked taken aback.

"You'd let me have them?" he spoke in a low, anxious voice.

"Yes." She rummaged in her bag for her notebook and handed it over.

"You can correct it all as you go," she said, and he managed a weak smile. He kept his face turned to the pages.

"I know you didn't do it," Emz volunteered. Logan gave an

odd laugh, and she recognised, almost too late, that it was part sob.

"It'll come good. The truth will—" as she spoke, he gave the terrible laugh, once more.

"Will what? Will be made up?"

Emz felt powerless; it made her feel wild inside.

"Can't you make Caitlin tell the truth?"

Logan's laugh was shrill, desperate.

"Someone should." Emz heard her own instructions.

"I'm never going near her ever again. Christ." Logan wiped his tears and stood up, gathering his strength. "I'm off," he said. He took an apple from his pocket; it was particularly red, and he offered it to her.

"Hungry? 'Cause I'm not." He tossed it into the air. Emz caught it and watched him move between the trees and out of sight around the Science block. In the near distance, a voice catcalled his name and there was laughter.

Emz stared at the apple. There was a message in it, but she could not fathom its meaning.

HER ESCAPE to Prickles was swift, and she wondered if Logan might have reached his home by the time she was standing in the kitchen waiting for the kettle to boil. She had taken the short cut through Leap Woods in an effort to still her racing mind and heart.

Someone should.

She owed him nothing. In the light of their more recent interactions, she might be gleeful at his troubles. Emz did not function like that. The whole situation with Logan distressed her. As she reached for the teabags another thought struck her.

Something did happen to Caitlin.

That much was true, Winn had found her in the woods and

there was no reason she would be there of her own free will. Caitlin was a townie to her core.

What happened to Caitlin?

Her thoughts were disturbed by someone calling from reception.

In the shop, Judith Killen, the stable girl from Caracole Stables, looked ill at ease.

"Any chance I can use your first aid kit?" she asked. "Only Greta has cut her thumb open on Pond Gate."

Winn bustled in behind her.

"Who's done what? Where?"

It was only a matter of minutes before Judith's group of pony-trekkers were crowded into the kitchen. Judith patched Greta, and Winn was handing out cake and tea. The pony treks often cut through Leap Woods, especially in winter. Judith felt that a ride was only a proper ride if it ran through countryside. There was little or no point trotting at the side of a road. All her trek routes took in as little roadway as possible and were, as a consequence, the most popular.

"The Crow House track is a ski slope by the way, Winn," Judith said as she picked up a wedge of Victoria sponge. "Want me to take a bag of grit up there on the way back?"

"No, don't worry yourself. I'll roll over that way in the Land Rover." She picked up a pen and inked in a reminder "GRIT" on her left hand. As she did so, she saw the smirched reminder "HORSE". "Which reminds me, Judith, you don't know anyone that has a really big horse, like a proper old-school draught breed?"

"Kent Willis has those Friesians, up at Willerwish?" Judith suggested. "They're quite chunky."

"But black," Winn mused. "This one is grey. Mostly."

"Doesn't ring a bell with me," Judith considered, shaking her head. "I can ask around for you," she offered.

Emz watched through the back window as Judith wrangled

the trekkers and their mounts. She moved amongst the horses with nickering sounds and sniffing nuzzles as if she was part horse and had considerably less patience with her two-footed charges. "Do you think…" Winn began, distracting Emz from her horse thoughts, "that there is any mileage in opening up the Orangery Tea Shop again?"

Emz was on alert.

"What made you think of that?"

"Oh, the Christmas brou-ha-ha. There's that Winter Fair coming up at Kington Tower Gardens and I wondered if we could do the same."

"Like a pop-up you mean?"

"Pop up?" Winn looked perplexed.

"That's what you call them, you pop up, do the event and then pop it away again. Not permanent. No commitment long term."

Emz could see a hint of anxiety in Winn's face.

"Is this to do with the Wildwood lot?" Emz asked and was alarmed to see Winn flinch at the mention of the Wildwood Society. "Have they asked you to do a Christmas pop-up at Hartfield?"

Several expressions creased their way across Winn's face and gave off a very mixed message indeed.

"What is it?" Emz asked.

Winn pulled a face.

"I have no idea what is going on with the Wildwood bunch," she admitted. "They rescheduled the meeting again. And they haven't paid the money they promised and so I… was wondering about a plan B."

"It's a good plan B," Emz said.

"Is it? Is it doable?" Winn wondered. "Would Anna be interested in something like that do you think? No, too busy at the Castle Inn, I expect. Foolish. Old fool. Forget I mentioned it."

And, on that note, she darted out to the pens.

3 2

BLIND SPOT

It still looked, eighteen months or more after moving in, as if Vanessa Way was camped out in the kitchen at Half-Built House.

"Are you sleeping in this lounger chair thing?" Anna noted the folded quilt, an old patchwork one from Cob Cottage.

"There are beds upstairs," Charlie chided. "I mean, it's like Goldilocks up there. What's wrong? One's too hard? One's too soft?"

"The night looks nice through this window," Emz chipped in, and Vanessa smiled to herself.

"Hey, at least she's home." Anna winked. They milled about the kitchen space, each at their own task.

"So what do you think of the pop-up idea at Hartfield?" Emz pushed a little. When she'd asked her in the car on the way over, Anna had not answered her with a straight "no". Now she crumpled her face in thought, and Emz recognised the positive signs.

"I could probably do it." She put the plates on the table in front of the window, Charlie stooping to prop up the dodgy leg with a wad of paper from the pile of work notes on the countertop.

"Seriously?" Emz had her fingers crossed.

"Yeah, why not? If Lella's thinking of selling up to this Herald bloke…"

"Ivan. Call Me Ivan," Charlie prompted, mimicking his serious tone. "If he buys the brewery too, I can join you in your new enterprise."

Neither of them managed a laugh at their own jokes, a fact noted by Vanessa.

"What Herald bloke?" she asked.

"Ivan Herald," Charlie said with utter seriousness slicing through the faked amusement of their conversation.

"He's some business bigwig. Owns a lot of property in Castlebury," Anna qualified.

"He's into some big regeneration thing that Aron is gagging to be part of." Charlie looked, to Vanessa's maternal eye, like her more troubled teenage self as she sat down at the table.

"Lella's thinking of selling up." Anna sat down, also looking troubled. "Casey's convinced, but it's all up in the air."

Emz sat down and was silent, which was even more worrying to Vanessa.

"It'll be a good thing. I love Hartfield," Anna brightened. As they ate, they discussed Winn's previous failed tea room endeavours, and as the chat snaked around Hartfield, so it touched on the bad luck of her previous tenant, Mrs Fyfe, after which name there was a silence.

"So how are things at Havoc Wood after all that?" Vanessa ventured to jumpstart the chat.

"All over the place," Charlie said.

"We can't find the Rider. The horse keeps wandering off."

Vanessa looked puzzled, and her daughters filled her in on recent events. She was taken with the passion they held, even in the light of their doubts and fears.

"You don't remember anything about Day's Ride, do you?"

Anna asked. Vanessa shook her head, stiffly, her eyes remaining on her plate.

"Anna has a theory…" Charlie nodded at Anna and reached for the garlic bread.

"Theory? Oh, yes. We've been thinking that it's lost its rider. I wondered if maybe it's waiting for someone."

"Like Uber, Havoc Wood style," Emz joked. Vanessa looked up.

"So have you only seen it at Day's Ride? Or does it hang out at Cob Cottage and wait for carrots?"

The sisters burst out, Anna giving a bright tinkling laugh, Emz snorting derision, and Charlie giving a decisive "Ha" to that idea.

"This is not some little pony, Mum." Charlie shook her head. "This is a magnificent beast of a horse. A great big grey one."

"He's been in and out the last week. Two, maybe three times?" Anna threw the figure out there for correction. Charlie's brow furrowed and Emz cut in.

"It saved Caitlin on one occasion. It's been down to the shore of Pike Lake, once. And there was the first night Charlie saw it. Three." Emz went over the incidences. Vanessa, thoughtful, made a mental note of each as the conversation drifted towards Caitlin and Logan.

"Caitlin wasn't on the horse? It doesn't belong to her?" Vanessa wanted facts. Emz shook her head and shared Winn's account.

"She says it came to Prickles, up by the pens, and then she followed it back to Caitlin in the woods." Emz was now looking only at her plate, her fork poking half-heartedly at the remainder of the meal.

"Protecting her," Anna said. "What do you think? We thought it might be a possibility."

"When did you think this?" Charlie sounded miffed.

"When you were off tracking it," Emz said. There were back

and forths about this possibility, amongst all the other possibilities, and the sense of positivity drained.

"You know, if it all gets too tiring, if you need some space, you can always come here."

Vanessa's suggestion caused a brief lull.

"Your grandmother chose this site specifically." The lull came to a distinct halt as it became apparent that their mother was about to share some information. Vanessa looked at each of them in turn.

"If you need to go somewhere, sometime. If the need arose," she chose her words, "to escape."

The silence began to feel as if time had stopped.

"Grandma Hettie chose where Half-Built House should be?" Anna asked. Vanessa nodded.

"I just thought you got the land cheap," Charlie shrugged. Emz was deep in thought and had turned to look out of the window.

"This is your space, too," Vanessa continued. "I don't want you to feel you have to wait to be invited. Cob Cottage notwithstanding, this is always your home."

Emz turned back to the table, her face bright with knowledge.

"It's a Blindspot," she declared with a grin.

CORNERS AND SKY

It was an awkward journey back to Cob Cottage, Charlie's car proving too small for the quantity of emotions being felt.

"Blindspot." Charlie had repeated the word several times on their way down Castle Hill Road.

"I thought Grandma Hettie told you." Emz felt out of kilter; Anna was very, very quiet in the back seat.

"Nope." Charlie ground the gears. "Never heard of a Blindspot. Not in Havoc Wood, at least. Anything else she told you that you forgot to tell us?" Charlie was rattled, crunching another gear as the traffic lights halted them.

"I don't know why you're taking it so personally." Emz, seated beside Charlie, was taking the brunt of her shortened temper.

"Because I'm terrified." Charlie was unemotional. "Because we need all the little tips and hints we can remember to stay ahead of Havoc Wood." She paused and then rattled at the steering wheel. "And because I can't remember *anything* she only told *me* about. No little secrets."

Emz, seeing her sister's hurt, dived in.

"It wasn't a secret. I just forgot about it. It never came up until tonight." She felt easier. "That's not keeping a secret."

Anna was very, very, very quiet.

"You seem to have your mouth zipped." Charlie glared into the rear-view mirror. Anna became even quieter.

"So what's your secret?" Charlie was forthright. Emz looked puzzled.

"She hasn't got one." Emz turned to her sister. "Have you?"

Anna was very, very, very, very, very quiet. Emz gasped as Charlie banged the steering wheel.

"I *knew* it."

"Seriously?" Emz was twisting in her seat, the belt slicing at her neck as she did so.

"Spill," Charlie commanded, pipping the horn for effect, the effect being that Emz jumped and Anna took a deep breath.

"The Paper Prophets," she confessed. Charlie and Emz looked confused.

"The who?" Emz asked.

"The cards. In Mrs Massey's deck. The Paper Prophets."

Charlie was nonplussed.

"Does that even matter? I mean, she's long gone," Emz reassured Anna. "What do her cards matter?"

"They're in my pocket," Anna said. Charlie gave a wry laugh and pipped the horn again.

"I haven't had them long, just since the other day. They were in a chest of drawers at Mum's house."

Charlie and Emz took in the same startled breath.

"I couldn't open the drawer," Charlie admitted with a glance to Emz, who shook her head.

"It punched me with its top drawer," Emz confessed.

There was a moment or two of less tense silence.

"Well, if Ivan Herald does buy the Castle Inn, you can make some dollar telling fortunes," Charlie joked. No one laughed.

"I don't remember the Paper Prophets. At all," Emz mused.

Charlie shook her head. "Didn't she teach you to play Three?" Anna half-expected the bewildered silence this question received. Charlie was shaking her head even more.

"What about you?" Emz focused on Charlie who kept shaking her head. "Are you sure there isn't something?"

Charlie pinched her lips tighter.

"There'll be something, something you haven't remembered yet, something—"

"Nothing." Charlie was certain. There was an uncomfortable silence as they rode along Dark Gate Street. The silence deepened as they pulled onto Old Castle Road and was a wall between them as they pulled onto the tarmac track to Cob Cottage.

"It doesn't matter," Charlie insisted as they headed inside. The way she threw her car keys into the bowl suggested otherwise. "Emz forgot. You randomly got given the Paper Cards. No matter."

Emz and Anna looked on with some distress as Charlie faffed too much with her laces when taking her boots off and then started cleaning things in the kitchen that did not require it.

"Shall we take a look at them?" Anna suggested, pulling the small deck from her pocket. Emz was eager, but Charlie was peering through the window.

"Who's that?" The other sisters moved to the window as Charlie slid her feet back into her boots and took her lantern from beside the back door. Ahead of her, a car had stopped on the edge of the dirt track and the driver was now unloading a basket from the passenger seat. The pale lantern light illuminated the woman's face.

Etta Boyle put her basket on the table.

"Mrs Boyle," Anna greeted her. "How can we help?"

Emz looked uneasy, Charlie suspicious, as Mrs Boyle unloaded three jars from the basket.

"Honey from the bees. Apple sauce and apple chutney I made last Apple Day."

Charlie looked at the jars with their bee- and apple-themed labels.

"You're here to sell us…"

"I'm here over Logan," Mrs Boyle stated and then looked at them. Charlie looked at Emz, and Anna turned towards the kettle.

"I'll make the tea."

"No." Etta was a little flustered. "You have to do something." Her voice was steady, but her nerves were catching her breath.

"Isn't that up to the police?" Charlie said. "They're investigating what happened."

"No, they're not." Mrs Boyle was determined, glaring at Charlie. "They haven't got, pardon me saying, a bloody clue. And John Williamson should have one since his family is old enough to know." She halted as if she'd gone too far.

"Old enough to know?" Charlie asked.

"To *know*." Mrs Boyle seemed to think this explained everything. A penny was rolling down a small mental hill in Anna's head.

"This is Havoc business," she filled in the gap. Mrs Boyle looked relieved.

"You've got to do something."

"The police are do—"

Mrs Boyle's sharp exclamation shushed Charlie instantly.

"It wasn't Logan," Mrs Boyle reiterated.

"We've talked about the Horse and Rider situation with PC Williamson. We haven't found a Rider, but we think the Horse protected Caitlin," Anna began. Mrs Boyle pushed hard.

"It's your job to find out. This is someone out of Havoc."

Charlie lost patience.

"No. It could be any perv between here and Castlebury."

Etta Boyle was shaking her head.

"No. Not this. It happened like this before, when my sister was seventeen and she was taken — your grandmother was the one who sorted it, and, I'm telling you, it wasn't no perv from Castlebury then."

"I still don't see how you—" Charlie began.

"Caitlin wasn't the only one. There's another girl — didn't report it but word got round town anyway."

Anna was white-faced. Etta Boyle realised she had made her point and continued.

"Bridget Whatsit from the council. Reckons some hippy weirdo tried to drag her off from the Highwayman car park, a good few days before this Caitlin thing." Mrs Boyle was becoming more fragile as she let go of the information. "Our Ade was in the Highwayman the other night, and they were all talking about it. She was laughing it off, said she kicked him in the bollocks with her boots." Mrs Boyle did not look edified by this tale of feminine strength. "Her red boots."

It was as if a red flag was suddenly hoisted. The Witch Ways had been drilled in the significance of the colour since babyhood, from rowan berries to riding hoods.

"Let the police fanny around town asking questions. This is your job. This is Havoc business." Mrs Boyle was visibly shaking.

"Would you like some tea?" Anna asked.

"No. I'd like you to stop the bastard."

ANNA AND EMZ struggled to keep up. Charlie set a brutal pace all the way to Frog Pond.

"Charlie…" Emz was out of breath. Anna was struggling behind. "Charlie, wait."

Charlie ploughed on, her boots chipping off bark from fallen logs, not answering.

"Where are we even going?" Emz said. Charlie paused for a moment at the top of a banking.

"To our only lead." And she marched onwards.

At Frog Pond, their stave was still standing, undisturbed. The sisters walked around the space.

"We don't know what we're looking for," Emz said, frustrated.

"No. But I think we'll know it when we do see it," Anna fudged the issue. Charlie gave a snort.

"Will we? Like we saw Mrs Fyfe?" She was leaning over the mossed stones, looking down into the water. "We Reached the other night, and this is where it led us, and this is tied into the horse. Maybe he's using the Horse as transport already. Who knows? But we have to try harder."

"The Horse isn't…" Emz began. Charlie held up her hand.

"Isn't? We have no idea. Either way, it's linked, protecting or whatever, the horse is the only link we've got to the perpetrator. If nothing else the Horse has seen the bad guy."

She disturbed the surface of the pond with a flick or two of her hands. "Come out, come out wherever you are," she said to the air.

"Nothing's moved or altered since before." Anna touched the stave, testing its surety. As she did so, a flicker lashed across her mind and she gasped.

"What?" Charlie looked up.

"Don't know. I saw embers." Anna pulled the slivered image back and forth across her mind's eye.

"Embers? Like a fire?" Emz asked as Anna shut her eyes, fastening her fingers around the stave, for the full blast of the Flickerbook.

"Peat. Earth. Embers. Heat." Just a suspicion of a face before her mind had to let the image drop. "Almost had him." She stepped back, flexing her fingers as though surprised they were not scorched.

"He's been here, but he's not been back," Emz said.

"Or, if he came back, he was warned off. So the stave has done its work." Anna's voice was hopeful. Charlie raked over some leaves. At once, a path lit up in front of her.

"Okay." She stared at the path, willing it to hold even as it was fizzling in her mind. "Embers. I see them." She looked swiftly forward, trying to see where the path was headed as it blistered and burnt away, and she had to shut her eyes.

"I think whoever it is knows we're onto him." She opened her eyes again. "He's hiding."

"We pushed him at the Reach," Emz suggested. "Frightened him off." The three sisters prowled the clearing.

"Might explain the Horse, too. He didn't have time to catch his ride," Charlie said and then started off in another direction.

"Charlie…"

Emz and Anna played catch up.

THE GREAT GREY Havoc Horse was waiting for them at Day's Ride, standing, magisterially, in the middle of the wide lane. When they emerged from their side of Havoc, it lifted its head and, with a scornful whinny, strode off.

"He's not even trotting, and we can barely keep up," Emz panted as the sisters tripped and sprinted in the animal's wake. Charlie was foremost, the path illuminating before her with a darkling sparkle. The path pulled her onwards. She could see a depth to Havoc as if she was in Havoc looking out through a doorway to Havoc. It was intoxicating; her heart raced ahead.

"Watch out," Anna warned as Charlie ran close to the wide-strutting hooves. She was heedless, the horse heading downhill towards Pike Lake.

"Emz," Charlie was breathless, not taking her eyes off the

horse, off the path it trod. "Short cut." She gestured down an old fox path. "Run back home. Get a rope." She dodged direction as the horse lurched through the trees. "Anna and I will herd it towards you."

Emz picked up the pace, running through the undergrowth, and, as she did so, feeling, once again, that fleet strength that had carried her through the castle, through town, to answer the call of Seren Lake in trouble in Havoc. She was balanced, wild, the thought struck her, like a deer.

She fetched the rope from the shed and was at the shoreline just as the Great Grey trotted majestically out of the woods. He looked refreshed and comfortable as Charlie and Anna, red-faced and panting, shooed and huphupped behind it. From Emz's standpoint it was clear this creature paid them no heed. He halted at the water's edge and began to drink.

"Now. Now." Charlie made lassoing gestures. Emz, looping the rope over her arm, approached the horse and hurled the rope across its back. As she did, the rest of it tugged itself out of her hands, burning her skin.

"Keep hold of the end of it." Charlie was losing patience. She reached down for the lost rope as it slithered out of her grasp. She looked at Emz.

"Keep hold of the end of it," Emz mocked, feeling vindicated. Anna tried a different tack, offering her hand.

"Don't let him confuse your fingers for carrots." Emz, who had always been a little afraid of horses, warned. Anna shook her head.

"He won't. Wusht. Wusht." Anna made the soothing noise and reached up to clasp the mane, her feet moving up onto Grandma Hettie's rock so that in one, two, three strides she would be up and on the horse's back. And straight over the other side. The horse began to nuzzle up to her as she lay on the floor, as if there were no hard feelings.

"Ow." Anna brushed herself off. The horse nickered, as if amused.

"What about trying to lure it inside Cob Cottage," Charlie wondered aloud. "If it needs to stay there, then the doors will shut."

As Charlie and Emz failed to lure and cajole the Horse any nearer to the cottage, Anna stepped out into the darkness behind and was gone for several minutes.

"Anna?" Charlie, distracted from the horse and its snooty demeanour, looked around for her sister. "This is no time for a pee. Anna?"

"She's coming back," Emz assured her as the Horse trotted between them, his head nodding as if in laughter.

Anna was carrying a stash of hazel wands from the back of the garden.

"Worth a try," Anna said and handed three staves each to her sisters. They approached the Horse, which was regarding them from the lakeshore.

There was a rhythm to their placing of the staves. Without conferring, they each jabbed a stave into the ground at the same moment, maintaining, unconsciously, their triangle of Strength. A bright lightness flooded through them, a sound of rushing air, like wings and something beneath it that was faintly musical.

The horse gave one serious nod and resumed the slaking of its thirst. The Witch Ways looked at each other.

"That felt…" Anna began the thought.

"Good," Charlie and Emz finished it. As if in agreement, the horse lifted its head and stamped a mighty hoof before beginning to crop at the small scrubby bit of grass within the circle of hazel staves.

"Now, let's hunt the Rider." Anna looked out over Havoc. "Where do we start d'you think? Frog Pond? Or what about up at Mrs Massey's old place? Remember the owl hooting when we did the Reach?"

"Town," Charlie said.

"Town?" Emz asked.

"That's where the women are." Charlie's logic was faultless as she started off along the shoreline towards Woodcastle. "That's where he'll be looking."

THEY EMERGED on the far side of Dark Gate Street at the northern end of the castle. Here, the streets were quiet enough, TV images twitched behind curtains and blinds. Security lighting flared as the Ways passed gates and driveways. No one spoke, all three alert to their surroundings.

At the Moot Hall in High Market Place, a group of women were leaving the yoga class. Most were heading for the car park at the foot of Barbican Steeps, and the Way sisters watched as they drove off. Anna recognised Kirstie and Hannah from the Craft Club walking away.

"Heads up, two o'clock." Charlie gave a nod; Emz looked puzzled.

"What?"

"I think they'll be fine. There are two of them." Anna looked to Charlie who was hawk-like in her observation.

"There are two of them now, but they don't live in the same house. Sooner or later, they've got to separate."

Anna paused as another of the town council staffers, Cressida, passed by alone and on foot. Emz had her eye on still another, Aurora Foundling from the florist shop, Mimosa.

"What about Aurora?" Emz asked. Charlie looked at Anna.

"Split up."

CHARLIE KEPT with Kirstie and Hannah until Kirstie said her farewells on Market Drab. Hannah hurried onto the small lodge at the top end of Lower Long Gate Street. Charlie watched from the corner as the lights went on and the cat came out.

As she turned up Moot Hall Lane, her eye was caught by a flicker of light. It was bright hot, brief burning. She looked towards it, reminded of something in Havoc. As it singed and faded again, further up the lane Charlie recalled the ember path she'd lost in the wood and her heart bumped. She watched. There. And again. She followed, unhurried and careful.

At Barbican Steeps, there was a path scorched into the stones, which turned to ash and blew away. She felt a shimmer of frustration. This person, whoever he was, was adept at concealing his tracks. A thought struck her, and she stooped to pick up a last handful of the ash before it vanished. Blackening her fingers, she inhaled the scent.

ANNA FOLLOWED Cressida who walked with her earbuds in, the music loud enough for Anna to hear the bassline. It was an uneventful journey, except for Cressida stepping into the path of a taxi, which pipped to an indignant halt. Anna hung back at the corner of The Crescent, watching as Cressida's dad put the bins out and welcomed his offspring home.

EMZ WATCHED Aurora Foundling stride home to the florist shop on Church Lane. She watched her unlock the door and head inside past a thick and tangled display of thorny twigs and branches that crowded the window.

As Emz moved away, she thought she heard the rustle and creak of boughs shifting and, on glancing back, was the doorway really decorated like that? Thorns and branches bursting at the glass? It was, Emz thought, very beautiful. Aurora had a gift for dramatic displays.

As she headed back to their rendezvous at Cob Cottage, a

dim memory flickered in Emz's head. There was something about Aurora, something from long ago when they were at primary school. She was in the same class as Charlie. Was that it? Something to do with Charlie, too? The details would not surface, and, as she crossed Dark Gate Street, her mind was pulled into sharp focus by the sight of the deer.

It paused in the middle of the road as Emz did. For just a moment, they looked like gunfighters in a stand-off, before the deer, springing high and fast, ran ahead of her into Havoc.

Emz ran hard, as hard as she had in the dream, and, once again, the fleetness of foot flowed through her. Her muscles stretched and powered her forward, so that she was almost toe-to-toe with the fleeing deer. The breeze rushed by, ruffling her hair. She saw Havoc in a different light, the angles altered and disorientating. Just at the break to High Foxes, as the deer darted into the trees, Emz, scared of her own speed, of the altered view of the wood, could not hold onto the wild running skill, and it fell away from her. She stood for some time at the side of the lake, trying to catch her breath. Was it a Strength? It felt odd, unlike herself. It felt, in fact, like the deer. She had an affinity with animals, that's what Grandma Hettie said, perhaps this was a new way it was manifesting itself.

With the thoughts buzzing, she walked onwards, greeted by a snuff or two from the Great Grey, still standing in his stave pen, before climbing up to join her sisters on the porch.

"Ash." Anna put out a finger to touch Charlie's smirched hand. "This was at the castle?"

"On the cobblestones at the Steeps," Charlie informed them. "It burnt the way it did in Havoc, but it didn't get lost in the leaves. It blew off the stones. This is the same person that we were following before."

Anna put her now ashen finger to her nose and sniffed, Emz leaning into Charlie's hand to inhale.

"Can you smell it?" Charlie asked. Anna and Emz sniffed hard and looked bewildered. "It's a strong scent to me. Frog Pond. There's the moss and the stones, that cold greenness." Charlie inhaled deeply. "It's Havoc all the way. And then, underneath, there's not just the woodsmoke…"

"… there's honey… like the scent we got from the warrior's head."

"Old Magic." Anna felt a chill at the thought, and Charlie read them instantly.

"Before you panic, remember that was a signifier for the Old Magic, whereas Mrs Fyfe's power had that sour apple scent to it."

Emz grinned.

"We're learning." She looked expectant. Charlie was watching Anna, who was sniffing at the ash like a hunting dog.

"What? Is it the raspberry jam or the vanilla?" Charlie asked. Anna gasped.

"Oh! Mrs Massey."

It WAS HALF an hour before the sisters found themselves at the tumbledown wall that bounded Mrs Massey's long-abandoned cottage.

"Interesting." Anna stopped short of going through what remained of the garden gate.

"What is?" Charlie was going to have no such scruples and was already tugging at the ivy that padlocked the entrance.

"When we did the Reach, we were drawn up to Frog Pond, and once we'd put the Marker down…"

"We were sent up here. I said about the owl hooting that night." Emz finished the thought. "Whoever it is knew we were onto them and moved house."

"Alright, Dr Doolittle. We'll know better next time. Anyway…" Charlie wrenched open the gate. "We're here now." The scent of vanilla and raspberry jam was joined by a strong waft of sunlight on a wooden garden table.

Anna was already moving to the apple trees and tangle of raspberry canes. Broken limbs and branches lay waiting, and she selected, carefully, three staves of apple, which Charlie twined through with the ivy she had uprooted. Emz, for her part, watched the trees. Anna was businesslike. Charlie took in a deep breath or two and shut her eyes.

"Can you see the path?" Emz asked as Charlie opened her eyes with renewed Havoc focus.

"No, but I can smell it. We're definitely on the right track."

Their voices were low and, while not brimful of confidence in their actions, their fears and doubts had altered shape, fuelling a questioning pragmatism.

"We put the stave in at Frog Pond. Now here." Charlie scanned the woods. "We still haven't caught up with him."

"But we're closing in," Anna said.

BACK AT COB COTTAGE, they were frustrated to find that the Great Grey Havoc Horse was not safe in its wood-staved pen after all. While Anna bottled her anxiety, Charlie exploded.

"For fuck's sake," she hissed, wheeling about for any sign of the beast.

"Calm down." Emz caught at her sleeve. Charlie rounded on her.

"Someone's got to panic. We're in the same mess again. Floundering about." Charlie waved her arms like a windmill.

"I meant calm down and look for the horse's trail."

Charlie's arms windmilled even more.

"Oh, yes. Calm down and let's do that." She was wound up, her voice echoing across the lake.

"You did it before." Emz was resolute. "You've been in charge all this evening."

Charlie stopped mid-windmill and looked at her little sister.

"Think about it," Emz said. "You picked up the ember trail, the ash scent, everything." Emz shrugged at all this. "Nothing in Havoc is a quick fix. Ever. Remember?"

There was a dangerous moment before Anna laughed, a light, ringing sound.

"She's got a point."

Charlie took a deep breath, shut her eyes, and then opened them.

The path the Horse had taken was starlight and velvet night, a sparkling frostburn that pointed in one direction.

"Day's Ride," she said. They all let the cogs of thought wind and grind.

"Out of Havoc?" Anna suggested. They all considered but looked at Charlie.

"We should go to bed. Get some rest. Pick up the threads again tomorrow."

It was a fitful night for all three, but most of all for Emz who rode the night in the footsteps of the dream deer, racing and racing, as if its life depended upon it.

34

A TWEEDY WAISTCOAT

Judith Killen had had a long day at Caracole Stables. She loved the horses, but she did not love Marlow Whitburn, her boss. It seemed to Judith, in general, but today especially, that Marlow felt being bossy was a skill, that it had some practical application other than to make people do the exact opposite of what should be done. It did not matter that this was a waste of time or the wrong tactic. No, Marlow wanted you to do it. Do it. Waste both your time and the horses'.

Sometimes Judith wondered. Marlow seemed to have been riding and keeping horses for about thirty years and knew bugger all about them. Like today when she'd been ratty with Damsel, and it was not Damsel's fault. The horse was not flighty with anyone else. Marlow spooked her. It was chiefly her personality, but it was also the way she flicked her hair about. Judith could see it plain. Marlow couldn't see it when it was pointed out.

Her reward for sharing her wisdom was a session of shit shovelling. Though, Judith would rather be at home farm with the manure and the other horses than running round the countryside with Marlow. It was very seldom that Marlow took treks out. She thought most people were beneath her attention, but today had been those arsey bigwigs from Castlebury, that bloke and his two women in bloody designer jodhpurs. Harlow. Herald. Whatever the hell name he had. Thought he was all that getting out of his Mercedes. Looked like a sack of King Edwards in the saddle.

She'd have her own stables one day. This thought brushed aside the dungheap of all the other trials of the day and kept her warm as she sat at the bus stop at the top of Castle Hill Road. Her stables would be nothing like bloody Caracole Stables. The horses she owned would be free to mix. There would be no separation into stables and being locked behind gates. It would be the way her grandfather Henry had always taught her it ought to be. Horses needed other horses.

"They're a herd animal," he had said. He had smelled of tobacco and saddle leather, and she missed him. She still lived with her mother in his old house on Old Forge Lane; not that that would be for much longer, as her mother had recently put the place on the market.

If she had the cash, Judith would buy the place out from under her. Her mother wanted to move to one of the new builds on the edge of Castlebury. Piss on that, bloody awful place. Not enough trees. No horses except police horses. That particular train of thought began to pull into a tunnel of darkness, and so Judith turned her mind back towards horses.

What was that?

"Hello?" She had seen a movement, just out of the corner of her eye. Was someone in the trees? No. It was probably just a reflection caught in the glazing of the bus shelter. Except that the only reflection was hers, and she looked frightened. Like the beginning of a horror movie really, which didn't help. Why did she think that?

Oh. No. There it was again, hanging about in the trees. A man. No coat, just a tweedy waistcoat and worn trousers. His hair salt and pepper, so that he might have been forty. Who was he? She didn't know him from town. Wait. Where was he? She twisted around. He had vanished.

"Hello?" She tried to sound like Marlow Whitburn, forceful and not to be messed with, but the hairs on the back of her neck were prickling like hedgehog spines. She checked her watch, which appeared to have stopped and, glancing up the road, saw there was no traffic, let alone the comforting lumber of a bus.

From the edge of her vision she saw, at the edge of the trees, a glimmer of red-orange exactly like the sparks from a wood-fire, and at once her feet were running along the road in the opposite direction. Fast. Faster. Her hand reaching for her phone, her phone falling, the screen cracking. She halted to snatch it up, not looking up, but looking sideways at his approach, because she could see him better that way. He was not even running. The phone blinked uselessly, and Judith turned and ran.

Into a muscular wall of tweedy chest, a scent of woodsmoke and honey, of forest floor and moss and water. A hand reached around her neck with ease; breath, cool at her ear.

"There is no running from me," the voice whispered.

35

THE HEART, ATTACKED

Vanessa Way had returned to the lab very late in the day, so late in fact as to be evening.

"Right you are, Professor Way." Greg was on the desk, keen to exchange a greeting. "Burning the midnight oil again?" He grinned as he swiped her security pass. He was a good-looking man, stocky in a comforting way. Vanessa wondered how old he was. He was just the sort of bloke that Anna should be with.

"You're not married, are you, Greg?"

"You proposing, Prof?" His smile was warm and winning.

"How old are you?" It was clear from his facial expression that no question was out of bounds.

"Age is not the issue, Prof. It's compatibility." He winked.

"My eldest daughter is nearly thirty," Vanessa said, struggling to keep the smirk from her face. Greg did not skip a beat, his eyes meeting Vanessa's with honesty and genuine interest.

"Oh, right," he laughed, honoured. "You're serious."

"Always, where my daughters are concerned." Vanessa was pleased to see Greg look moved. There must be some way she could engineer an encounter for these two. As she pushed through the big black doors of the Dark Lab, this task slid into place on one of her many mental to-do lists.

ELEANOR AND VANESSA were going over the handover data from the afternoon shift.

"It's been a recurring issue all day, even though you haven't been in the building," Eleanor said.

"Campus wide or…"

"Just us." Eleanor looked harassed. "I'm not happy. Outside of the Dark sessions we've always had a steady calm that gives us a good baseline for your interference."

Vanessa looked at the jagged and abandoned readouts and felt her own mixture of excitement and unease.

"You're thinking," Eleanor observed. "Share those thoughts."

"I'm thinking perhaps, this time, this isn't all one way. This isn't just about me going there, it might be about others trying to come here."

Eleanor paused in her own thoughts and adjusted them to this new theory.

"Okay. Is that a good thing?" Eleanor looked uncertain.

Vanessa shrugged.

"It was always a good thing…" she hesitated. "Now, I'm unsure."

Eleanor nodded.

"This is a strain on you. I don't want to end up destroying all the work we've done so far." Eleanor was calm and reasoned, except for her eyes. They were a beautiful walnut brown and were, Vanessa saw, wild and bright with worry. "Perhaps we should call a halt for a week or so? You should rest."

"There is no rest," Vanessa confessed. "Every time I shut my eyes…" Her eyes dropped to the handover data, the spikes and etchings of activity. "There is no stopping," Vanessa said. "This is a build-up of energy. This is a bigger connection than that simply generated when I'm here. This could be a linkage or a loop that we might be able to use."

Eleanor relaxed a little.

"A lifeline. A rope thrown at us," she nodded.

"What about the surges and outages? Did you get timings?"

The two women looked over all available data.

"This time..." Vanessa pointed to a range of spikes on the most recent session. "What coffee did Rufus have?" Vanessa asked.

"What?" Eleanor said.

"It was a mocha, one of the big ones with chocolate and cinnamon."

Rufus spoke from the doorway. Vanessa and Eleanor turned. He was carrying a cardboard tray from the canteen, and the scent of cinnamon wafted over them. Each member of the project had learned the importance of scents in recreating the optimum sleep state. Cinnamon and ginger, chocolate, allspice, were good, washing powder and commercial perfumes too synthetic, interfering with Vanessa's sensory landscape.

Eleanor rigged Vanessa to the various machines. It was engineering of their own devising, and Rufus had christened the main contraption "Mr Mesmer". Through pressure points and low frequency sound, it helped to induce a sleep state. Since her first Arctic incident as a student, Vanessa had found sleep difficult. The various sedatives and soporifics were of little use and proved less so during her experimentations. The machines were a different approach, using the senses and inducing a hypnotic state. The central machine was also the beacon, ready to signal the way home should the unconscious Vanessa wander too far.

Never far enough. That was Vanessa's thought. Over the years, always, something wrenched her back. Or perhaps, she now thought, it pushed her away.

Tonight. It was different at once. She closed her eyes and the simple darkness was filled with filigree shadows. She was deep in the trees, branches clustered and gripped at her. It felt like a cage, and her heart bolted a few beats. The icy rime on bark and branch held her breath in ghosts as she turned, this way, that. She was hyper aware of the creak of branches. Of ice. It was not a cage. She understood in an instant, the lacework light, the twigs and whips and limbs were a hiding place. Hiding her from what?

In the near distance a call, and the branches before her snapped open, revealing a path, glittering with frost. Vanessa did not think. Her feet carried her quickly into the dappled shadow that littered the floor.

She was broken up, disguised by the shadows along the track. Leaves, mouldy and frozen, muffled her footsteps as she sped onward. She looked ahead to where the forest ended at the lake's white edge.

The ice creaked as she ran, the sound like hushed breath. A glance over her shoulder revealed the cohort of Riders, the horses snaffling, the metallic chinks and pings of bridle and bit echoed out across the crusted lake.

She was running as fast as her heart could carry her, the hooves in pursuit, a dissonant arrhythmia, threatening. Her lungs clutched at the bitter air, and, above, the aurora lit the sky a leafy acidic green. Inside her chest, the thunder vibrated, rumbled through her into the ice, the sheet of white trembling with its force. Vanessa felt her hair crackle with static as the thunder cracked once more, the horses unafraid, Riders on the storm. She could hardly breathe, the breath crystallising in her lungs, the breath from her lips making fragile, lucent formations that shattered before her.

The lightning tore at the sky, the aurora flaring against it. Vanessa felt her feet slide, uncertain. The lightning forked, and, as it reached down, she reached up towards it.

"Alive." The word cracked through her with the glare of the Dark Lab lighting. An alarmed sound, a siren here, a warning there, the scent of heated metal, of sweat, of anxious faces crowding in.

ELEANOR, ashen-faced once more, was shaking.

"You don't understand. Professor Way…"

"I was technically dead." Vanessa was matter of fact. "I understand."

"For five minutes," Rufus interjected. "You were dead."

Eleanor could no longer speak. Her shaking hands wiped at her face.

"You don't seem to understand," she managed at last.

"Alright. I was properly, physically, totally dead for five minutes." Inside, Vanessa felt illuminated, a consequence, she thought, of the lightning strike. Eleanor and Rufus exchanged a worried look, and Vanessa was aware she was not reacting rationally.

"I've decided that this is not the route we should take." Eleanor's voice was stony. Rufus remained silent. Vanessa thought of a white lake, of the ice kicking up beneath her running feet. She knew the direction, the route to take.

"I'm not sure, if this happened again," Eleanor was struggling to hold it together, "whether we would be able to bring you back." Her voice cracked. Rufus was still silent, observing Vanessa.

"It was a bit iffy," Rufus confessed. "This time."

Vanessa did not respond; she was looking at the array of printout, the lines jutting and jagging above the white paper.

"Vanessa?" Eleanor could see she was distracted. "Vanessa, I think we need to call a halt. A temporary halt."

Vanessa reached out a finger, began to trace the line of the first encephalograph.

"Vanessa? A temporary halt? Yes?"

Vanessa Way took in a relaxed breath.

"This…" she traced onwards, "this is Far North."

Eleanor watched for a moment, then gasped. A ragged, epic landscape written into their equipment. Not data. Skyline.

SPOOKED BY A PAPER BAG

Judith Killen was surly with her replies. She was not going to cooperate. She was furious with her mother for calling the police. PC Williamson was staring at the blank page of his notebook, trying to order his thoughts.

She looked bad. She knew that much from the mirror; the terrible cut above her eye had required a butterfly stitch, and her face was bruised. She could not hide that, though her heavy Caracole Stables sweatshirt was covering over the heavy bruising on her right arm. It felt painful to move it, but the shoulder was not dislocated, they'd said as much at the A&E.

"You're rather bruised," PC Williamson downplayed her injuries. "How did that happen?" he asked.

"Fell off Whistledown yesterday afternoon. He got spooked by a paper bag at High Foxes." It was a genius of a lie, utterly plausible. She felt better.

"This is bollocks," her mother cut in. "I'm telling you, she didn't come home. She was three hours late, and we were out on the lookout for her gone nine." Mrs Killen was clearly distraught. "Found her up at that back road going to Rook Ridge."

"I got off the bus at the wrong stop," Judith insisted. "I was walking home. End of." She glared at her mother.

"This is that bloody Boyle lad, this is." Her mother was hysterical. "He's the one as did it, bloody perv." A little bit of spit landed on the table between them.

"It was *not* Logan Boyle." Judith shot her mother a look and then turned to PC Williamson. "This is nothing at all to with 'the Boyle lad'. I never saw him. He's got nothing to do with it."

PC Williamson nodded.

"Can you describe the person who attacked you?" At the question, Judith realised she'd been caught out in her defence of Logan Boyle. Judith shook her head.

"Nothing?" PC Williamson was kind and careful. "Tall? Short? Thin? Fat?"

Judith shook her head.

"No. Nothing. I'm sorry. But I am telling you straight, it wasn't Logan Boyle." She banged her hand on the table for emphasis.

PC Williamson took his cue and, as he was leaving, handed Judith a card.

"When you're ready to talk about this, just ring me." He gave her a sympathetic smile, and Judith relented. After all, she was angry at her mother for bothering him.

"Well? What was that?" Her mother was like a yapping chihuahua after she closed the door behind him. "What were you playing at? You proper showed me up, that's all I can say."

Judith grabbed her jacket.

"No, Mum. You showed *me* up," she barked. "I told you. I said straight. I didn't want police. It was nothing to do with the police. I told you."

She left to a chorus of complaints, her mother's indignant screeches following her to the very end of the garden path and only being drowned out by the rusty squeak of the gate.

It was a long walk to Old Castle Road, Judith's breath

catching in her chest, tightened with anger. Why couldn't her mum just let her deal with it? The sooner she could move out of there the better. She was going to harass Marlow Whitburn next week for a raise. The snooty cow knew she was worth it, and she was going to get first dibs on that flat she was doing up over the stables, too.

Judith could hear her anger in every step, every grunt of physical effort until she turned in at the tarmac road that was swallowed, almost immediately, by the crowding trees.

Today, they did not scare her. Havoc Wood scared most people because they were generally afraid of anything that wasn't brick-built or offering free wi-fi. Aunt Peg had taught her better. Aunt Peg knew what was what. How many times had she been down this path with Aunt Peg and her trolley shopper, filled with bread from the wood oven? The new bakery was a bit shit since her aunt died; but then, if Judith thought about it, most things were a bit shit since then.

The ground beneath her feet shifted to gravel and then the proper raggedy dirt track, at the foot of which sat Cob Cottage.

You could go to the back door. Aunt Peg always had done. But Hettie Way wasn't here anymore, and Judith knew her manners. She'd been a couple of classes above Emily Way at secondary school, so she didn't know her. She was a stranger.

Judith took a deep breath as she rounded the house and saw the Great Grey cropping the grass. It was, by far and away, the most magnificent, the most beautiful horse she had ever seen. The sight shook her. She felt her heart fluttering, and, at the sight, it was hard to tamp down all the emotion she felt. The Horse lifted his head, gave her the nod, and, at his signal, she stepped onto the porch. It was clear that no one was home, but she knocked anyway. The horse watched her. She could see his reflection in the round window.

She knocked once again, more quietly, and then turned away. She was properly shaking now. The pain in her arm was a low-level thrum. The horse whiffled down his nose, and she approached. He stepped between the tree branches, ranged around it like a half-finished fence, and muzzled at her hair.

The tears rose. She wiped at her face, the salt of the tears stinging at the cuts and soreness. The horse's huge and stately head nodded at her once again, stepping forward to loom over her, so that her face was set against the strong-scented coat. Was there a better scent in the universe? Judith Killen doubted it. Her hand reached up to fasten itself in the mane, to slide down and pat the lustrous grey. The tears slid with it. She stood, the horse's neck arched around her as she sobbed her heart out.

Judith sat on the porch for a good hour. She didn't mind the wait. She felt cooler and lighter. The door opened behind her.

"Oh, can I help?" asked Charlie Way.

PROPER HANDS INSIDE MY HEAD

The Great Grey had watched them all head off into the woods. Judith was giving instruction but not leading: that role fell to Charlie.

They paused at a clearing. There seemed several ways forward and the Witch Ways were patient with Judith.

"This way." She indicated a twisting path that led deeper into Havoc and was not well trodden, even by Hettie Way.

"Charlie?" Anna checked in with her sister. Charlie nodded and dropped onto her haunches.

"Yep. Trail's burned, same as before." She reached her hand deep into the leaf litter and it came up smirched with ash. She sniffed. "Definite." She stepped forward. "Put me right if I seem to be going wrong, Judith," she said. Judith nodded. She had, Anna noticed, become much quieter the farther they ventured into the wood. They walked for some minutes, Emz gazing around the wood as if she'd never seen it before.

"What is it?" Anna asked.

"I'm not sure," Emz said. "I think I dreamt I was here." She looked disturbed by the thought.

"He carried you this far?" Anna asked Judith. She was

thinking of the distance between the bus stop on Castle Hill Road and was working out the physical strength of such a feat.

"I wouldn't go with him. I tried to run but… It was weird… He kept cutting me off. Every time I turned, he was there." Judith shivered. "He only put me down when the horse appeared." Judith looked around and stepped forward towards a scratched-over bit of ground.

"Wait." Charlie, who had been scouting ahead, came tripping back. "What horse?"

"The horse." Judith looked at them. "The one by the cottage just now. The grey."

The Way sisters exchanged a look.

"Tell us what happened with you and him and the horse," Charlie asked.

"The horse came up from the lake, and the man threw me down here." Her voice was cracking.

"But…?" Charlie began. Anna shook her head. Judith took in a ragged breath.

"He wanted the horse. He kept… he wanted… I don't know what he did."

Emz handed her an almost-clean tissue to wipe her eyes.

"Tell us anything. Doesn't matter if it doesn't make sense," Anna said.

"Nothing in Havoc makes sense." Charlie rolled her eyes.

"I was… it was like he was rummaging through my memories, like proper hands inside my head. I couldn't keep track, like he was jumbling stuff about, looking for something, and he couldn't find it." She was feeling stronger, angrier. "Like being drunk. Or like the time I fell off Horatio and dislocated my shoulder, and they gave me gas and air. Disconnected. Like that."

Around the scrape, the Witch Ways had, in the manner of breathing, assumed their triangle. As they did so, the trail lit up for them. The embered path the assailant had tried to scorch out showed up visible, and the incident with it, a blurred maelstrom of movement like a video edited at hyperspeed. The Ways watched.

"Any ideas?" Charlie was asking herself as much as her sisters. The trapped memory of the incident flittered on, the assailant, angry, throwing Judith down as the horse strode towards him.

"What next, Judith?"

"The horse kicked him. Then it stooped so I could get on its back and took me up to Hackett, so I could get out of the wood."

"That is the fastest way out from here," Charlie confirmed.

"The horse let you ride him?" Emz asked. Judith nodded. The Way sisters made a note of this new information.

"You alright going to Hackett? Only we'd like to trace where the horse went after he dropped you off."

The trail was clear. Both the embered path the assailant had tried to obliterate and the one the horse had trodden, a frosted black shadow track that glittered. It was, Charlie thought, a thing of beauty. It had nothing to hide, and from Hackett they were unsurprised to find the horse heading back towards Pike Lake and the cottage.

As they emerged from the trees, the Horse looked up from its makeshift, and clearly useless, magical corral and once again nodded, with what could only be described as wisdom.

"He saved me," Judith whispered. "He saved me."

As they moved down to the shore, the Horse strode over to meet them. He snorted, pushing past Emz to sniff and nuzzle at Judith's face and hair, and, as it did so, Anna had a blast of thought.

"You're the horse Whisperer," she said. The horse snorted at her. Judith shook her head.

"I'm good with horses."

"Grandma Hettie called you a Whisperer," Anna smiled. "Trust me."

"I came here a lot when I was little. With my Aunt Peg." There was a moment of silence. "She was old school. She knew about Havoc. Which is why, when it happened…" She faltered.

"Come inside." Anna gestured to the cottage. "Have a cup of something and a bite to eat."

As they wandered in through the door, Emz paused on the porch to look down at the horse. Something was tugging hard at the edge of her mind, but she could not pull it free.

3 8

A BORROWER BE

Borrower was tired in his very bones. There was almost nowhere that was open to him. The Gamekeepers had staved him out of Frog Pond and, now, the deserted cottage too. He had scorched over his tracks, but the Map had found them and put her hand in them, so those paths were dead ground.

It was slow torture, the like of which Hettie Way would not have countenanced. Except, as he held himself steady in the tall elm, he recalled Hettie's countenance very clearly and the wrath it visited upon him for venturing to fetch himself a wife under her watch.

He was shaken. He had taken the horse Whisperer, and she had not done his bidding. He had given her a chance, and she had fought him. When he reached in to rummage in her skull to borrow her skills for himself, he could not take them. All that he wanted slithered from his grasp, and he felt where he was pushed at, tugged back by the scruff of his mind.

He could find no reason for it. The girl, when he rattled through her senses, shaking so hard that the charms and protections might fall out, possessed no power of her own, was allied to nothing and no one. All that tumbled and knocked about in

219

her soul was human. There was nothing to signify the protection of another of his own kind.

He drew the conclusion that the wood itself worked against him, part, perhaps, of an unknown legacy of lingering punishment bequeathed him by Hettie Way.

He breathed like the breeze, his shoulders settling back into the support of the three topmost branches. From here, he could see clear to Ridge Hill, and, in the bowl of the land, he saw the lake glimmer, the lights winking at Cob Cottage. His mind wandered there.

They were novices, were they not? Might it be possible to borrow their skills? To take one of them for a wife and throw over Havoc Wood?

His grin stretched across his face. This plan was much better than any that involved running away.

The eldest was too old, and he did not wish to borrow the heavy veil of grief that Fate had woven for her.

The middle one, the brewster, the Map herself, was too harsh, and he didn't require her skills. He knew his way around the wood.

The youngest. Ah, yes, a wife to be worn in, raised up above her siblings. He had much to teach her.

More important, she had much to give him; the heart of Havoc Wood, beating and bloody.

39

DEER DREAMING

In the light of recent incidents, Charlie ran Judith home and when she returned her sisters were already deep in discussion.

"Why do you think the staves don't hold the Horse?" Anna asked.

"He's a good guy," Charlie said. "He doesn't need to be penned up."

"And it doesn't need protecting either," Anna said.

"He saved Judith. And seems to have saved Caitlin, too, though she'd never say it." Emz fitted in the last flimsy pieces of their jigsaw. Charlie looked at them, expecting more, but they stayed silent.

"I know what you're thinking." She looked at Anna, who seemed to tighten her lips even more. "You're thinking the staves didn't work on the assailant, that he's still out there."

Anna gave in, nodded.

"We didn't stave him," Emz said. "We only used one at Frog Pond, one at the cottage. We've never had the chance to surround him."

Anna looked relieved at this thought.

"He wants the Horse, and he can't have him." Anna mulled it over, her brow furrowing. "Why hasn't the Horse helped us find him?"

"It's not its job." Charlie tugged her boots off and sat down at the table.

"But he protected Judith and Caitlin. He interfered," Emz said. "Why not go all the way and bring us the villain?"

"Because that's our job," Anna said. "Because, whoever he is, he's part of Havoc."

Charlie nodded vigorously.

"Exactly. Anyway, for what it's worth, this other stuff is incidental. The Horse isn't here just to save those women. I still think he's waiting for someone."

"Someone who might come from Day's Ride?" Emz said. Charlie shrugged.

"Possibly. Who knows? There are lots of ways into and out of Havoc. Could come from anywhere. We don't know."

They both looked at Anna. She was deep in thought and didn't notice until the silence became obvious.

"What?"

"You could ask the cards," Emz said. "The Paper Prophets. They might help. Isn't that what they are for?"

They cleared the table, Charlie chucking her discarded boots into the hallway and Emz hanging up the jackets from the backs of the chairs, as Anna cleared away the supper dishes and wiped the table with a cloth. Then they all sat, in their usual triangle: Anna at the middle facing directly out to the window and the view, Charlie on her left, Emz on her right. Anna reached into her trouser pocket. The Paper Prophets felt warm.

"Do we have to join hands or switch the lights out?" Charlie teased. Anna stretched the elastic, sliding it over her hand like a wristlet so it would not be lost. She was about to deal a card.

"Wait." Emz reached out. "Shouldn't you ask the question first?"

They paused.

"Is the Great Grey waiting for someone?" Anna spoke carefully and, after a breath to let the question settle, she dealt three cards face down. She took another breath, exhaling to calm herself before turning the first card.

The Pike Amongst Weeds. The background richly green grey, stranded with weeds, twisting and twined and, only just visible, the bronze-speckled Pike within. She was trying to recall its meaning.

"Oh." Emz sounded eight again, her voice softly in awe of the beautiful illustration. Anna concentrated and turned the second card.

Lightning.

Charlie was silent, looking at the Pike, then at the Lightning as if she was trying to do a crossword puzzle. She said nothing. Anna said nothing.

"Aren't you going to say anything?" Charlie asked, fretful. Anna shook her head.

"Wait." She took in another breath and resettled, turned the third card.

The Maps and Compass.

She looked at the three cards and felt her mind trip over itself. This was not how it had been with Mrs Massey, and so she took in another calming breath and thought, not of the cards and her search of her memory, but of Mrs Massey and the parlour. The nap on the velvet tablecover. Jam. Cream. Her mind unflustered itself.

"Yes," Anna said. It seemed clear to her. Emz and Charlie were patient, waiting for clarification. "Something, someone possibly, elemental. It's their Fate, this person. They're going home."

"Which way?" Charlie asked. "Is this an into-Havoc or an out-of-Havoc thing?" She thought the cards looked spooky and was not clear why Emz seemed so keen. The colours were too rich, like old paintings.

Anna considered. For her, the compass was spinning again, and it was unnerving. It meant something. She felt the weight of it, pressing, and yet it was hard to identify.

"Through Havoc." She understood that much. "They've been found."

"They." Emz was eager. "Who is they?"

"You've asked the question wrong." Charlie leaned back. Anna felt her eye drawn to the spinning compass; the pattern of filigree lace made by the shadows of trees freckled the maps beneath so that she could not see where they led. Old maps. Old writing. And the lightning was striking a whited-out lake.

"No. The cards have answered the question. Anna asked, 'is the horse waiting for someone', and they've said yes." Emz pointed down at them but did not touch them. Charlie was looking only at Emz's face. The Maps and Compass in particular was making her feel odd, the funny little compass and the piles of maps that led to too many places. The routes and byways made you feel lost. Anna put them back into the deck and shuffled it.

"Go again?" Charlie asked. Anna nodded. "Be more precise. What is it that we want to know?"

"Who is the Horse waiting for?" Emz said. "Then we know who or what to expect. Guest, Poacher, Trespasser. We'll know where we are then."

Charlie looked as if she doubted that outcome very much, but she nodded. Her arms were folded. Emz leaned forward.

"Who is the Great Grey waiting for?" Anna asked the cards and at once dealt three onto the tabletop. She held her breath this time and turned the first.

Lightning.

Charlie's arms folded a little tighter across her chest.

The Castle.

Anna stared at the card as if she could see someone in the tower. She held her breath for the last card.

The Black Blank.

Anna held her breath as the black altered itself again into the stylised image of a heart, something bloodied and animal. At the edges of the heart was torn fur, grey and black. The aorta twisted out of it, the open end of the artery pointed towards her. Anna hesitated. She had seen this before. She recalled the scene pictured at the end as through a telescope, dared to look again. A vista: a white lake and a black wolf. The prints in the snow were bloodied.

"The Wolf's Heart," Anna said aloud. The words whispered into her head. She heard them very clearly and had no idea of the meaning. Emz and Charlie said nothing. The heart folded itself into the black. Anna put the cards into the deck, slid the elastic band over them, and replaced them in her pocket.

"So." Charlie did not unfold her arms. "We know where we are then." She looked at the space on the table where the cards had lain.

"The Wolf's Heart." Emz said it over, and Anna wished she would not. "Is it something to do with Cry Wolf d'you think?"

"Nope." Charlie was certain but offered no alternatives.

"Did Grandma say anything about wolves? Other than…"

"Is it Dad?" Anna dealt the idea like an extra, Fate-filled card. "Remember? The old dreams, a black wolf?"

"On a white lake," Emz rallied to this cause. "You think Dad is coming? Is that who the Great Grey is waiting for?"

Charlie snorted.

"Good luck with that." She was agitated. "A wolf. A wood. We just need a red riding hood." She stood up from the table. "I'm going to bed."

"But what about the Wolf's Heart?" Emz asked. "What do you think?"

Charlie halted in the hallway.

"I think we'll know whatever it is when it's breathing hot, bad breath down our necks. As usual." And she slammed her bedroom door shut. Anna was also heading towards her room.

"Anna?" She turned to Emz. "What if it is Dad? It could be Dad." The youngest sister glittered with excitement. Anna was guarded.

"Nothing is certain, Emz. We don't know. Let's just sleep on it," Anna said. "Goodnight."

IT WAS NOT A GOOD NIGHT. The moment she fell asleep, Emz was in the deer dream. It grazed by Cooper's Pond and, as it did so, rather than be a spectator chasing behind, Emz stepped into the body of the beast, its heart a drumbeat powering the limbs. Emz felt the wildness course through her, setting her blood on fire. Uncontrolled. Seared with adrenalin. Flight. She was pursued.

She jolted awake. Emz reached for her grandmother's raincoat, folded herself smaller beneath it, and drifted back into sleep.

It was instant this time. She was leaping, branches whipping as she fled between them.

Fear. Deep in the bones of the deer, bright and fierce. It seized upon Emz, and she was one blink from waking but more springing steps held her in the dream. It asked, for help. The eye of the deer, glittering with an odd light. What was that? She leaned closer to see.

A glow of embers. The deer faltered. Its rear haunch quivered and Emz's dream self felt for the scar. The fear fell away. She held the deer safe with just the touch of her hand. She knew this place. This was not Havoc. She saw where they were in Leap Woods, at Barkway.

Emz turned. The predator vanished. Her eyes scanned the wood, the strips of the trunks, the reaching arms of the trees, the leaves dappling and falling so that nothing was clear to her, and yet, there. An eyeblink and the face was gone, unlike any face she'd ever seen. She could not hold it, the shadows flattered and shattered, and she woke.

AT BREAKFAST ANNA was forensic in her questions about the deer dream in a blatant effort to deflect any questions about the Paper Prophets and their divinations.

"How long have you had it?" she asked as Emz cleared her plate.

"Now that I think about it, since before Caitlin was attacked, so a week or more."

Anna nodded. "And you're sure you were in Leap Woods last night?" She wanted the details. They needed details.

Emz nodded. "I think I know Leap as well as Havoc."

"And it's recurring, but it isn't always the same?" Charlie was grabbing her keys and was already zipped into her jacket, the collar hiding most of her face.

"Yes. It's the same deer but a different…" She stopped. Anna and Charlie paused to watch the revelation pass across her face. "Hunt. The deer is being hunted."

"By our friendly neighbourhood villain." Charlie folded her arms once again. "If the embers are any clue."

"They are."

Charlie was edgy.

"Right. So what's the plan?" she asked. "I'm not sure if I can get off early today."

"I'm going to have a scoot round Leap Woods. I'm in school this morning, but I'm going over to Prickles later."

"Be careful," Anna warned.

"In the dream I think he was scared of me."

They let this new thought sink in. Charlie unzipped her jacket a little.

"He knows we're onto him," she said. "Definitely."

.   .   .

EMZ WONDERED why she even came into school. Of course, the A-level minimum requirements of the Wildwood Society popped into her head, but it seemed the only course she was really studying in the sixth form was anger management. The second she stepped through the door, she was assailed by the tangles of the black web stretching out above her. They oscillated a jagged rhythm of the lies being told.

"… Judith Killen, the one at the stables." As Emz came through the door to the common room she knew it was a mistake.

"You're joking me?" No one was even whispering the gossip. It was hissing and biting around the place.

"Seriously."

"Seriously what?" Emz broke in on Kelly and Luna's chat. They were gleeful at a fresh place to spread their news.

"Logan Boyle attacked another girl." Kelly relished the words. "That Killen girl from the stables. Raped her and left her for dead in the woods. Same as Caitlin."

Emz felt the charcoal of her Strength inside her burn up to daylight heat. Whereas previously she had been unable to control it, letting the energy burst from her into the nearest inanimate object, this time was different. The charcoal glowed whiter and whiter and she held the energy, let the heat and light forge her.

"No, he didn't," she began. Luna snorted.

"That's what you know." She was sneery, a knowing look exchanged between her and Kelly. "Just 'cause you wish he'd fucked you in the woods."

The charcoal was vivid, diamond edged.

"He did not attack Judith Killen," she said. "In fact. It was nothing to do with him. She told the police it was not Logan. Fact. Evidence."

Luna backed down, cowed by fact, but Kelly's eyes flared for a fight.

" Get you, Logan Boyle's defence lawyer, someone is—"

"Lying. Slandering. Deriding." It was unlikely that either girl would understand these words, but Emz kept on. "Accusing. Defaming. Shaming. Sneering. Slating." The words were spilling and spicy. Luna and Kelly's smiles were sealed and tight, unamused as everyone began to look round.

"Smearing. Smirching. Mudslinging. Insinuating." Emz concentrated her gaze on the two girls and reached for their real faces. Kelly, whiny and downtrodden, her cheeks stretched thin over sharp bones. Luna, vain and preening. And written into their eyes, Emz saw their darkest dreads, their sorriest deeds, and pushed at them.

"Badmouthing. Slutshaming. Backbiting. Bitching. Shit stirring." Silence. The room crackled. Not everyone stared, some, Mark Catton amongst them, looked down in shame.

In half an hour, Emily Way was cutting down along High Foxes on her way to Leap Woods.

40

TWIG CROWN

It was a rough breakfast shift at the Castle Inn with a welter of picky ramblers arriving, freshly frosted, from Rook Ridge.

Casey was rattled and quiet, a fact that did not register with Anna who had her own whirlwind of thoughts. It was the smash of crockery that broke both from their distractions.

"Bugger." Casey, Anna noted, was teary-eyed at the mishap, her hand rushing to shove back her short hair in a flustered gesture.

"I'll get the dustpan and brush." Anna scooted past Casey, her hand touching her shoulder for just a second as she did so. The Flickerbook of memory rifled through Anna's head. She reached for the brush without flinching, and a glance at Casey clarified that she had not noticed the mental exchange. Anna handed her the dustpan, and, in silence, they cleared away the shards.

"Sorry." Casey's voice was hardly more than a whisper.

"What is it?" Anna asked.

"What's what?" Casey flipped the bin lid closed in order to not have to look at Anna.

"What is it that's bothering you?" Anna stood, shielding Casey from the rest of the kitchen. The space they occupied was framed by ancient beams of oak. At the edge of her mind, Anna felt dappled shade, frosted leaves the colour of amber and rust. The wind whispered.

"Casey...?"

Casey was trembling.

"I've done something wrong." Her skin paled. Anna shook her head.

"I doubt it."

"No. Seriously, Anna." A tears fell from her left eye, her quivering hand reaching up to swipe it away.

"You've done nothing wrong." Anna picked over the terrible pieces she'd been given from Casey's head. Forest. Embers. "Come on, Casey. This is me. It's my turn to help you."

Casey looked at her.

"Few nights ago… Mitzi set me up on a blind date."

They did not move from their space, Casey's voice low and then breaking as she told the story. "… and I didn't report it." She was struggling. "That lad from the farm, the one everyone's blaming. He didn't do anything. And I didn't come forward."

"You're not in the wrong." Anna reached out a hand to Casey's shoulder. "Hey, come on." She kept her voice steady as she felt the memories lurch forward. If it was a Flickerbook, she should be able to turn the pages. She should be able.

She hugged Casey as she cried it out, days' worth of anxiety and guilt.

"It's okay." Anna smoothed Casey's pale hair. "It's going to be okay."

With the breakfast done, Anna poached Casey some eggs.

"Not eaten since," Casey confessed. "Nothing proper." She thought about it as Anna poured tea. "Had half a piece of toast yesterday. Thought I was going to hurl."

Her hands had stopped shaking, but her smile still had a wobble to it.

"D'you want to go home? I can cope with the lunch rush. We're not busy."

Casey shook her head.

"Nope. Rather be busy, not sitting at home thinking about it." She sipped her tea. "I should go to the police."

"I'll come with you, if you like?"

ANNA HUNTED Lella down in the reception office.

"You can't go out," Lella snapped.

"It's important." Anna had not gone into details but had said they would both be back in plenty of time for lunch.

"I don't care. I've got the accountant coming in. We're getting the books ready, so I won't be able to man the phones or the bar."

Anna looked at Lella's peevish expression.

"I doubt there'll be a rush between now and lunch," she countered. Lella's peevish expression faltered and revealed her underlying anxiety.

"I doubt it, too."

As Anna and Casey left, Anna turned the sign on the door to CLOSED.

AS CASEY GAVE her statement to PC Williamson, Anna stepped out and walked up to Church Lane.

As usual, Mimosa's window display was wild and creative. The thorns of the whitewash bramble crowded the window and door. Anna couldn't see how it helped Aurora's business. No one wanted whitewash bramble bouquets, did they?

The thought did not trouble her as she spotted the ladder outside Mari's new shop.

"Hey." She stepped inside. The interior was a stripped-back contrast to its former self. A pot of limewash was sitting on the sheeting covering the flagstone floor.

"Hello? Mari?" There were voices from the rear of the shop. Anna stepped to the kitchen doorway.

"Mari?"

Outside in the small garden she could see Mari and Matt Woodhill looking up at the building. Mari waved to her.

"Anna!"

They were moving back inside. Matt nodded to Anna and made his farewells.

"I'll get the paper quote to you ASAP. Let me know what you think." He ducked out of the shop.

"Renovations," Mari said. "It's all go."

"The new signage looks good," Anna said as they moved back onto the shop floor.

"I'm full of optimism," Mari said. "It won't last."

Anna smiled to herself.

"Plus, just as I'm setting up to take Betty's into local handi-crafts, bloody Roz Woodhill decides she's opening her gallery in town." Mari's face assumed its familiar cheery grumpiness. She rolled her eyes. "Only bloody typical."

"In town?" Anna could not think where the new gallery was. "You sure?"

"Yep." Mari started to sort her brushes out, kicked a bit of sheeting back into place. "Over at the old Plainsong Chapel."

SINCE ROZ and Anna were not particular friends, she had time, during her swift walk to the chapel, to think of an excuse for dropping by.

"I noticed the renovations…" It was flimsy, but it got her through the door, bearing the sign OPENING SOON.

Roz was subdued, and it pained Anna. She had lost her

confident manner, and her face, while never the smiliest of countenances, was stark and serious.

"You'll have two galleries then. Expansion." Anna's breezy interest made a brash echo in the chapel's interior.

"Oh, no. Let the lease go on the one at Knightstone." She looked smaller, thinner. "I'm concentrating on this place. New opportunity. Nearer to Castlebury and home."

"Shorter commute," Anna said.

"Exactly," Roz smiled. "You'll have to come over for the launch." She reached onto the long trestle table behind her for some tickets.

"Oh, great. Bit of excitement in Woodcastle for a change." She was cheery, but Roz's face fell a little further as she turned away. There had been too much excitement at Halloween. Anna pursued the matter.

"I'm glad I caught you. I was wondering, you know, if the Craft Club were meet…"

Roz stiffened, and Anna regretted the blundering question.

"Oh. No. Not." Roz managed, shaking her head.

"Oh, I just saw Mari, and so I thought…"

"The others can meddle with that if they choose." Roz's smile was haunted. "I'm too busy." She looked around at the artworks already out and others waiting to be unpacked. "Super busy."

"I can see."

There was nothing more to say.

As ANNA HEADED BACK to the police station, she thought over all that had happened after Apple Day. Roz, she could see, was physically fine, no lingering after-effects of the hideously broken ankle, but Anna didn't know her well enough to ask what she might remember of the whole incident.

The after-effect, the cessation of the Craft Club, bothered

her. Roz had had a passion for her Craft Club interests. Being possessed by Mrs Fyfe had been a lesson in the Occult, one that she need not have learned.

Anna felt guilty, as if it was not Mrs Fyfe but Anna Way who had robbed Roz Woodhill of her twig crown.

FOOTPRINTS

The problem of the quest for the Havoc attacker was a bee trapped against the window of Emz's head.

She was concerned with the fact that Caitlin had been found in Leap Woods, and that she and her sisters did not make patrols there as a matter of Gamekeeping course. In order to remedy this, she made her simple trip to the hide into a swift patrol. She looked for embers or any sign that might have been left.

By the time she reached the rear edge of Cooper's Pond, she was disconsolate. She did not have Charlie's pathfinding skills and so the trail was cold. Her mood was shifting towards irritable when a thought occurred. She did not have the Map skills, but she had Reach. She wasn't sure if this was something they could only do properly together, but it was worth a try. She stepped off the trodden path and, standing deeper within the trees, took a deep breath.

It was like flicking a switch. At once the wood was altered. If she looked up, Havoc was beyond, the trees tinted at the canopy level with a faint smoke wisp that trailed out towards Mrs Massey's old cottage. Smoke made her think of the embers she'd seen in the deer's eyes, and, at once, she focused on Leap Woods and picked up the cold smoke filtered through the trees. It was thin and uncertain, but it was there. She followed.

The deer dream chimed in her head. The smoke trail turned her this way and that, exactly as in the dream. Her heart was racing as she stepped down at the shore of Cooper's Pond. Where had the deer splashed? Just over there. She moved to the spot and the dream began to replay itself. She ran on, gathering speed, rocking up at last, breathless and sweating, at exactly the clearing she had seen in the dream. The smoke thinned and drifted, hardly more than a breath.

At her feet, the patch of ground where she had halted, last night, and faced her pursuer. She saw at once the real prints, the neat notches of a deer and the brief dance of fear it had printed into the mud.

She looked around to the trees that had hidden the pursuer, had shielded that real face, the shadows of which deepened in her memory, trying to pull at the shape of the skull and jawline.

She walked around to the hide, attempting to knit her thoughts together. The attacker came out of Havoc. His ember trail had shown up as smoke in her Reach. The dream of the deer? It was real. She had the hoofprints to prove it. So what did that mean? The deer had shown her something? She dredged the dream back. The scar on its hindquarter. What was the significance of the scar? The threads wove and snapped as she opened the hide. She would take it all back to Anna and Charlie and they could pick it over together. She picked up a few bits of sweet wrapper and discarded worksheets and began closing up the shutters.

She'd reached the last of them when the door opened behind her, a rectangle of mizzly November late-afternoon light. Emz turned.

Logan Boyle stood on the threshold. Neither said a word, even as the mizzle became a more insistent rain, the drops catching in his hair, making a rattling sound on his waterproof jacket.

"I—" he managed the sound, then drew in a breath. "I heard what happened."

Emz said nothing. Her heartbeat was clogging her mouth, grasping at the air in her lungs.

"Mark said," Logan still faltered at the threshold, "I thought… I wanted to…"

"They were being bastards. Like normal." Emz's voice was husky with emotion. Logan took a step forward.

"I wanted—" his voice cracked. He took a breath. "To say thank you."

Emz was glad of the bench in front of her and the press of it against her shaking legs.

"Mark said what you did." Logan circled the point. "So, I—"

Emz felt the rain blowing in on the back of her neck from the open lookout.

"Thank you." He put his hands in his pockets, but the crackle of his waterproofs did not disguise the crack in his voice.

"You can't thank me for the truth," Emz said.

"I'm trying," Logan shrugged. He did not make a move to leave.

"I'm sorry," he said at last. "How it all went down. Before."

Emz nodded.

"I know," she confessed.

"You're not the same," Logan said, "as them." He nodded in the general direction of Woodcastle.

"No." Emz hoped the hide was dark enough to hide the fact that she was shaking. Logan took one step forward. Emz moved, her primal brain operating the controls, but she staggered back, caught. The pocket of the black waxed raincoat snagged on the edge of the bench.

When she looked up, Logan was gone.

4 2

PRIORITIES

When she arrived home, the sound of raised voices pushed thoughts of Logan out of Emz's head, the argument rising out of Cob Cottage like bitter smoke.

"Because Cry Wolf needs three of us." Anna's voice, usually so calm, even in anger, held an odd tone. Emz heard it clearly as she strode up the shore to the porch. It was bird-like, a call like a crow. "You can't keep doing this, Charlie."

"Keep doing this? Keep doing? It's tonight. It's just this once."

"To add to the other tonight-just-this-onces." Anna's swift attack. "We're all in this. We are together." Her tone was as hard as the stone at the waterline.

"Anna, this is one night." Charlie responded with frustration. Neither sister acknowledged Emz as she walked in. "I have a reason."

"And I have a reason for asking you to stay." Anna was insistent. Charlie railed against her.

"Tonight I need to do this one thing that is *not* about Havoc." Charlie's hand was slicing at the air between them. "One night."

"We have a job to do."

"Then do it." Charlie was unmoved. "You'll manage."

239

"Managing isn't good enough." Anna's voice held an eerie calm. "Not if we're going to help Caitlin, Casey, Bridget, and Judith."

"Who?" Emz heard the list of names.

Charlie stared, Anna matching her harsh gaze as she spoke.

"Other victims. I found out today Casey was attacked, to add to the rumour around town about Bridget Quinn being jumped at the Highwayman. That's why finding this man is our priority."

"Not. Tonight." Charlie's hand was a guillotine blade coming down on the table so that the cup nearest to her over-balanced, rolled perilously to the edge. "Tonight, I have promised Aron, and that is all there is. If you had had something important to do with Calum, then you would have chosen the same."

"Charlie." Emz glared, sensing Anna shutting down beside her.

"Tonight is that important. It's not my fault she won't listen." Charlie would not retract, held her eldest sister's gaze. "I have to."

There was a cavernous silence ended by a nod from Anna.

Charlie, released, was out of the door in seconds. No one spoke, the sound of Charlie's car growling up the track to Old Castle Road, growing fainter and fainter. Anna made a move to go to her room.

"There's nothing stopping us," Emz said. "Let's go." She handed Anna her jacket from the back of the chair.

The two sisters did not speak as they patrolled Havoc Wood. Emz trudged under the weight of her day, Anna the opposite, lightfooted and swift with emotion.

Havoc creaked and rustled around them as they made their way along their usual tracks, heading down to the edge of Thin-Through, the terrain hard underfoot with the last frost, the trees bare, looking, it appeared to Emz, starker than usual.

At Quinn's Gate, Anna came to a stop, her breath coming in

short, harsh bursts that did little to disguise the roiling emotions. Her eyes were too bright in the autumnal night, the beam of Emz's lantern catching at her jawline making her face seem wild and raw. Except, as Emz looked, her Strength pulled focus. She had not looked at Anna's real face in a long time. It was not simply a courtesy to those she loved and lived with, it was, Emz was beginning to realise, how her Strength worked. At this moment, her Strength revealed Anna's face, unbidden. It was older, thinner than Emz remembered. Her eyes were a danger to look into but carried in their depths a torch of light. Her jawline was more angular, no softness in the way it curved into her neck like a thin blade. It was not an ugly face. It carried its scars. It warned you.

"We've come the wrong way." Anna's temper had died and been replaced by frustration with herself. "We… I should have taken us up the ridge."

Emz looked at their surroundings, another raggedy edge of Leap and Havoc striped with thin elder trees.

"Where are we? The back end of Stride?" Anna asked. Emz nodded and a thought struck her.

"We never stopped here, did we?" she said.

"Stopped? What d'you mean?" Anna was puzzled. "When?"

"We've walked this way hundreds of times with Grandma, but this is one of those places that we never stopped. We never had a picnic or a breather here." She looked around at the stony ground, the thin trees crowding in on them. "Do you see anything?" she asked her sister, as she herself surveyed their surroundings.

"Like what?"

"Can you put being pissed off with Charlie on hold for a minute and concentrate?" Emz snapped. There was a moment of standoff. "There are two of us. We're not useless." Emz was restless, something pulled at her. At first, she thought it was the emotion of the day rattling around her, but, as she berated

Anna, she understood that the wood was reaching out. "Feel for it." As she spoke, the wood rustled with the cold night breeze and prickled at her. She switched her attention away from Anna and their argument and let her Strength connect with the wood.

The effect was instant. The beam of her lantern sparked against the air; veins in the few remaining leaves stood out as the amber and copper and bronze of the dropping foliage illuminated the wood.

She could see the wispy, smoked trail of the Havoc attacker, a handprint on an oak, a bootprint here and here and here, showing the rat run he had made through Havoc. It was not the route that Charlie might have seen. It was the remains, the archaeology of him. As Emz walked forward picking up the traces, she understood.

"He's here. He's in Havoc, and he's been here a long time." The Strength hummed in her mind like an old tune. She turned to Anna.

Anna was looking in the opposite direction.

"We need Charlie," she insisted. "We can't do this."

"We can." Emz could see the trail heading into the direction Anna was facing. There was an indication, a glow of embers, that hinted it had been recently used. "What's that way?" she pointed. Anna considered for a moment.

"Takes us to The Brush and…" Anna's mind had caught up with the track. She turned to Emz with a quick glance.

The stave they had set by the gate at Mrs Massey's cottage was still in place. Emz could see it gave off a pale light, like sunlight through a leaf. She and Anna were breathless from their hurried trek, but now they felt they had picked up the scent.

"We've kept him out of here." Anna's face lightened. "I can feel it." She looked to Emz for confirmation and found it. She could see the traces of where he had been, a frustrated circumnavigation of the cottage. Emz turned as Anna shut her eyes, and she felt the Reach push out.

"Anything?" she asked, as the thrum of it died away. Anna turned.

"This way."

It was an assault course, instinct and insight pulling up this track, along that trail, up this path, but not once finding the culprit.

"Oh!" Anna exclaimed, throwing a stone in frustration. It bounced off a fallen trunk with a hard, broken sound. "This is useless."

Emz, too, after nearly two hours of wandering, had lost heart.

"He's hiding." She felt a sharp prickle jab at her fingertips, like an allergic reaction. "In the dream…" she was dredging the images up, "in the dream he could hide himself, camouflaged," she admitted.

"Good. *Stay hidden!*" Anna shouted at the trees. "There's no place for you here." As the words left her, a fierce squally wind blew up, whirling a cloud of leaves, branches rattling above them like beseeching hands, twigs breaking off, the movement spinning out from where they stood.

"That was him." Anna darted to the spot. "Damn it, that was *him.*"

"It's the trees, carrying your message," Emz said.

"Not a message." Anna turned to spit the word between them. "Let them carry the Spell."

THEY MADE their way home to Cob Cottage.

"If we'd Cried Wolf…" Anna and Emz were not in disagreement. "It's so obvious. If we'd just done it."

"Tonight we should think of the Other places. Like Stride, like High Foxes. All those places that we brush past. They're different. That's what Grandma Hettie taught us by not stopping there." Emz was trying to be practical. "Charlie will be back tomorrow."

"What if tomorrow's too late?" Anna had a wild look, too close to her real face. Emz felt afraid. She had nothing to reply, but the gap was filled by a deep, rumbling whinny. The Great Grey stood on the path between them and Cob Cottage. It shook its head, its mane releasing a powerful musk of woodsmoke, honey, and horse.

"We've got help," Emz said, and turned onto the porch.

From inside, she watched as Anna approached the Great Grey, her hand settling on his neck, and then her cheek resting against him. Emz felt a pang of jealousy. There was something about the horse. She hoped he would stay with them. She hoped he had been sent, not to wait for someone, but to take up residence and help. She felt there was evidence he had already done so. There was also the glimmer of their father too. This flame of hope flickered and dodged in her heart.

Outside, Anna let herself rest against the horse. The scent was strong and reviving and then the cold bit at her, awakening her ravelled senses. She Reached to feel the heart of the horse drumming in the cave of its chest. The frost glittered like broken sunlight, and the Flickerbook of it opened.

The sky expanded, taking down the trees to a distant skyline. At one side, a range of mountains like icicles, Pike Lake widened out, a crust of diamond ice formed across it, and there, at the far edge, a black wolf, waiting.

A shock. Anna felt the breath freeze in her lungs, and she could not release her hand from the horse's neck. The horse breathed at her, the air condensing, scintillating with light. The wolf approaching, a steady pace until what had been shadows became shoulders, strode into the shape of a man.

Far. He walked, never drawing near until the ice cracked with a sound like the water tearing itself apart and, as it split, something landed at his feet. A heart, bloody but still beating, punctured by pins.

The drum of the wolf's heart matched the drum of the Great Grey's own heart and Pike Lake thawed and pulled her back. Her own heartbeat, too fast and frightened.

Once more the horse breathed at her, the warmth from its nostrils reviving her. She took a step back. The Great Grey bowed its head once to release her hand and trotted away into the trees.

Emz had been talking for some moments about the deer dream.

"It's real," she concluded. "The deer is real. Charlie saw it. And I know it's connected to the attacker." She was tracking around the kitchen, fiddling with little chores, as she thought aloud. "I need to keep a notebook at the side of my bed, need to write down the routes it takes me. I think it might be giving him away. It's some sort of marker, maybe. But I can't work out what the scar means?" She looked towards Anna who had not moved, was staring into the window of the woodburner and had clearly not heard anything Emz had said.

"You alright?" Emz was concerned.

Anna nodded. "Yeah." Her voice a whisper. "Cold." She stood by the woodburner.

"Want a drink?" Emz asked, making for the teapot. Anna nodded but instead made a move for the small cupboard by the scullery door. Emz watched Anna and turned to fetch the old glasses from the top of the dresser.

Who knew where the whisky had come from? It had been in the cupboard for as long as the Way sisters had been alive. Grandma Hettie had kept it for 'emergency use', while never being specific about what constituted such an emergency. The liquor was perfumed, they now smelt, by woodsmoke and honey, but they swigged it down, a shot each.

Black wolf, white lake.

"So what do you think?" Emz asked.

"About what?" Anna looked suddenly present.

"About the deer in my dream. About the fact that it's a real deer."

Anna was not listening again. Emz waited a moment. Her sister was far away.

"Remind me, what do you dream about when you dream about Dad?" Anna asked, refilling their glasses.

"What does that have to do with the deer?"

"Just tell me."

Emz looked at the shot glass, at Anna, who was waiting. The liquor's scent was heavy and comforting.

"I dream of a black wolf, on an ice-white frozen lake."

Anna nodded.

"Did you see something? Did you see Dad? Is he coming?" Emz's face was contorted by the strong alcohol.

"Sorry. No idea," Anna admitted and knocked back her second shot. It was more fiery than the first, liquid bronze plating her gullet with heat. She poured a third one. Emz was wide eyed.

"Nightcap." Anna knocked hers back. "Help us sleep."

Black wolf, white lake. More real than all the times she had dreamt the same. *Black wolf, white lake.* A heart, pierced by pins. What did it mean? Anna Way thought she might never sleep again.

THE ACE OF HEARTS

Charlie had been waiting for some time outside Aron's flat. She couldn't even get into the communal hallway tonight. She had been waiting by the harbourside, watching the gulls on the water and letting them take away her thoughts.

"Hey." His voice made her turn. He was standing with his hand outstretched, his charming smile on his face.

She didn't like his charming smile, she missed the smile he had had as a teenager, the one that lit up his eyes. She looked into his eyes and he looked away, started moving towards the swing bridge.

"I was enjoying the view." She couldn't think of a better opening gambit for a conversation. She didn't want to start with "you're late", as that sounded like picking a fight, even though it was simply a statement of fact and might lead to an interesting story as to why he was late. He smiled once again.

"Come on. Let's go." He leaned in to kiss her cheek and then began what seemed like a frogmarch.

They moved up towards Old Town with no further communication. It was difficult to hear above the roar of the rush hour traffic. Charlie felt the tight way he held onto her, his hand cold and thin feeling. As they waited at the foot of Parker Street for the lights to change on the crossing, he leaned in again to kiss her.

They did not go straight to Pandemonium. Instead, wordless, Aron guided her part way up the hill to St George's and turned in at the old wrought iron gates of Brandon Chase. Charlie's heart started on a slow, deadly beat that robbed her of her proper breath. In the back of her head, a bell was tolling, the sound ringing out over the lake of dark sadness.

They walked along the path to the grotto, and they said not a word.

The grotto, or the 'grotty' as they had christened it when they were teenagers, was a folly constructed of old shells and flints and concrete and it lurched from repair to repair, bits of it occasionally falling down on visitors' heads as they negotiated the dark, damp maze of the place. Many turned back in fear of the spiders in the pocked and low-slung roof. If you were brave, and Charlie and Aron always had been, then you eventually emerged in the Palladio, a little domed room that looked out over the ornamental lake.

Beneath the dome, mouldy and mossed, the panes of glass in the roof long since cracked and broken, Aron pulled her to him, his mouth planting on hers. He pulled her closer, the kiss deepening as he pushed her back against the wall where the paint crimpled like old skin. His cold hands cupped her jaw, moved to her hips, her back, stroked at her hair. It didn't matter that she couldn't breathe. She saw all their moments in that kiss, and they all ran down to the reflection of the lake in his left eye.

"I thought we were going to Pandemonium?" Charlie hid the fact that she was shaking. She had felt more at ease last night at Frog Pond.

"Thought we'd have a minute or two to ourselves, you know?" He smiled; the edges of it were fraying, becoming his old smile. He put his hands into his trouser pockets, looked out over the water.

"Why not…" Charlie heard herself playing the game, "… knock Pandemonium on the head? Go off by ourselves. Go to the Night Zoo?" Her words sounded like a playground chant, learned by rote.

"What the fuck is the Night Zoo?" Aron turned to her, his face furrowed and, she realised, thinner than of late.

"It's late night opening… at the zoo," she finished rather lamely. "I saw the poster the other day. Or not that, something else."

He shook his head. "Night Zoo? What the fuck?" He gave a world-weary laugh and then glanced at his phone. "Anyway. Time is clocking on. Let's go." He offered his hand.

"I'm serious. Let's not go." Charlie knew this was pointless. She could see a very clear and distinct Map written into the knobs and nobbles of rock above Aron's head leading straight to Pandemonium; however, it did not hurt to try to defeat Fate. "Let's go back to yours."

"Don't do this." He shook his head, not angry, rather weary.

"Do what?" Charlie was surprised, very often the hint at a free evening naked in front of his fifty-inch TV persuaded Aron from any pastime or pursuit.

"We're going tonight. It's important." She could tell how serious he was. It was shocking to see.

"Okay." Out of the periphery of her vision, she saw the Map above his head, how it inked itself onward and turned, not towards the harbourside flat but off, up towards The Lea Meadows at the edge of the suspension bridge. Why would he go that way?

"We need to go. You have to change." He took her hand again and they wound their way back into the gardens and out through the gate at the top of the hill.

.   .   .

IF VIEWED SIMPLY AS A BUILDING, the Georgian townhouse that held Pandemonium was what an estate agent might call "sought after". As Charlie and Aron approached, the beauty of the building was not lost upon her, the way that the sash windows on each level looked out with life. The soft sandstone steps that led to the double, black-painted front door were inviting. Anyone would want to know what the building was like inside. Charlie recalled each room and staircase as it had been that fateful Halloween. She'd been left to wander, Aron too busy with his private card game.

It might have been her go-to place if not for the memories attached to it. She had been peeved with Aron for bringing her there and then abandoning her, but, on entering, she had been intrigued by the place, and there had been redemption of sorts in the discovery of the Ceilidh and the live fiddle band at the very top of the house. She had enjoyed the revels, the breathless dancing, the fiddle playing the bright and intricate music. It had been a double-edged sword. She had felt guilt that she had enjoyed being abandoned, being away from Aron, and that led to the edges of her inner lake of sorrow. Worse still was the aftermath, that, having walked back with Aron, they were greeted with the news of the tragedy of Ethan and Calum. It seemed too terrible. It felt to Charlie that Pandemonium was a place to which she ought never, ever venture back.

Pandemonium was not like the other nightclubs in Castlebury. It was so utterly exclusive, exquisite, and mysterious. Rumours flew and whispered about the anything and everything that carried on there. It had an epic scale to it. Charlie had girl friends that longed to be taken there. She ought not to be so ungrateful.

No. She was ungrateful. She didn't like the place. The left-hand side of the double door had opened to admit them, the doorman giving a serious nod to Aron as they stepped into the plush hallway with its dark grey wallpaper, its antique furnishings. The door was closed behind them, the doorman leaning to Aron to exchange a word. What the word was, Charlie didn't take note, she was distracted by a sudden view through a door at the end of the hallway. Where the hallway was dark and elegant, the rear room was stark and pale, the bare wood of the back-sash windows bordered by stripped-back shutters. Beneath the window, a leather and metal couch slung with a sheepskin. There was a scent of coffee, bitter as dark chocolate. A shadow moved across the polished wooden floor and the door shut, the dark grey sealing the space. From here, it was as though the door vanished. Only the shadow of it could be seen lurking against the wall beneath the tall arc of the staircase.

"This way," Aron said, his eyebrows flashing upwards as he tagged her at the elbow and headed up the stairs. He waited for her on the first landing. He took the stairs two at a time up to the second landing and was opening a door at the back of the house. "Here we are." He let the door swing wide, ushered her inside.

The room was a thin rectangle in shape with three vast windows that ought to have looked out onto the garden and the city beyond. Here, the shutters were closed and were painted in a dark blue-black. Fabric draped across high brass curtain poles and dropped to the black-painted floor. The furniture here was all antique, a wingback leather chair, a velvet upholstered chaise. Up against the wall was an ornate cabinet, the like of which Charlie had only previously seen on a landing at Hart-field House.

Aron was moving to another door and opening that one. Charlie followed him to the threshold. He entered the sump-tuous bedroom and turned to her. He looked on edge.

"What do you think?"

"Of what?" Charlie asked, not venturing into the space. The bed was a four poster, draped in a heavy grey and gold brocade. It looked like something from a fairy tale, as if, at any moment, the Beast might arrive. The mirror on the far wall added to the effect. Its frame arched upwards, the glass within foxed and tarnished.

"Of your room." Aron was stretching his fake smile over his face. "Surprise," he said, spreading his arms.

"My room?" Charlie thought of all the stories she had heard about the private rooms available at Pandemonium. She looked at Aron and, as she had suspected, he looked away.

"What's going on?" she asked, taking a step into the room. As she did so, Aron moved to the bed. There was another dramatic dress draped over the covers.

"This is, I hope." He lifted the gown on its hanger. It was, this time, black silk, and, here and there, small constellations of beads winked in the light from the lamp. The skirt, she noted, was made with black feathers glimmering with a forest-green iridescence. She was jolted, thinking back to the Halloween outfit she had worn the last time she was at Pandemonium, which included a set of black angel wings that she'd impulse bought from a nearby vintage shop.

All her instincts were at her shoulder, whispering of possible escape routes because, Charlie darling, something is off, something is odd, something is not quite right. She looked at Aron and saw all that was odd, off, and definitely not right. Her heart creaked like old wood.

"What's going on? What is this?" she asked again, this time with much the same authoritative tone she had used recently to their Havoc visitor Ailith. Aron faked his smile and moved behind her to shut the door. Charlie stepped to open it. His hand stayed hers. They wrestled the door handle for a few stupid moments.

"Stop." Aron was stronger. Except, Charlie knew he wasn't. Inside, her Strength creaked like seasoned oak. She was a fingertip away from wrenching the handle from the door. "Chaz. Chaz." He wedged himself between her and the door, his free hand moving up to her neck, leaning in to kiss her, his mouth moving over her face. Charlie pushed him away, hard enough that his back met the wall with a heavy thump. He looked rattled.

"You bolt and that is it. End of." Aron shifted the fake smile from his face and replaced it with a glare. Now he was the cocky teenager, except Charlie saw through him. He was afraid, there was a wildness in his eyes that she had not seen since their schooldays.

"You need to put the dress on."

"*You* need me to put the dress on," Charlie challenged. Inside she could feel resistance. Anger was filling her mind like smoke. She saw the wild terror flare in his eyes, and he looked away from her with a wry laugh, shook his head, could not, she saw, look back at her.

"Jumping off The Ark was quirky. Interesting. You bail here, you will make me look like a wanker. Just do it." Now he looked at her, she saw where his face was thin and tired, his hands shaking.

"What is going on?"

Aron gave a sharp laugh.

"Put the dress on and find out." He wrenched the door open, shut it behind him. Charlie's heart felt like a balloon bobbing in her chest. There were no tears, only a white-hot rage.

She looked around for a moment or so, checked out the reflection of the room in the giant mirror, tried the shutters and found them shut fast. She tried the door. The hallway outside was softly lit and, at the opposite end at the top of the stairs, Aron was talking to a doorman.

Charlie sank onto the bed feeling tetchy. It was a princess and the pea kind of bed, rather thick and overly high. She leaned back to think and, as she did so, the glamorous dress slid to the floor rather drunkenly. She jumped to pick it up. If she didn't damage it, it could be returned. Aron could not afford this dress, Charlie was certain. She'd cost him with the gold dress doubling as a scuba suit. Tonight she had better be careful.

Touching the dress was a mistake. Charlie had intended not to change, not to wear the dress, not to play whatever this game was, but the dress was persuasive. The black silk was slightly rough to the touch, raw and holding darkness. The feathers were sleek, like a bird's wing, forming an elegant, curved silhouette. It would not hurt to try it on.

The neckline of the dress was high on her collarbones, the sleeves slim and long. She felt graceful and lithe as she moved in it. A glance in the mirror at her hair led to a brief flurry of damage limitation. There was a brush on the dressing table, and she loosed her hair from its habitual messy bun. It was a matter of moments before she was not Charlie anymore. She looked at this new self and was not sure she liked her. She glared at herself. There were no dressier shoes apparent, so she put her boots back on. Grounded. Rooted. Feet on the ground. Charlie felt a charge go through her as she tied her laces. She looked up. What *was* that? Not electricity. She had not been staticked by her bootlaces or the dress. More. She recognised it at once as a Havoc Wood feeling, and she sat for a moment, still hunched a little forward as if tying her boots, as if she didn't want whatever had warned her to see she had been warned.

Warned. Charlie wasn't even surprised at the thought in her head. The rest of her day, her last few weeks, even, had been filled with this unease and to finally confront it felt like a relief.

Except for the panic and fear, of course, because if you were being warned then there was something to be worried about, something that would have to be dealt with.

As she headed out into the hallway, the feathers in the skirt ruffled with a sound like jackdaws lifting from the branches of the elms at Top Hundred.

· · ·

THERE WAS a chink of glasses behind a black door and a strong scent of cigar smoke that could not mask the oakmoss and vetivert she could smell from the mingled aftershave in the room. All the scents and wafts were expensive. She could see the vestibule directly ahead, the sparkle of its stained glass, and the sleek door beyond, painted matt black on the inside. She was walking towards it when the doorman stepped out of a small front parlour.

"Good evening, Miss, pleased to meet you. I'm Jonas. Anything you require, simply ask me. This way, if you please."

His hand, like the rest of him, was giant, a paw that appeared to usher her sideways but, effectively, blocked her exit. She looked up at him, his vast muscled frame fitted perfectly into a crisp suit, a shirt whiter than snow. His skin was a deeply burnished brown, his eyes a deeper hazel, and serious. She glanced to the parlour, saw the side table, a book face down upon it.

"It's just through here." His voice was soft and educated and insistent. "Mr Herald is expecting you." He smiled and took one step forward. Enough of a step to persuade her to turn towards the door. "You're in the Montpellier Room this evening, Miss."

His giant hand turned the knob; the door swung open. Charlie took a step forward and the door closed behind her.

"Hello, Charlotte." Call Me Ivan moved from his post by the window beside Aron to greet her. "And how are you this evening?" His smile was genuine and nervous. His hand brushed at her elbow to guide her towards a small side table.

The room was a barrage of scents and aromas; the champagne she was offered was redolent with lemon and oak, and it floated above the beeswax scent from the furniture that mingled with dry, harsher, and more ancient niffs and whiffs from the fabrics. Old smoke, spilt wine, old men. A waft of river water through the small crack in the sash window at the front of the long thin room made her look out of the window, try to see any slight glimpse of Woodcastle in the blue dark. Streetlights winked on and obliterated distance.

"Hey." Aron, looking white-faced, his fingers fiddling with the button on his suit jacket, came to stand beside her.

"You look beautiful," Call Me Ivan said. "I hope the dress pleases you." Again the smile. Aron fiddled with his cuffs now, cleared his throat. Charlie understood that the dress was not Aron's choice. She said nothing. Her mouth was dry. Charlie had not drunk the champagne, and she put the glass down to make a ring on some hideously pricey mahogany side table. There was an awkward silence.

"So, since we are all now gathered, shall we play?" Call Me Ivan turned to Aron, who was already moving towards an elegant card table set up in the centre of the room. There were three chairs.

"I don't play," Charlie mentioned. Call Me Ivan smiled and began riffle shuffling the cards. As he did so, Charlie felt as if someone had just turned up the volume on every particle of her body. She struggled to focus; the sound of the deck made a noise like leaves rustling at Hackett, and Aron pouring more champagne made a sound like the brook at the foot of Banner Hill.

"The cards have been unkind to your man here, of late." The cards, arcing and roiling, a murmuration caught between his skilled hands. "He has dug himself quite a hole… a grave, you might call it."

He did not look up from the cascading movement of the cards. "If we take a quick inventory of the losses…"

Aron flinched by the sideboard, still keeping his back to them, saying nothing. His head bowed. Call Me Ivan continued.

"His car. His goods and chattels… his flat. Did he tell you he's been couch surfing for the last week?"

Charlie thought of the night at the marina when she could not contact Aron, when the flat had been dark and out of reach.

She thought of the Map written over him tonight, heading to The Lea Meadows instead of home.

"So, in order to get himself out of this pit, Aron offered me one final wager, for the ultimate stake." Call Me Ivan stopped shuffling the deck and looked up at her. "You."

Charlie's heart battered in her chest. There was a smothered snuffle from Aron at the sideboard.

"He knew I had seen you here the last time, that particular and terrible Halloween. You wore your wings," Call Me Ivan said. His eyes glimmered and he looked back to the cards, his fingers working them so that they snapped and cracked once more. "Then… there was your swan dive off The Ark." Call Me Ivan took a sharp intake of breath and shook his head in wonder. "And yet… before we have dealt a hand, everything is already lost. Your man here has no heart."

Call Me Ivan stood, moved around the table to stand before her.

"But I suspect you already know that."

Call Me Ivan's voice was soft and there was a note within it, singing out to Charlie, but she was unable to hear it clearly over the percussion of her heart.

"Go or stay? Love or leave? The only player at this table is you." His voice had lowered to a whisper. She did not move, kept her eyes on the deck. Was his hand shaking? She was shaking. He offered her the deck. "Everything depends on the turn of a card."

She looked into his face. His expression threw her. The arrogance and authority she anticipated was absent. His eyes were bright and nervous, and bewildered thoughts scrabbled at Charlie. He looked away, reached to pull the top card and looked at it, took in a deep breath. Charlie felt she might memorise the pattern on the back of it. Leaves, branches, twined and endlessly furling. She looked over it into Ivan Herald's face.

"We don't often have a chance to save someone we love." He

was direct, locking her gaze. His eyes, green-flecked, his voice a deep and resonant note that took her breath. What was happening?

"If offered such a chance, I would take it," Call Me Ivan said.

Words failed Charlie; her mind was a jumbled torrent of grief and confusion and fear. She could just about manage to breathe in, and the scents in the room began a chemistry deep within her. She turned to the door, but before she touched the brass knob, she knew it was locked.

"I would not risk my soulmate at a card table." Call Me Ivan's voice caught at her. She took her hand from the doorknob and placed her palm on the door itself. The wind through Havoc Wood sighed through her mind. In the mirror on the wall beside the door, Charlie could see Ivan Herald. He turned the card he had picked, the single red symbol catching in the golden light of the lamp.

"I believe in Fate, Charlotte. In the Ace of Hearts."

Charlie breathed in, drew in Strength. Her free hand was shaking. She raised it, flattened that, too, against the door.

"Unlock the door." Her tone was as firm as the wood itself, grained with its strength. She had no need to concentrate, the idea was there. Through her palms, she felt it in the architrave, sensed it within the wooden beams running like a skeleton across the ceiling, beneath her feet in the planks, polished and treacled brown with age. Ivan Herald took a further, hesitant step towards her.

"I believe in the wild card."

The note sang out once more as he spoke. Her breath stalled. Charlie pressed harder against the wood.

"Door." Her voice was a low whisper of leaves in the birches at ThinThrough. She looked at her hand, the fingers like branches from the bough of her arm, from the trunk of her body. The Strength rushed through her. The door released an angry groan. Beneath her feet the floorboards shuddered, as if a lorry was passing. Ivan Herald took a step towards her.

"I would stake my life." Her eyes were drawn to his reflection in the mirror beside her. His voice, cracking a little at the edge, the note within it bewildering. A warning? An alarm?

Charlie did not turn or move, she breathed in. The breath rippled out through the floorboards again and, once more, the door creaked a sharp, fractured sound. She turned the knob. The door swung open.

She saw the Door Giant tug his reading glasses from his face, move into action to bar her way, but the door to his small parlour swung shut in his face, slammed as the main door moaned, mournful, as it opened to let her out. It was bitter cold as she walked down the steps. There was a streak of frost, a thin strand of glistering ice that caught at her mind, and she was following it, not listening to hear if anyone followed her. Not caring. Blank and bare. The wind of Havoc Wood was pushing at her, helping her stay upright as she cut down the side street. Here, the Old Chapel Art Centre and its darkening trees that shushed and whispered her onwards, and, further up the hill, the caged-in garden elms and limes and beeches of Milton Square. The frosted path winked ahead of her with its delicate starlight, and her feet stepped on, on, moving her homewards.

It was after midnight before she reached the edge of Castlebury, and the long dark road to Woodcastle lay ahead. She could already see where the streetlights gave out and, in the last fifteen minutes or so, had been aware of a dark car pulling up from Castlebury behind her. It was careful and sleek, and she was probably imagining it.

The frost had continued out of town, and she watched where it turned to cross the road and moved into the trees at the edge of New Road. Operating on instinct still, Charlie moved with the frost. It might be warmer within the trees, and she could cut across country that way and no one could follow her.

The effect was not instantaneous. Rather, Charlie had to walk a few hundred yards into the shelter of the trees to trigger it. Where she thought she would come up towards the back end of the Hartfield estate, the most far-flung edge of meadowland, instead she moved through the trees and felt the woodland shift and realign itself. No. That was wrong. She was realigning, adjusting her view. If she turned here, to the left, she would be at ThinThrough in ten minutes.

The wood began, at once, to work its magic. The ground softened beneath her feet, each step lifting the damp perfume of leafmould. Above her, the bare branches locked twigs to protect her. An owl hooted greeting.

It was the fox that finished her, the way that it tracked along at five trees' width, watching her, halting and waiting. It was like an ember in the darkness, the vivid burnished pelt, its easy rhythmic gait. Charlie felt her emotional carapace cracking. She was not going to be able to hold it together, nor was she going to be able to tell her sisters what had happened. As she broke out of the cover of the trees, she halted by the lakeshore for a moment to try to gather herself.

It was done. That was a way of thinking about the whole terror of it. It was done. Aron. Done. He had not lost her in the card game, but he had lost her. She saw where Ivan Herald had really played an excellent hand. Oh, the trump card, the bitter Ace of Hearts. There was no gambling debt equal to what had just happened. A gusting sob of grief ripped from her; she folded herself over and tried to take deep breaths. They were all shallow and shrieking, so that she sounded like some odd kind of wading bird at the water's edge. At last it subsided, and she breathed in deep. She looked up. Across the sheen of Pike Lake winked the gold dots of light of Cob Cottage.

44

BLACK CROW

Clearly, Grandma Hettie's whisky had been too strong. Anna, weary, had fallen into a heavy sleep that was thick with dreams. It felt so tiring, that it was not a dream at all. She looked back over her shoulder to see Cob Cottage, aware that her body, the tired, run-ragged part of herself, was flat out in bed.

Yet, here she was, running through the wood. Running? No. Her pace was light and swift the way it always was when she was angry. She had covered a lot of ground, knowing the territory better barefoot.

In the trees she sensed the deer, watching the white light of it, soft as the moon, race along ahead. Except that the white light was Emz, her breath coming fast as she leapt and trotted through the wood. She did not remember Emz having four legs, but it seemed not to matter as they raced on together. Ahead was an ember, scorching a path. An old path. His old path. His old Havoc. The deer's moonlight shadow spread like a pool, and Anna could see where the ember raced to be ahead of it.

She saw him, peppered hair, weathered face. Not unbeautiful. The tweed of his waistcoat made of threads of fire and lichen and ivy. Always he kept a step ahead, but only just. They were after him, and he knew it.

An explosion of black feathers, as if a murder of crows had fallen out of the sky.

"Wake up." The feathers battered and rustled. "Wake up." The crows cawed, and Anna's arm was tugged, yanked at, so that her mind flew back to the sleeping body. Wide awake in an instant, she half tumbled out of bed.

"Charlie?" Feathers, a black gown made of crows? Anna fumbled for the bedside light, almost knocking it off, Charlie gripping her arm.

"Now. We do it now." Charlie was dragging her from the bed. Emz, shell-shocked and pale, was already in the doorway, her jacket pulled on over her PJ's, lanterns at the ready.

Charlie brushed them aside.

"We don't need them." She marched forward, her feathered gown beautiful and confusing.

"Am I asleep?" Anna rubbed vigorously at her face. "What's…?"

"We're going to Cry Wolf." Charlie pushed Anna onto the porch, throwing her jacket after her. Emz was ahead, already stumbling down the steps.

"Which way?" she asked as they continued their frogmarch to the shore. Anna was disorientated, her feet bare. Was this still in the dream? She was heading in the direction of the dream.

"This way." Charlie was striding ahead, Emz also on the trail.

"It's the Other places," Emz said. "That's where he's been hiding." But Charlie did not respond, picking up the pace. Anna noticed that Charlie, too, was barefoot.

"High Foxes. Stride. Hare's Ell," Charlie intoned before her voice lowered to a growl. The sound reverberated beneath them as Charlie, raising her arms like an opera diva, let out a raw howl.

It was feral, clawing at her sisters so that their throats

yelped, and the sounds rose from them to join it, a dissonant harmony that skittered over Pike Lake.

At once the air stilled, the sisters' breath forming glittering clouds. Charlie was drawing in breath, a deep sound pulling through her, hollow as the wind.

At once, Emz saw the smoke rise through the trees.

"There." She was running, Charlie and Anna with her, the howl skirled out once more and, as the sisters ran, each taking up a point of their triangle, Anna was aware, from the very edge of her vision, that they were not alone.

They howled onwards, up into the narrow-cut valley known as High Foxes, a place often visited and patrolled but never halted at. Here the trees were ragged and gnarled and, Anna knew, the most ancient, threading their way through a cleft of rock. Here, there was only one way down, one way out.

Their bare feet were sure as paws. Emz felt it; the ground knew her, she knew it, and boots ought to be a memory. On and on they stalked and alongside, between the trees, the glimmers of other creatures. Anna glanced to one side to see a flank, a pelt of brown and grey and black that was more than a shadow, less than… than what? The word howled from her. *Wolf.*

The sound they made rang itself off the stone of the valley so that the whole of Havoc hummed with it. Never. It had never been like this. Charlie beyond and ahead of all of them, like a raptor in her black feather gown. There was no stopping; the howling took hold of Anna, rushed her into Emz's wake of whipped-back branches, the singed glow of the embers through the trees, the trace element of their prey.

They were gaining on him. Branches snapped and he fell from the trees, scrabbling up the closest trunk, hefting himself onto boughs, as if he thought they were his confederates; but he had lost his way. The trees scratched and scuffed him.

"Bring him down." Charlie's voice was gruff and unlike herself as she pushed forward. The black feather gown seemed to lift her as she clambered into the nearest tree. As she hauled herself up into the branches, the feathers were torn and snatched away, the skirt tearing, but she was unconcerned. Beneath her, Anna and Emz moved under the trees. They could see where the tree limbs moved beneath the Ember man's weight. The smoke plume curled and twisted, darkened to black. Emz knew he would vanish into it, make himself one with the smoke. Charlie's progress towards him was terrifyingly swift, her feet leaping, her arms catching at branches, swinging herself round limbs so that he was pushed, this way, now that, and all the while she howled onwards. The sound carried blood and teeth. Emz raced to keep up, Anna rushing ahead to cut him off, their hearts pounding with a rich decoction of excitement and fear.

Anna was breathless, her lungs tight, her howl a harsh rasp of throat-calling fear, and the wolves she could see in the shadows ran in closer, pulling more darkness. Deeper and deeper the shadows set, Anna witnessing where the trees were being blanked out, closing in on the hunting party.

She could not stop. Her bones rattled over the ground, but her heart pumped her feet forward. Pounding. Pacing.

They were at the edge, the clipped bowl of land always known as the Bear Pit where, in older times, there had been fighting; bears baited, men bare-knuckled and bloodied, dogs scrapping to the death. Now, Emz felt it, felt that much worse had happened here. This was the blood bowl, the sinkhole for revenge and retribution and nothing, but nothing, escaped. Charlie leapt, a wired black bird, clawing at the Ember man so that his breath fell out of him with a dry sound like death. The two tumbled, the branches snapping and cracking. Anna and Emz, open mouthed. Anna turned, her arm reaching out.

"No." The word a skinny breath, snatched by the wind through the trees. She could not move to stop her. They would fall all the way down into the pit. The sisters, shocked, eyes wide and watchful, as they saw Charlie's hands at his neck, her face wild, her teeth bared as if she might kill him. As she lunged forward for the blow there was a cracking sound, and a figure in black stepped out of the shadows, leaned hard against a holly bough. The branch snatched Charlie backwards, the dress snarled in the glossy leaves, the spines pinning her, so that the Ember man dropped alone, landing like a cat, before fleeing in a flurry of smoke and dead leaves.

Charlie cried out. The holly bough bent downwards, and she was dropped to the ground at Bear Pit. She reared upwards, her voice rising into the howl once more, but the sound tore, the wolves, the shadows, the ghosts of all the wolves that had ever been hunted through Havoc Wood halted, and the note rang through them all, a slow, mourning lament.

Anna and Emz slid themselves down the smoothed-out edges of Bear Pit to reach Charlie, unable to approach through the wall of sound that called out of her. The high, pierced whine of it strained against them until, out of breath at last, Charlie gasped an inward breath and broke down.

Emz and Anna folded around her, the tears like a tide salting the earth beneath them. Sobs and shrieks shuddered through her, all the more frightening because Charlie never cried.

Her eyes were glittering, her chest heaving and exhausted, her lungs barely able to draw the air in so that she fell at last, ribs lurching, a broken bird in Anna's arms. Emz, holding her hand, never letting go, the fingers closed so tight around her own that she thought they might break.

It was a long time before the tears dried and the sobs subsided enough to let Charlie breathe properly. She released Emz's hand only long enough to wipe at her face, giving a long, tired sigh and taking in her first, calmed breath.

"We need to get back," Anna said, and began helping Charlie up. With Emz on the other side, the two half-carried their sister back home, to Cob Cottage.

45

A BORROWER, A THIEF

To Borrower, it was delight and desolation in equal measure when the Gamekeepers gave chase.

Delight. In the darkness of it, in the Old Magic breathing once more through the wood, held in the jaws of the wolves; the lost and the hunted, the ghosts of Havoc pursuing him, the three witches part of their pack, the driving force crackling through the trees. Havoc, his home, his hearth. He understood the mistake he had made, the grave he had dug for himself.

He had been one footfall from the clawing, dirt-blackened fingers of their magic as it felt for the scruff of his neck, dragging him down from elm, oak, ash.

Stronger than Hettie Way, and not simply by the power of three, the hard stone of the matter was that Havoc was layered through them. He felt it in the way it reached for him like the fungus and roots of the place.

He had been panting hard, stepping from bough to bough, leaping, slipping, this branch saving him and that one whipping him on. On. On. Their wildness tracked him. He had never been prey. It exhilarated. His blood, slow and still as Frog Pond itself, was in spate, rushing to the dam of his heart. The magic, the rich savour of it, edge to edge with his own, clashed with a spark like sunlight, and he finally he saw it. Where he had lost the prey, that it should have such a consequence.

The Elf Shot. Fashioned by his own hand, glinting with the Forge's light. Hot. Searing. Where had it gone? He had pulled up higher into the oak to chance a look.

They had almost been on him, the wolves howling their betrayal. There. He had seen the flicker and furnace of it around the young one's neck. That was what bound him to them.

On he had sped. Finally, he understood. This was how she had borrowed his moonlight. She had taken his Elf Shot, the thief. His chest rumbled with laughter and choked with despair. He was not making an escape. He would go to earth.

The trees curved away from the bare ground; he had to cross the amphitheatre of Bear Pit to reach the stand of birch trees that would save him. The wolves had gathered in the shadow of the trees and then the Crow Woman in her feathers had taken flight and the Snare was done. Her hands had reached behind the black-edged blade of her Strength, shaving at his neck. He had lunged forward, straining to reach the birch trees, glancing back to witness where the holly snagged at her and she fell.

He ran without stopping until he reached High Foxes, and he lay down in the hollow tree until his heart had ceased its thunderstorm. The girl was a thief. His thought bobbed and dallied like a leaf caught in the low pool at Wild Way. A thief who had dared to steal from him.

His mind roved back to early autumn with the leaves turning, when the woman had come to the cottage and the Gamekeepers had first Cried Wolf. They had hunted their own prey then, a man, clumsy and stupid. Borrower recalled his own chase; the plump deer had escaped, and he had lost the shot, embedded in the beast's flesh. It was of no matter, except that this girl had taken it for her own. It was theft, he was sure, to take the shot from his prey. She had borrowed moonlight, borrowed the deer. The audacity both impressed and infuriated him. How dare she? He would teach the girl a lesson.

He would take back what was his and he would take her for his wife, a suitable bargain in payment for the borrowed moonlight. It was a good match, her magic conjoined with his. He pushed doubts aside. Once she was his, he would have mastery. With a Gamekeeper, no less. With a Way for a wife, he would take the Wood.

They were both of Havoc, who was there to gainsay it? Which is when the shadows lengthened and his memory flickered over that last glimpse of his flight, where the holly bush stood. Beside it, her old coat crackled, night black, and starlit, was the shade of Hettie Way. Warning or watchful? He could not say.

46

A DOOR CLOSES

At some point the Way sisters had fallen asleep. They were tangled together like roots on the wide and weather-beaten sofa. The dark floral upholstery, faded here, worn there, made an odd optical illusion. To an observer, the old blowsy roses and their thorns, twisted about the three sleeping figures, held them safe.

Anna was folded at the corner, her legs knotted into Charlie's. Charlie's arm wrapped around Anna's waist, her head bent into the crook of Anna's neck. On the other side, Emz was curled at Charlie's back, her arms holding her sister's waist, protective. Snoring sounds made them appear to be purring and Anna, blinking awake, sat for a long time watching the dawn pink the sky and feeling the comfort of both the old sofas and her sisters. She could smell Charlie's hair, a soft cloud of the shampoo she always used, the traces of cigar smoke, and of the underbrush of Havoc. Her mind filled with feathers, and she held tighter to Charlie, kissed her hair.

"You're awake then," Charlie said.

"Are you?" Anna ruffled Charlie's hair and the two began to shift position, Emz groggy, but rousing.

"What?" She scrabbled up. "What's the time?"

"Time for breakfast," Anna said, without a glance at the clock.

"Not hungry." Charlie stood up, careful not to look at Emz or Anna. She saw the reflection of the three of them in the round framed window. Three swift steps took her to the hall and three more before the bathroom door shut behind her and the shower began to rain down.

"She alright?" Emz and Anna looked towards the bathroom.

"What do you think?" Anna gave a worried shrug as she moved to the kitchen. "Did you see Grandma Hettie?" Emz took a chance.

"When?" Anna was cagey, pricked at by a memory of the cracking sound of the shadow at the Bear Pit.

"By the holly above the Bear Pit last night. I think she stopped Charlie."

Anna took in a breath.

"Or saved Charlie," she suggested.

"Maybe it's both," Emz said. The sisters were quiet for a moment.

"Either way, I think I'd like to go and pay a visit to Aron," Anna jabbed the spoon into the porridge oats, "and rip off one of his arms to use as a baseball bat to stove in his head." The words were small and calm and powerful.

"What about this Ivan Herald bloke?" Emz said. "What sort of person does that?"

"A rich and powerful one." Anna sounded weary. "Anyway, I don't care about them. I care about Charlie, and we need to focus on her." Her voice dipped to silence as the bathroom door clicked open.

"Bathroom's free," Charlie yelled before her bedroom door banged shut.

"What do we do?" Emz asked.

"We get ready. We go to work," Anna suggested, and for the

first time Emz felt uncertain of everything, of where she might go and what she would do.

Charlie dropped Emz off at Leap Woods.

"Don't look so worried," Charlie said. "I'm fine." Her voice cracked, though her face remained businesslike. Emz made to speak, but Charlie shoved the car into gear. "I will be." Her voice was still giving her some trouble, but Emz ignored the cracks in it and nodded.

At the traffic lights Charlie wiped away her tears, because Aron Thorne did not deserve them.

BANISHING SPELL

Winn was off to the rescheduled meeting with the Wildwood bunch and would not be back before lunchtime. Emz busied herself with cleaning, mopping over the toilets and sorting through the gift shop, aware, at all times, of the wood outside snagging at her mind. It was more powerful a sense than she had ever had, and the mundane tasks served to help her rearrange her thoughts, and mentally prepare for whatever or whoever was out there. There came a moment when she felt she might burst if she didn't brave the wood and so, she understood, it was time to head out.

Emz was aware of the different way she was moving through Leap Wood. Before, she would let go. There was freedom in the trees. Now, she was thinking on two levels — aware of a discarded energy bar wrapper here, but also of the sudden flurry of coal tits over there on the far side of Cooper's Pond that crackled with Havoc magic. They had spurtled upwards into the higher branches and were now fluttering away into denser trees beyond, and so Emz found her footsteps had naturally turned that way. A flock of starlings rolled and curved through the air, shifting from the reed beds near Quarry Tump into the cover of the sycamore and oak beyond.

Something was coming and the wood knew it, made way. Without arranging her thoughts, she focused on the dark charcoal inside her and a couple of breaths made it glow. She held it, ready. The trees seemed to lurch towards her, two boughs springing downwards at her, a storm of leaves enveloping her. It was wild, raw, colour, crackle, scent. Her piece of charcoal slipped from her mental grasp for a blink. A scent of woodsmoke and honey, but also of earth and deep water. The embers of the waistcoat burnt at her, flaring and scorching, and, at once, her charcoal lit up inside and she let the power rise, free. She stood within its force, saw it barrel from her, blurring out the embers in the man's waistcoat so that he was undisguised. Thin, wiry, afraid, he pulled back. She watched the strain in his muscles, his feet digging into the litter of the wood as he struggled to turn from her. She looked at his real face, even as he struggled to turn it from her, to hide, his arm lifting as best it could, a hand stretched out, no more than an inch from his body, as if to push her away. His fingers scratched at the air, at her own neck so that she bent them back.

His face. She had never seen one like it. It held something of a fox in it, a pointed skull, a wide smile of jaw. It was not old in the common sense of wrinkles or grey hair, and yet it was an ancient face. In his eyes, a glow of long-kindled fires banked against a harsh winter. A heart beating an old rhythm, his own skin stretched over the drum of it, enough to make you dance. The wildest wind for breath that blew her, softened against her so that she had let him go. And the moment she did so, he fled.

Emz stood for a moment. She was out of breath, tired as if she'd been running, and an ache moaned through her. Tears pricked at her eyes, and she had to sit for a moment on a nearby stump. Emotion washed over her, but she couldn't recognise it. Not quite fear, almost sadness, a long remembrance. She wiped her eyes, took in deep breaths. As she put her head in her hands, the memory raged forward of a day long ago when she was small, a memory of a man sprawled on his back on the shore of Pike Lake, of her hand on his heart, of Grandma Hettie's hand on her shoulder so that she knew she was safe.

48

A DAY, DISTANT

Borrower had seen his mistake too late. He had already been twined around her, the leaves, which should disguise him, instead being burnt against the bright charcoal of her Strength. He had imagined nothing like this. His own embers flared and scorched against her, but she took his power and threaded it into her own, turned it against him. His only hope, it had seemed, was to take back the Elf Shot and use it against her. His body had lurched and hit the force of her like a wall. He had been an arm's reach away, but, try as he might, his hand had only lifted so far, every muscle straining. He felt where the oldest, darkest piece of himself took over to protect him, to tear himself free of her.

Her gaze had taken away his disguise. She looked at him in a manner that no one had looked at him in a long trail of years. As the daylight heat of her Strength had seared, it revealed the way they were linked, and he saw that the Elf Shot was nothing, a token only.

The day lay distant where he had been spat out by Pike Lake, and the child had revived him, and Hettie Way had let him go.

He saw how she had woven him into the wood, that the gift that Hettie Way had allowed was also part of his punishment.

As that memory had stretched, the young one had let go, and Borrower fled.

He needed the deer. It was no longer simply his lost prey; he saw that it was his lifeline. He would hunt it down. He would eat the deer's heart and, in so doing, steal the magic contained within, the healing she had gifted it.

He laughed uncertainly to himself. Was it not the perfect revenge? To steal her own kind of Elf Shot? He would use the Gamekeeper's own power to protect himself: it would enrich him and help him, after all this time, to flee Havoc Wood.

49

THE RED THREAD

The Ways had been discussing Emz's too-close encounter and were all on edge. They had been knitting together the facts, and the deer, now, seemed key.

"How? It's just a deer." Charlie was defensive. "I don't get it."

"Emz dreamt it. You saw it. I dreamt it." Anna's face crinkled as she recalled the dream. "Last night. Cry Wolf night… I was barefoot, following the deer. It was leading me." She looked at Emz. "It had a white light to it, and I thought it was you."

"The white light or the deer?" Emz wanted to be clear.

"Both. I saw the deer, I saw the light and associated it with you, connected to you," Anna said. "Then there was the ember trail but that was when Charlie woke me."

Charlie stiffened a little. Anna and Emz were leaning in, palms flat on the tabletop. "That settles this. The deer is definitely important." Emz said.

Charlie was arms folded, legs crossed. Suddenly she unfolded and reached to the neckline of Emz's t-shirt, pulled at the length of leather thong looped through a small triangle of metal.

"What's that?" Charlie asked.

"It's a bit of metal that Carrie—" Emz began. Charlie, shook her head, reached forward to tug at her t-shirt.

"Not that. That." There was a red welt at the base of her neck. Anna leaned forward with a worried look.

"What?" Emz reached up. It did feel sore.

"It looks like a burn." Anna touched the red marking, and Charlie stepped up to retrieve the small hand mirror from the dresser drawer. Emz took a look.

"What the…?" The mark sat where the thin leather rested on her skin.

"You allergic?" Charlie picked up the thong. The shard of metal glinted and cast a shadow across the table. It was, she saw at once, no ordinary shadow. It was a complex, tree branch image, an ancient map of Havoc. Charlie took in a breath.

"What is it?" Anna was distracted from Emz's injury.

"The shadow." Charlie watched the shadow move as if shivered through by the wind. She felt her Strength take in the pathways it revealed, the routes and byways. Anna looked at the shadow, saw a small arrowhead shape, daylight searing through like a spotlight.

Emz saw the glint, the white heat of its forging speaking to the charcoal sparking inside her.

"What did you say this is? This is Carrie's?" Anna's fingers reached to touch the shard, but, at the last moment, she thought better. Charlie reached for the leather thong, dandled the Elf Shot in front of her own face, peering.

"What did you see?" Charlie asked her. Anna shook her head.

"Daylight. An arrow." They looked at each other, Charlie's glance daring her. At once, Anna reached for the piece of metal. The moment her fingertip touched it, the Flickerbook rattled and unfolded in front of her. She gasped, let the beauty and the danger ride over her, leaving a scent of woodsmoke and honey.

"It's a piece of shot, shrapnel or something, that Carrie took out of a deer in September. Round about the time Seren arrived," Emz said. Charlie and Anna were rapt, watching the now quiet scrap but feeling the after-effects of Map and Flicker-book like the aftertaste of wine. "Carrie thought it might be a martial arts thing. Hunters shot the deer with it."

"You mean like a flying star? One of those ninja things?"

Emz nodded, felt at her neck, at the thin, sore line the thong had made.

"I kept it because I thought it was beautiful." She looked at it now, uncertain. "I don't get it. I've been wearing this for a while, and it hasn't done this before. Why has it burned me like this today?"

"You said the Ember man, or whoever he is, reached for your neck." Anna was very calm, her mind reeling with images of Casey quietly sobbing, of Judith Killen tearful on the trail of her assailant. "Maybe he was reaching for this."

There was a silence, the shard glimmering and fading with light as if it were alive.

"I think it must've been him who shot the deer, back in September." Emz wanted to grasp one fact. Others began to bustle forward to join it. "It was hurt. I helped Carrie in the infirmary." Emz took the steps, slowly, aware where they were leading. "She took this out and I…" She stopped.

"You used your Strength to heal the deer?" Charlie ventured. Emz nodded, recalled her hand and its heart, steadying the beat, and, as she did so, her memory juddered further backwards. Emz gasped: Grandma Hettie's hand upon her shoulder, reaching down from the past.

She looked at her sisters, "I have seen him before." The memory was vivid. "Long ago. At the edge of Pike Lake." She felt the heart in his chest and the beat it had taken from her hand, greedy, before he had been up and off, away into the trees, and they were glad he had gone.

"Long ago? What, like when we were kids?" Charlie asked.

Emz began the recollection. "I was small. Four maybe. He

was on the lakeshore. Flat on his back. He'd come out of Pike Lake."

There was a breath and then the sisters picked up the old thread.

"It was pouring that day," Anna said.

"And she made us go out anyway," Charlie nodded. "Absolutely hissing down."

"He was unconscious. Grandma Hettie knew what she was doing. What I could do for him."

"Yes. And then he ran off into the trees." Anna recalled him, racing away.

Charlie nodded. Her mind folded out the Map of the path he'd taken that distant day.

"She asked me where he'd gone. To the East."

"Frog Pond," Emz said.

"You're connected. In some way," Anna offered.

"In some way?" Charlie scoffed. "She made the man's heart beat. No wonder he couldn't steal his Elf Shot back."

Charlie was folding her arms once more as the thoughts crowded and clicked.

"His what?" Anna's palm was flat on the surface of the table, as if touching wood would earth her, keep her safe from this conversation.

"Elf Shot." Charlie was zipping up her sweatshirt. "That's what it is. Shot by an… well, anyway. You know what I mean." She looked across at her sisters and their wide-open, disbelieving faces. "Oh, come on," she chided them. "It's definitely come straight out of Havoc." She gave a savage nod to the artefact.

"And so has he," Anna said.

"Because I kept this?" Emz felt a dead weight of responsibility, her heart falling through her chest, a vision of Logan Boyle wronged and outcast, lit by the shimmering silver of the Elf Shot.

"No idea." Charlie was pragmatic. "Let's be honest, you've had this... how long?"

"Since September. Since Seren came. That same week."

Charlie pulled a face.

"So, no immediate effect."

There was an audible sigh from the three witches.

"We've got the bits here, we're just not seeing them." Anna's voice drifted with her thoughts. The deer healed, the Ember man healed. Elf Shot. "It feels wrong. I don't think it's as simple as just the Elf Shot." But she couldn't put the pieces into the right places.

"Why not? He clearly wants it back," Charlie argued. "Maybe it's like she's nicked his door key or something."

"I think she's right. We can all see the power in it," Emz said. They looked at the fragment. Anna was tense.

"No, not his power." She shook her head.

"What then?" Charlie asked, grumpy.

"Your power." Anna looked at Emz.

"Mine?" Emz looked scared.

"You healed him all those years ago, and then you healed the deer which had been shot by him. I think that's a bigger connection, stronger, than this... this is just incidental, a side issue."

"You think that's how he's got out of Havoc all of a sudden? He's using something from me?"

Charlie gave a groan, rested her head on the table. "Bollocks." Charlie shoved her hands into the pockets of her sweatshirt.

"We've messed up everything." Emz felt light as an autumn leaf, as if every bit of her had worked loose.

"Again." Charlie spat the word.

"No." Anna was shaking her head. Charlie took in an angry breath, but Anna held up her hand. "No. This is Havoc Wood. This is the job. We put Mrs Fyfe right. We put Ailith on the right track. We Bone Rested a warrior. We helped Seren."

Charlie and Emz looked at her.

"There is no way that Grandma Hettie would have let you heal this man's heart at the lake that day, without good cause," Anna reasoned. "No. Way."

"She's right." Charlie nodded "She knew her stuff. If you weren't supposed to heal him, she would not have let it happen."

"Whereas she actively dragged us out into the rain that day," Anna said. "She knew what was happening... or what had to happen." Anna looked at Emz.

"Exactly," Charlie said. "If he was meant to be dead, we'd have stayed home, and the crows would have eaten him. If you think about it, it's Gamekeeping 101."

They let this logic sink in. Emz felt better, more grounded.

"He's out of Havoc, but he belongs here. In a way that Mrs Fyfe didn't." A thought occurred. "So last night, with the feather dress and the holly tree..."

Charlie did not wait for Emz to finish her thought.

"Grandma was there. That's why she stopped me killing him."

Anna gave a gasp of surprise.

"Trust me." Charlie gave a sigh.

"But in stepping into Woodcastle, he's crossed a line." Her voice grew stronger. "So we have to Gamekeep."

There ought to have been a moment of breakthrough, a sense of triumph. Instead there was an awkward silence.

"Any suggestions?" Charlie asked.

BORROWED MOONLIGHT

There was a clearing, just East of ThinThrough at its border with Unseelie Maids. Here, Havoc was gnarled and raggedy, and the deer that roamed it gathered to spend their nights. In winter, Borrower could sit in the Old Elm tree and see where their breathing made a cloud above those wild and wayward trees.

This clearing was his first choice to begin the hunt. The deer must be with the herd. It needed its fellows for warmth. If he took the deer, if he stole its heart, then what might he not borrow? The thought stopped, crackled at the edges with fear of Emily Way's Strength. He stopped his mind, let the wood into his head, let the wind guide his feet along Whitethorn to the pinch of rocks at Hare's Ell, on through the scar of crumbling chalk, the way cloaked with shelves of wort and moss, the thinnest and thorniest of trees here.

For just a breath, he thought of hiding here, tucking himself into this thorn and holding his breath for a hundred years; but, in a step or two, he had scented the deer, and he could not resist.

. . .

THE WAY SISTERS had a bony skeleton of a plan. As they moved down to Pike Lake, the Great Grey stopped snacking at the grass to give a deep, rumbling nicker.

At the sound, Charlie Way looked for her fear and found, in its stead, a powerful whirling sensation in her chest, as if her breath was being made into a storm. She glanced at Emz, saw the Strength sparking from her, starlit and glittering, black velvet; she had seen this before when they were up at Day's Ride. She looked towards Anna, gilded, shimmering, and, this time, instead of doubting herself, she wondered what they saw when they looked at her.

"Remember, we don't Reach. He'll see that coming, like before," Anna warned. Charlie stepped forward, one foot in Emz's path, one in Anna's wake. At once, her own Strength surged, and, as she looked up, Havoc lit up with every pathway, footfall, and hoofprint. She breathed in the rich scent of the dark edge of Havoc, watched for where it winked with a lantern of embers.

"Unseelie Maids," Charlie said, and looked at Emz. "You ready?" Emz did not look ready. She was fussing with her boot-laces and watching the tree line.

"No, wait…" Emz untied her laces as the deer stepped out of the trees. She slipped off her boots, balled up her socks, and threw them down.

"Emz?" Anna was anxious.

"Now I'm ready." Emz ran forward, her bare footsteps matching those of the deer. Charlie and Anna fell in behind.

Boughs bent, limbs sprang. Havoc Wood had never seemed so alive. The shimmer of the last leaves, the shadows and light all drawing down to Emz as she leapt, surefooted, deeper and deeper into Havoc's heart. They were turning away from the well-trodden ways, and the air was different. Charlie, with her heightened sense of smell, could sense it at once, and Anna, pacing up behind, was inhaling the woodsmoke and honey that drifted towards them, stronger and stronger.

Ahead, they could see the tawny red-brown of the deer, the white flash of tail as it yawed and bobbed on its journey. There was no sense of panic to the creature. It paused in places, nose twitching, eyes wide and taking in the Way sisters, until, Charlie saw, Emz urged it on with a heavier breath, with a hand flicked this way or that.

At Unseelie Maids, the trees were slender and magisterially tall. The deer slipped between the trunks with Emz close behind. Charlie thought of their task, her heart sledgehammer-hard in her chest so she thought her ribs would crack. It took effort to focus, but, as she did so, the wood lit up once more, and she picked up the trail of the Ember man: there was no disguising it. She saw where he would go, that Emz and the deer were, as planned, drawing him down.

"This way." She took Anna's hand. "It's quickest."

At Frog Pond, Anna tugged their stave out of the ground. It released with a shimmer that darted across the water and crackled against the shelter of the black rock beyond. When the River Rade was in spate, there was a waterfall. Tonight it was jewelled with green splashes of navelwort and harts tongue fern. In the near distance, Charlie and Anna could hear the trees bend and swag as Emz and the deer brought their quarry. They were springing a trap, and it had to work. With a jolt of fear, Charlie thought of the moment in the castle at Halloween, when Anna had taken the step forward, had bitten into Mrs Fyfe's last poisoned apple. She glanced over to her sister. Anna looked certain of herself, holding the stave like a weapon, waiting. Charlie took a deep, calming breath.

It happened in moments, the deer darting suddenly above them. In pursuit, the Ember man could not stop. With an angry cry, he tumbled through the air. A gasp of breath, a flurry of embers from his waistcoat as he plunged, feet first, into the water. There was a hissing sound, and all was still. Anna and Charlie watched as the deer pattered down the path towards them, and Emz appeared on the rock above.

"Where?" Anna asked. Emz scouted the water.

"There." She pointed. Anna saw the water flicker and bubble as Emz headed down to join them. Charlie was already picking her way over the rocks and stones to the flat stepping-stone. Here the water was deepest, but, in one decisive movement, Charlie reached down into the water and dredged him out. He struggled, but her own Strength tamped down the embers with small bursts of soot as she lifted him like a fish onto the stone before her.

He lay, wet and winded, and, as he gasped for breath, Anna saw Grandma Hettie's ghost looking down from the edge of the rock above, giving a nod.

Anna joined Charlie on the rock. Reaching down, she grasped the Ember man's hand. She felt where he resisted and pushed back hard. She felt him give in as she opened the Flickerbook.

The images dazzled and astonished. Colour. Wildness. Dark-hearted, wild-headed magic rattled down the centuries at her, beautiful and daring and glittering with danger; but she saw the fear and the flight, too. The grey sky of loneliness lowered over him, and she held tighter, sharing the grief. The small and familiar fingerprints that marked his heart. The Ember man gave a weak gasp.

"Borrower," Anna said, the name written in the margins of the Flickerbook, the skills he'd stolen, the pieces of broken hearts. He took in a deep breath and let her Strength take him over. It was irresistible to her, to ride the landscape contained within him on borrowed horses. Havoc as she had never seen or felt it. She drank it in and then, gently, let him go.

He stood, triangulated between them. Charlie could see him lit by staves that stretched around Havoc, the bounds beyond which he must not pass and where they were broken. She saw her grandmother's shade walking these Bounds.

"The Gamekeeper bound you and you broke those Bounds," she said.

Borrower snarled, a sound so animal it made the Ways feel like mice beneath an owl's gaze. Charlie stood up, put a foot on his chest to hold him. The Bounds were clear in her head. Borrower howled and shifted beneath her foot.

"I bind you as before." Her foot pressed just hard enough, and the words whispered into her head like an old, half-remembered story. "Go on your way, the one marked."

"Not until you give me back what's mine," he turned to glare at Emz, "thief."

Emz reached the Elf Shot from around her neck, dangled it before him.

"This is the tithe we may take." The words came to her mind like birds roosting. Borrower was shaking, his eyes intense with fury.

"No. Liar. You borrowed moonlight," he demanded. A look flickered between the sisters, and Borrower began to laugh, a low unpleasant sound. With a rough shove, Charlie ditched him back into the water, her fingers knotting themselves tighter into his hair.

"Borrowed moonlight? What's he talking about?"

"Not a clue." Anna was pale and tense. "Emz?"

Emz was silent, her thoughts focused.

"Emz?" Charlie urged. "What is he talk...?"

Emz raised her left hand. Inside it, an orb of soft white light glowed. Anna gasped. Charlie's mind spooled backwards to a search for Seren Lake, for the light she had taken as phone light or flashlight.

"After the deer. With Seren," Emz explained. "I didn't know

what it was. Why it happened." She let the light play in her hand for a moment. "I thought it was something to do with my Strength. But it felt wrong."

"Does it do anything?" Anna asked. "I mean other than look pretty."

Emz rolled the light around. It was soft and appealing and lit their surroundings with a clear brightness. She used her Strength to look into the heart of it, to feel around it.

"No. It's just light. Useful." She thought about it. " But not powerful. Not like a weapon. More like a tool."

"We're on a learning curve," Charlie reassured her. "You weren't to know."

"What now?" Anna asked. "Is it a debt? Do we have to repay it?"

Emz was calm, staring deep into the soft light. Her fingers curled and explored the light, and she gave a short laugh as it revealed its secrets.

"No. It's part of our connection. That's why I could borrow it from him." Emz looked down into the water at him. "It's ours to share."

Charlie shook her head.

"He's been attacking women in Woodcastle. Emz borrowed a bit of moonlight. We're repaying nothing."

"And he broke his Bounds," Anna nodded. "But, still, what do we do next?"

There was a moment of deep silence.

"Pull him up," Emz said, decisive.

"You sure?" Anna asked. Emz nodded. Charlie wrenched Borrower back onto the stone; his unsettling laugh burbled out with the water he had swallowed.

"I borrowed moonlight for Gamekeeping. For a search and rescue." Emz kept her voice steady, focused on the moonlight.

"It's mine. Return it." Borrower was braver, twisting away from Charlie's grip, straightening his waistcoat. The embers flared and banked. In Emz's hand, the moonlight no longer felt odd or wrong. Her Strength glowed within to match its cool silver, and it revealed the secret.

"It's not yours," Emz said. "You borrow it too." She did not look at him. Charlie and Anna saw the remark hit home, how he pulled away from the truth of it.

"There is an ancient bargain, made between my father and your great-great-grandam. You would be wise not to…"

"Careful, faerie man. I might take back what is mine." She held out the other hand and made a loose fist. As she did so, his breath stalled. Emz released her fingers at once. Borrower's face was chalk white, a shaking hand reached to his heart. The wood darkened, and a cold, whispering breeze breathed through the trees. Charlie's stomach lurched. She saw Anna take an uncertain step back as Emz leaned into Borrower's odd, foxish face.

"The power in the deer's heart is not yours to take." Emz's voice was so unfamiliar it made Charlie afraid. "Honour the bonds and bargains. Be Bound, Borrower, or I will take back what you *owe* me."

Their eyes locked for a flashing moment before Borrower bowed his head in assent. The cold breeze blew out, the shadows shifted back.

"You cannot take women from Woodcastle," Charlie decreed. As she said it, she felt the air twist. Borrower turned, gave her a single, sorry nod. "If you want a wife, find her in Havoc." At once Charlie regretted the words, the way the air twisted a little tighter for a second, and she was disturbed by the quick and greedy glance he cast at Emz; but Emz herself was unfazed.

"Flee." Emz breathed the word at him. Charlie felt that twist in the air once more, like a struggle for breath, and with a crack of twigs, Borrower was gone.

. . .

ANNA, Charlie, and Emz looped back to Cob Cottage via the bounds their grandmother had set for Borrower, their thoughts weaving the repairs, picking up the magic Hettie had put down.

"You were scary," Anna said. Emz laughed.

"I was scared," she replied.

"But we did it," Charlie sighed. "We managed it." There was a lightness to their mood. "Now we've just got to sort out the Horse." There was a new energy in their footsteps.

"Interesting that he couldn't borrow the Great Grey, and we know he tried," Anna mused.

"Yeh, it's a bit like a cat trying to catch a badger. Give it a go, but ultimately…" Charlie said. She could feel where their mutual fear of the Wood dissipated like smoke. Anna smiled.

"I've had a mad thought." There was a hint of laughter in her voice.

"Well, the bar isn't set very high on that one," Charlie teased.

"Spill," Emz encouraged.

"Remember when it thundered? Grandma Hettie always said it was the Night Horses galloping to Havoc." There was laughter from Charlie and Emz at the recollection.

"I haven't thought about that in forever," Emz said. "You think the Great Grey is a Night Horse?"

Anna shrugged.

"Who knows?"

"Anything is possible. We live in Havoc Wood," Charlie said.

"It's still waiting." Anna grew a little more serious.

"*Is* it waiting for Dad?" Emz asked, and this thought sobered them. Charlie shook her head, a sour look on her face.

"Don't get your hopes up." And she picked up her pace, pulled ahead on the path, and did not look back. They returned to Cob Cottage in silence.

AFTERSHOCKS

E mz had accepted the lift from Charlie simply to spend time with her. After their recent adventures, she'd thought Charlie might need company, but, on the journey, Charlie was silent, dropping her at the school gates with a simple "see you" of farewell. Emz had seen how Charlie was after Aron's betrayal and seen her reaction to Borrower. It made her uneasy that there was nothing more heart-searching to be said.

She had been focused on Charlie and forgotten about Logan Boyle. She glimpsed him now, heading around the side of the school towards the yard and the entrance to the sixth form block.

His drinks can was dropping out of the vending machine as she passed. There was no one else around and, as he had already glanced her way, Emz braced herself for his speaking to her. She did not brace herself for him blanking her.

He moved quickly past her, down the stairs, leaving his can in the bottom of the machine. Emz looked at it, looked at the stairs, and her unease quadrupled. By the time she reached her

Maths lesson, only to watch Logan leave as she entered, it had increased to the power ten.

She watched him leave the common room when she entered, dodging by her as if she did not exist. She watched him make a detour away from the Science corridor as she strolled up towards her Environmental Sciences lesson. She watched through the lab window as he walked the long way round to Physics.

He spoke with others, so she understood it was not a universal situation. She witnessed a brief smile here. A laugh there. Nothing approaching his normal interaction with fellow students, but it was obvious that everyone was rewriting and erasing the lies and rumours of recent history.

She understood that she, too, was being rewritten and erased. It was like being stabbed in the heart with a pencil; a thin, pointed object being pressed hard into her chest, until she could not breathe.

When she could not breathe, there was only one place to go. So she went there.

THE LAND ROVER was parked up, but there was no sign of Winn. Emz busied herself with as many trivial tasks as possible in order to block thoughts of Logan. She headed outside to refill the bird feeders and let her mind drift.

It ran, on small hooves through the trees, and she looked up. What was that about? She brought her mind back to the business of the bird feeders, but it twitched at the edges. She let it go once more, following the deer in her mind until she saw that it was running to the narrow cut in the rock at Hare's Ell. She tugged at it, made it turn back, and, as she did so, was aware of an ember path, fading to cinders.

She pulled the deer towards Leap Woods.

All that had happened, the great torrent of events since

Grandma Hettie's death, washed over Emz, and she shuddered a little.

The woods were bare and beautiful. Emz looked up to the bronze and lemon tones of the left leaves, the sky winter-grey above. Her breath clouded into the air. She was on the edge of something; she felt it keenly. She wasn't sure if she was afraid. Would she fall?

As she thought it, the jackdaws rose in a great chattering flurry around her.

Fly.

WINN WAS ON THE PHONE, signalling like mad for Emz to hurry back along the path. As she entered the education centre, she could hear that it was Mrs Dalrymple on the mobile and there was a problem.

Mrs Dalrymple was old school, a map reader and nature lover, and so the coordinates for their location were very precise. As Emz and Winn jumped into the Land Rover, Carrie was already on her way from the other direction at Willowhip, where she'd been on a call out at White Houses farm.

The wound was vicious, the leg bone exposed, the tawny fur spattered crimson. As the women gathered around, Emz felt the charcoal begin to heat within her. Charlie, she knew, would be able to pick up the tracks of both the fox and whoever had laid this snare. Anna could, most likely, reach into the fox and flick through the book of its memory, which might not be useful in snaring the poacher, but she could perhaps read something in the snares' wires. The fingerprints left there could give up their owner. Emz reached in with cutters to snip the wire free as Carrie cleaned and stitched. The fox, wild with fear and pain, settled at a touch from Emz, and as her fingers brushed at the fur, she thought of the fingerprints she was leaving on the fox, if she might dream as it dreamt, run where it ran. She let the thoughts of the running deer and Havoc Wood smother the fox's pain and sense of danger. It barked, growled low, allowed Emz and only Emz to pick it up, patched, and put it into the dog bed in the back of Winn's Land Rover.

Mrs Dalrymple was livid about the incident and speculated on the identity of the culprit.

"We'll find him," Emz stated the fact. Mrs Dalrymple looked taken aback.

"You'll liaise with the Wildlife Officer in Castlebury?" she asked. "I've already spoken to him about the threat to the badgers at Willowhip, and he's not interested."

"She's a Gamekeeper," Carrie said, as Emz and Winn prepared to head off. "In Havoc Wood."

There was just a glimmer from Isobel Dalrymple. She nodded.

"Knew your grandmother. Lovely woman." Isobel and her rambling companions headed off. Carrie rummaged in her bag and handed over a phial of antibiotics.

"I've got more back at HQ," she said. "I can drop them in later on my way home."

It was an hour later, the fox settled and sleeping in the infirmary, and Emz was standing at the back door looking out into the encroaching evening. Carrie was strolling up the path, hands deep in pockets, a tired trudge to her step.

"Hey, how's our patient?" She stepped inside, put the medication on the worktop.

"Settled in," Emz said. "What do we owe you?"

"Nothing. On the house. The batch is almost out of date. I'd have to toss them from the surgery, so consider it a charitable donation," Carrie said. "I don't think the date stamps will bother the fox." She gave a vast sigh.

"Thank you, Carrie." Winn came in from shutting up the education centre. "It is very much appreciated."

"Good. Good. Right." Carrie was definitely out of sorts. Emz peeked at her real face, saw distress and anxiety.

"What's going on with you?" Emz asked as Winn put the kettle on and Carrie made no move to leave.

"Oh, the usual." Carrie shrugged deeper into her waterproof.

"How's your equine project shaping up?" Winn asked. "I hear you ruffled Marlow Whitburn's feathers…"

"Oh, don't talk about Marlow. Anyway, that's the least of my worries. We've been told the surgery building has been sold, and we've got to find new premises." Emz felt the hairs on the back of her neck prickle, and Winn took in a small breath. "I don't know, one minute you feel you've got all your ducks in a row, next thing, someone's shooting at them."

Winn offered the last piece of fruitcake. Carrie took it.

"I'm having a pizza and a glass of wine when I get home." She munched at the cake. Emz's gaze met Winn's.

"Erm." Winn was flustered. "Erm, Carrie… I… erm…"

Carrie looked up.

"Lush cake, Winn."

"Yes. Thank you. Care to come and take a look round Hartfield tomorrow?" she blurted out. Carrie stopped munching for a second. She swallowed hard.

"Sorry?"

"Would you care to look round Hartfield tomorrow," Winn asked. "There is a range of outbuildings, land attached. If you…"

Carrie's eyes had widened, and for a second Emz thought she might be choking on a sultana. Her mind was ticking.

"Seriously?"

Winn nodded. Seriously.

"I've had a set to with the Wildwood Society, so I've lost some funding."

"Oh my God, oh my God, why didn't I think of it before?"

"Well, you know, have a look around first and see what you…"

"Oh! You do weddings. We could do the carriages." Carrie was already making plans. "With my sister. Oh, yes. Yes. Why don't we go now?" Carrie put down the last of the cake and hugged Winn. "Oh, thank you. Thanks so much, Winn."

As they headed off towards Hartfield, Emz, feeling the wire of the snare curled into her pocket, headed home.

IN THE GATHERING TWILIGHT, Anna turned the snare wire in her hand.

"Pockets. Dirty pockets," she said, and passed the coil of wire to Charlie.

"Weed. Rollups. Extra strong mints," Charlie contributed. They were poised, at the edge of Havoc and Leap Woods. Emz nodded, and they Reached.

It was a breath or two more before the trail, greasy and rubbery, lit up. Emz Reaching for it first, taking the thoughts of pain from the fox and placing them into the landscape like a beacon.

"This way." Charlie was striding forward. Owls watched. Badgers in their setts listened to them pass overhead.

The Gamekeepers were after someone.

PIN WINSTANLEY WAS ABOUT to drink his pint. He was rolling up a little spliff for later. He usually stopped off at the Towler Inn at Castle Hill, most often when he'd been out in Leap Woods setting his traps. It was usually quiet, with no TV on, and tonight the only music was that mandolin and fiddle couple from Knightstone who were quite good. He'd have a quick pint and then back to his boat, moored up on the Wisheart Navigation.

Three women entered, bringing the chill of the late November night with them. They looked stuck up, so he was surprised that, after a glance around the place, they came to sit at his table.

Well, stand at his table, glaring at him.

"Did you shove that table at him?" Anna asked Charlie as they cut down to Cob Cottage from the edge of Castle Hill. The stars were out, and the air was fresh and bright tasting.

"Yep." Charlie hiked onwards, leading.

"How though?" Emz asked. It had been impressive the way the round top pinned him back into the seating. It had been discreet, too, only Pin Winstanley and the sisters witnessing the trick.

"Not sure. Works with wood. Got to be wood I think." Charlie's face tensed a little at a memory of doors and frames and a poker table.

Anna gave a chuckle; small, but perfectly formed.

EMERGENCY LIGHTING

The skip lorry pulled out of Half-Built House loaded with the remnants of Vanessa Way's possessions. Some people considered a good clear-out to be cathartic; not Vanessa. That night she sat on the reclining couch in front of the window and watched the shadows and light dance across the floor. The intricate filigree drew her gaze no matter how she fought. She was pinned into the lounger, unable to take a step off, lifting her feet up under her body and remaining watchful.

The house felt cold in its bones. The ice, Vanessa noted, crystallised on the inside. She reached up to the patterns, and, as she did, she saw the map, the paths of it spiralling towards her, carrying threat.

Beneath her the floor altered, blown by a cold wind.

ELEANOR LOOKED tired in spite of the mug of coffee she'd drunk.

"Did you even go home last night?" she asked, frowning at Vanessa. Vanessa nodded.

"Yes. Promise." She could see the strain, the toll being taken on her young colleague. "I had domestic stuff to do. A skip lorry, no less."

Eleanor managed a smile at this.

"Good." They were going over the data and calibrations from the previous session. Vanessa noticed that Eleanor kept to strictly numerical files, nothing graphic that might show up the pinnacled landscape of Far North.

"So, MRI." Eleanor tapped at her keyboard.

"Today?" Vanessa raised her eyebrows. "I thought that it was rammed solid for the next three weeks."

Eleanor's face pinched a little more.

"It was. Dr Littleborough had one of her subjects pull out, last minute."

Vanessa nodded.

"Good. Good."

"Yes," Eleanor sighed.

"WE GOOD?" Keith's voice over the tannoy as the machinery began to click and whirr, and Vanessa was moved into the cylindrical chamber. She had noted, as Eleanor wired and blocked her, that the machine was white as snow.

The sound she heard ought to have been the clinical metallic battering that she had heard in previous experiments. It had always reminded her of hammering, as if the Gods were tempering the steel of humanity. Today, the hammering slipped quickly into the beat of a drum. Drums. As she moved through the white plastic, it chilled and morphed and was ice.

She was falling through the canopy of a tree and she reached to stop herself, but she could not, and the ice gave her up with sound like blades. Vanessa slid through the trees, the lace pattern of light marking her skin, felt the inked runes at her neck darken.

She landed heavily at the edge of the lake, her body skidding over the surface with the momentum of her fall. Across the white expanse, she saw the dark shape separate from the horizon. She picked herself up, began running across the white ice to greet the black wolf.

THE ALARMS SOUNDED out on deaf ears. In the initial incident. Explosion, electromagnetic pulse, it was not certain; the skeleton staff assigned to Dr Vanessa Way's laboratory were knocked unconscious. The lab, sited in the Dark Lab wilderness of the De Quincey Langport campus was off the main grid, and no one had thought to check the protocols in place for this sort of meltdown. In the cafeteria, half a mile away, people busied themselves choosing soup and snacks, grumbled at the lack of choice of carbonated drinks.

In Vanessa Way's laboratory, the inhabitants were as still and silent as Sleeping Beauty and her servants in the castle.

Thorns might have grown up around the low, skinny, black-clad building, but for the emergency lighting, which suddenly flickered on, unsure of itself.

The light glittered over ice crystals creaking across the surfaces of the laboratory. Plastic and glass pinched and patterned until, with a gasp, Eleanor woke. As her eyes opened, as she took in breath after clouded breath, the ice melted and vanished, leaving no trace, save the cold, dead drives of the desktop computers.

THE BLACK BLANK

THERE IS NO TIME

The morning mood in Cob Cottage was as bright as the golden November light that filtered in through the windows. The Ways were busy with breakfast, the rustle and chink of cereal and spoon.

"What are you up to this morning?" Anna asked Charlie as Emz joined them at the table. Charlie looked at her sister with a wry smile.

"You can ask me, you know," she said, her voice light and easy. Anna looked caught out.

"Didn't want to risk it." Anna toyed with her muesli. "I feel so hyped up after catching that Poacher. Then I thought of you and…"

"Aron?" Charlie said the name with no emotion.

"You okay?" Emz looked worried. Charlie nodded.

"Yes." She ate a spoonful of cornflakes. "And no, obviously. An odd mix," she considered.

"Angry," Anna offered. Charlie pointed her spoon in agreement.

"Tick."

"Sad," Emz offered, and Charlie nodded, a shadow passing across her face.

"Big tick." Her voice faltered. She scoffed more cereal, and Anna poured coffee to fill the silence.

"I'll get over him." Charlie was sure. "I know it. Time will do that." She looked at Anna who nodded. "But knowing that doesn't wipe out the—" She couldn't go on. Under the table, Emz stretched out a booted foot to rest on Charlie's boot. Charlie gave a thankful smile.

"I'm glad it happened the way it did," she confessed, her spoon now stirring at the softening cereal.

"Glad?" Anna asked.

"Brutal," Charlie said. "Final." She took in a deep breath. "So there's no going back."

"You heard from him at all since?" Emz asked.

Charlie shook her head, and they ate in silence for a few minutes.

"So. Hyped up on Poacher, eh?" Charlie swerved their discussion sideways.

"Aren't you?" Emz asked. Charlie shook her head.

"No. I'm still wondering about the Horse."

They looked out of the window. Charlie had put out a string of hay earlier, donated by Carrie. The Great Grey was disinterested in the offered feast, head raised as if listening, looking out across Pike Lake.

"Now that the Borrower situation is solved, we can focus," Charlie said.

"Find the Rider," Emz finished the plan. Anna felt an odd shiver, recalled the Flickerbook of images she'd seen from the Horse, mixed with something else, something nearby, a reminder in her head. What was that?

She was restless, cleared away her dishes, the sound of cutlery and crockery jarring instead of comforting. Charlie and Emz followed suit.

"What time do you finish?" Charlie asked.

"Not late," Anna said. "We're closed this evening. Private function and caterers."

Charlie nodded.

"Emz, need a lift again? I'm going your way." And Emz agreed, yes, because it was understood that her sister needed the company.

Anna watched them drive away. As she did, she focused on the nagging feeling, like a whispering inside herself, like someone trying to catch her attention. It was odd, but also not unfamiliar, and so she trusted it.

She looked out at the Great Grey. He was still watchful, intent, showing no sign of being interested in either the hay or the residents of Cob Cottage.

She pulled on her jacket. As she did so, the whispering intensified. It was a second's thought before she unzipped the inside pocket and took out the Paper Prophets.

They felt warm in her hand and the whispering stopped. She slid off the elastic band, and the cards felt jumpy, as if, should she loosen her grip, they would fly from her hands. She turned to the table and, after a single shuffle, put three cards face down.

The first was the Black Blank. The paper framing the dense emptiness, except that, somewhere in her head, Anna felt starlight. It was so intense a sensation she had to look up, check the roof was still on, that it was still daylight.

She turned the next card. No. That couldn't be right. The Black Blank? With urgency she turned the third. The Black Blank. Not right. The room grew colder. Had Charlie and Emz left the door open?

Anna felt the tug of the other cards in her hand. She turned the next. And the next. Slapping them down in any order on the table. Each one. The Black Blank. Fear cast its cold shadow. Ha. It did not matter how many times they chastised Borrower, how many Poachers they caught, how many Warriors they Bone

Rested, or Mrs Fyfes they thwarted, there was always, always, more.

Fear. She knew where she was with fear. Her heart raced as she picked up the cards and shuffled them once again. She recalled the riffle shuffle Mrs Massey had done and thought that might take practice. Holding her breath, she dealt the cards onto the table, face up, in two rows: one of seven, one of six.

They were all Black Blanks, but, in a breath, they began to alter. The sense of starlight filled Anna, and, as she watched, it filled the blackness of the top row of seven cards. A night sky, starlit and no longer black; rather, it shimmered with ghostly green light.

The bottom row of the black cards turned white, a wide expanse of ice that she recognised as a lake. She looked to the right, to the furthest edge of the ice, to where a black wolf walked towards her.

The cards flickered and fluttered, the old images. Hearth and Heart, Maps and Trees rewrote themselves. The starlight faded, and the whispering stopped.

Anna, hand shaking, gathered the cards, pulled the elastic around them, and zipped them back into her pocket.

She stepped out onto the porch and breathed in deep, still shaking. As she stepped down to the shore, the horse turned, watched her progress, and, when he saw her hand reach out, he moved into her, his shoulder against hers, his breath on her neck as the Flickerbook opened.

A white ice lake, a black wolf. A heart pumping. This seemed so familiar. Not just here. Not just in the cards. In her dreams, all her life, her dreams of her father, a lone black wolf walking across a frozen lake. What did it mean? With another breath, the horse halted the Flickerbook.

"What is it?" she asked. "What is it?"

The horse gave only a low nicker in reply.

. . .

ANNA THREW herself into her shift at the Castle Inn in an effort to push the images of the cards and the Horse's flickered message into the edges of her mind.

"I need lunch for four in the Knight's Hall," Lella commanded. She was overdressed, heavily made-up, her hair scraped and gelled into a tight chignon that gave her face a gaunt and pinched look.

"For four?" Anna confirmed.

"Yes. I've got a guest coming at 1:30, and if Casey can serve champagne cocktails at about 3:45." Lella was looking at her watch. She was carrying a leather document wallet and a gold pen in a gift box. She swung out through the doors without another word.

"Dodgy." Casey frowned at the space Lella had occupied.

"Dodgy? How?" Anna felt prickled at.

"She's up to something." Casey cleared down the countertop.

"Like what?" Anna's mind reeled, skidded over an ice-white lake.

"Like selling this place."

LUNCH CAME AND WENT, Anna plating up the special Lella lunch and coping with a tourist party from Castlebury. Their bright purple minibus pulled in at 1:30, and the tour operator wondered if they were too late for lunch.

The dining room buzzed. Anna chopped herbs and poached salmon, and wine scented the kitchen, and all of this everyday stuff kept the black wolf at bay.

"I said it was off." Casey was wired as she slammed into the kitchen. "We've got to join them. Bring champagne for the big announcement."

Casey was fetching glasses. Anna took the champagne from the chiller and followed her into the Knight's Hall.

It was called "hall", but it was long and thin and low beamed. The titular Knight had been found buried under the hearthstone in the seventeenth century. Today, it was bare of all tables, save the one Casey had set. The tablecloth was crisp white damask, so white in the late afternoon light that it caught Anna's breath.

Lella, pink with wine, was overly bright as she introduced: "Ivan Herald, the new owner of the Castle Inn."

Casey and Anna were united in silence as the two other guests, accountant and lawyer, gave a brief round of applause.

Lella smiled so far Anna feared her face would split in two.

"I'd like to assure you both that, other than the change of ownership, everything about the Inn will remain the same." Ivan made his statement and smiled, in particular, it seemed, at Anna. There was a silence.

"Aren't you going to say anything?" Lella looked wild eyed, her lipstick smudged by food and wine. There was a sound like a sail cracking in a high wind as Anna peeled off her pinny.

"I quit." And she was out of the door before she had time to breathe in.

AT DRAWBRIDGE BREWERY, Charlie Way had immersed herself in perfecting a new brew. It was deep ruby red, so that poured into a glass it would look like jewelled blood. She'd begun the wort yesterday and now poured some off, scenting for what might be missing. Nothing. It held all the flavours she required of it, the barley roasted, the hops a special batch from the far side of Castlebury at Tucker's Stretch Organics. There were other things in there, bits and branches she'd snipped from the garden at Cob Cottage last night, too wired from witchcraft to sleep. It had been boiling and brewing all day.

Ryan entered the workshop.

"Mike says he's off to Keelham, and he won't be back till late so will you lock up?" It was a game of "Mike says" in the last few days, she noticed.

"Yeh. Not a problem." She poured Ryan a glass from the wort. "Have a quick swill of this." He took the small glass and sniffed.

"Is it new?" he asked, sipping at it. Charlie nodded, and his eyes widened.

"Christ on a bike," he said.

"Bad?" Charlie wrinkled her brow. Ryan shook his head.

"Lush. Or it will be when you've brewed it up in the big one." He finished the cupful. "Keeps going, du'nt it?" He licked his lips. "You got a name for't yet?" Ryan was keen for Charlie to name a beer after him.

"Drown Your Sorrows," Charlie said.

"YOU DID WHAT?" Charlie had come home feeling less hyper but keen to head out and fulfil their quest for the Rider. Emz was waiting on the porch for them both, ready to go. However, one minute of conversation with Anna concerning her day had had a mood-altering effect.

"It seemed right." Anna looked edgy. Charlie took in a deep breath and then hugged her.

"You did not have to do that. Not for me." Charlie held her sister tight. Held the tears in tighter.

"I did it for me too."

"Selfish," Charlie teased, secretly touched by her sister's gesture of solidarity. "How's it feel now?" She knew without asking.

"Terrifying." She gave a squeaky cheer. "But freeing." She looked at Emz and Charlie. "And something will turn up."

"Or pop up," said Emz.

"You could go back to Popjoy's," Charlie joked.

"No, I mean pop-up. Remember? Winn and the Orangery?" Emz said. Anna gasped.

"Oh, yes. Perfect timing."

"Go and have a chat," Emz suggested, Anna already nodding and looking enthusiastic. Charlie shook her head.

"Maybe not tonight, though. Tonight we need to do a proper full Strengths search for whoever this Great Grey is awaiting."

"Let's go." Anna was fired up and positive.

THEY WERE LIGHTING up their lanterns. The November twilight had cloaked Pike Lake in a soft grey, blurring at the edge of Woodcastle, so that it disappeared. The Great Grey was restless as the Witch Ways walked down to the shore.

"Hey boy," Charlie said, the horse nickering in low urgent tones.

"Something's spooked him." Emz was at once watchful, looking into the densest trees behind Cob Cottage for any sign of incoming trouble. Charlie was scanning the trees to the West.

"Someone is coming," Anna spoke. The sisters turned.

A woman was walking along the shore of Pike Lake. She was wearing a long dress and what looked like a cloak. Her long hair trailed in the breeze, and she was carrying a basket.

"Mum?" Emz stepped forward. "It's Mum."

The sisters walked down the shore to greet her.

Vanessa Way looked more beautiful than they had ever seen her. Her skin was pale and had a luminescent quality to it beneath the stark, rich black of her hair.

"Your hair looks amazing," Emz said. "You never wear it down."

Vanessa reached to hug Emz, putting the basket down at the feet of the Great Grey as he trotted towards her.

"You're not in the car," Charlie stated the obvious.

"I am the Wolf's Heart." Her voice was off, with a hollow tone to it that struck all the sisters at once.

"Wait. What?" Charlie, flustered, her face pinched.

"Mum? What did you say?" Anna, pale as the moon. Emz did not speak. She was looking, without thinking, for her mother's real face, but it was only this; nothing was hidden from Emz, and, as her mother turned to hug Anna and her hair fell back over her shoulder, Emz saw the black markings inked into her neck. She gasped at the memory of parents' evening back in October, the glimpse of her mother's real face. As their mother pulled out of the hug, Anna saw the markings too.

"Wait… wait… you got a tattoo?" She reached a hand to her mother's neck. Vanessa tossed back her hair and laughed. It was a sound chinkling with ice.

"I am the Wolf's Heart." Vanessa's eyes widened in pleasure and delight. There was a twist in the air. The sisters felt it as though Havoc Wood skewed into sharper focus.

"What?" Charlie looked around. The edge of Pike Lake was there and also elsewhere. Was this Pike Lake? It made her nauseous.

"I am the Wolf's Heart." Vanessa seemed light, bright with the idea of it. Anna felt the ice bite into her.

"No. No, not that. No." Anna clutched at her mother's arm. Vanessa's hand folded around hers.

"Yes. I am the Wolf's Heart, and he sends for me," Vanessa was eager, "because it is now, and there is no time."

"No. No." Anna stepped forward to the edge of the lake, her hand raised in protest. "This was in the cards. The Prophets. No." The starlight above began to cloud over. Vanessa took her hand.

"I am the Wolf's Heart, and he needs me." She kissed Anna's hand. "Your father needs me. They are coming for him. They will take me. There is no time." She turned to tie the basket to the saddle of the Great Grey. Anna was frozen with fear, her breath coming in sharp, stabbing pains.

"Wait. Wait. What?" Charlie had lost all her other words. Emz stood rigid.

"This was always how it was to be." Vanessa took all their hands, Charlie pulling away.

"Wait." Charlie's tears spilling over. Vanessa held her tight.

"I didn't know when. It was always that there was no time."

"No. No." Anna reached for her mother's skirt as the Great Grey stooped a little to let Vanessa mount to the saddle.

"Wait. Where are you going?" Charlie grabbed the reins. Anna could not let go of the handful of handwoven dress. Emz stood in front of the horse.

"There is no time," Vanessa said, as Pike Lake began to crack and groan. Their breath was frosted, glittering sparks that broke against the air.

"Far North." Charlie saw the frozen lake, the compass spinning before her. The dark velvet path stretching in only one direction. Anna turned, saw the black wolf waiting in the far distance. A mournful sound fell from her, animal and wild.

The Great Grey moved, unbidden, with his burden, his hooves clodding at the shore and then crisp against the ice. The Ways could not move, Emz's face blurring with tears, Anna reaching her hand forward, Charlie panting hard as if she'd been running, small angry sounds punching the air in front of her mouth.

The sky widened and stretched away from them as the Great Grey broke into a canter, a gallop, his hooves kicking up the ice. As Vanessa moved further across the lake, the cracks and chasms chased through the ice, shattering the surface, as Pike Lake, black deep, blue cold, took over.

The world weighed heavily into place, the Way sisters at the water's edge unsure, uncertain, bereft.

. . .

BEHIND COB COTTAGE, headlights showed through the trees. PC Williamson bumped off the tarmac onto the gravel and finally the dirt track. He thought of his Grandma Violet, and he wanted to have brought a basket of stone scones, a brick of fruitcake, anything, anything except the message he carried, the news he must now break.

Helen Slavin

Crow Heart

1

THE GLINT IN A GIRL'S EYE

The road from Highfar had been a long and stony one for Thinne and his apprentice, Nuala Whitemain. Horses lamed, coach and cartwheels splintered and cracked until Thinne almost thought someone worked against them. It would not be surprising. He had stolen this girl away from Havoc Wood on the promise of teaching her dark things. The longer he spent in her company, the more he understood that he had not made a good bargain. Thinne had taught her well, but she had learned too quickly. She was not wild. She was measured, calculating. She outstripped him, and he was careful not to reveal that he was aware of this. He had to watch her, like prey. No, it was worse than that; he might be prey.

Polly was the landlady at The Gilded Boar, a stout woman not given to easy smiles. She was used to drunks and vagabonds, and little shook her, which was why it was so disconcerting to Thinne to see fear trembling through her as she spoke with him.

"You and the girl are to be out before nightfall." She put her hands on her hips in an effort to hide the tremor. It did nothing for the quiver of her lips, so she pinched them together, her direct gaze holding his.

315

"I've booked and paid for…" As he spoke, she was already taking coin from her apron pocket. He did not take it. Polly placed it on the table before him.

"Before nightfall." Polly drew in a breath for courage. "You are not to come here no more."

Thinne was not popular, but he paid his bills. He had been a regular at the Boar, even back when her father ran it, and she was a small girl clearing tankards. Of all the inns and taverns he stopped off at along the many roads, this was his favourite by far. Polly minded her business and cooked good food. The rooms were scented with lavender and rosemary, and the linen had not been slept in by a previous guest.

"We have always got on, you and I. You run a good place." He kept his eyes on hers, hoping that there was some bargain he could salvage. He tried to recall anything he had ever heard about her, if there was anything he could use against her, but Polly was wise and careful. He needed his rest. This was the only place he ever truly rested. He decided that this was the best hand to play. "You must know how I value my stays here."

Polly shook her head.

"No more." She was firm, but all of a sudden, her eyes could not land on his, so he kept staring, like waiting for a fish to hook. She might relent, realise what a poor bargain she was making in rejecting him. Her eyes peered once more into his own, struggling against the fear. "Not no more." She rallied.

"Tell me." Thinne was stern. Polly stood up straighter.

"I will show you."

Thinne had never ventured through the small wooden doorway at the back of the parlour. This led to the private territory of Polly's own quarters and the laundry and kitchen. Polly shut the door behind them and called up a small flight of stairs.

"Nimmy."

Quick as a dog, the girl responded. Thinne needed only one glance at her face, the left eye clouded over.

"Step closer." Thinne reached a slender hand to the girl's face, his fingers touching her chin, angling her face this way, then that. Her heart was skittering in her chest, the other eye swivelling to not look at him.

"Look at me." His fingertips pinched lightly at her chin to add to his command. The girl looked at him. Thinne's heart dropped into his boots, but he kept his face calm.

"Your girl done this." Polly's voice was low and afraid.

"What bargain did you make?" Thinne asked the girl, hoping it might be something he could alter, possibly to his own advantage. It might be wise to show his power to Polly, hoard her fear for future leverage. Except at this moment, he was unsure of himself; his own fear, very often a cowed and shrunken thing, was snarling at him. The girl spoke, but her voice was a whisper like the wind, catching in the air, and the words whisked off before the ear could hear them. Thinne felt around for the spell of it; it was unlike anything he had ever taught Nuala Whitemain. He withdrew his shaking hand.

"Can you take it from her? She's not right." Polly was concerned for the girl's welfare. In a few short moments, Thinne had come to understand why the woman in the ticket office at Dogday Station had crossed the tracks to avoid serving them. He recalled the odd demeanour of the girl at The Tin Rabbit a week or more since, and he was afraid.

"Yes," Thinne lied. "Give me tonight." He bargained.

"Only tonight." Polly was unbending.

Night fell and he wore the darkness like a cloak; here was a skill he had kept from his devious apprentice and was grateful. He did not have to wait long in the shadows of the courtyard.

The serving girl walked across the yard and stood by the well. Her eyes were open but, he knew, unseeing. Nuala stepped from the shadows opposite, except, he saw with a start, that she too wore the darkness. The breath stopped in his chest. Had she seen him enter the yard?

She approached the girl and took something from her pocket as the girl, still upright but sleeping, lifted her hand. Thinne could not believe what he was seeing: Nuala's careful pricking of the girl's thumb, the polished pearl glint of a needle made from bone. Nuala stepped up onto the wall of the well and reached to hold the girl's head in her hands. The girl's jaw fell slack at her touch, and Thinne watched in horror as Nuala leaned down to whisper the summoning into the girl's mouth.

He had not taught her this. All his errors and mistakes fanned out before him like the worst hand of cards as he cast off the darkness. Nuala, startled, let the girl go.

Thinne snatched at the girl's soul as it left her body. She slumped, the essence of her thin and draggled, so that Thinne could see where Nuala had taken from her before, had asked this essence to run her errands. He did not dare to think what kind.

Nuala, enraged, flew at him, snatching at a wisp of soul even as Thinne wound it round his fist. He took breaths from Nuala's lungs, pinched a beat from her heart.

"The apprentice owes the master." His voice was guttural and rasping at her to keep her at bay, but the old trick no longer touched her. He felt the cold fingers of her magic flex themselves around his heart, the beats drumming out of him. His breath quickened; he felt his heart struggle against this arrhythmia. He had not taught her this, only chastised her with it. He saw where he had failed, that he had never broken her, that all her punishments had been lessons, teaching her the trick of them. It took all he had, borrowing some of the serving girl's soul, to reach within his chest. Even as he fought, he saw where she watched him still, taking his knowledge even as they fought, twisting it to herself. Just when he was uncertain whether his heart or the magic would break first, she staggered back, her face white as her hair.

Thinne caught at her coat, tugged her from the ground.

"You will offer up your heart." He commanded now. "You will pay what is owed." His breath was cold as stone and scented with graveyard dirt; the shadows deepened around them. Nuala writhed, slipping the sleeves so all he held was her coat as she released a blow of magic strong enough to throw him back against the low wall of the well.

He watched her go, witnessed the ragged darkness of her footsteps and did not give chase. Let her run. The only place that would have her was Havoc. Let Granner and Hettie Way see what a monster they had made. He would bide his time. Perhaps when she was Queen of Havoc after all, and he would claim his debt. One day. When he was desperate.

Today he skulked away from The Gilded Boar, the serving girl's soul not returned after all but ravelled into his pocket. He wore it ragged running errands, wringing all the power he could until, one sunset, his weary maid of all wicked work gave a sigh and sank into the boards of the cheapest room at The Tin Rabbit, a small heap of dust to be swept away by other servants, unawares.